EX,
Why,
and Me

EX, Why, and Me

Susanna Carr

KENSINGTON PUBLISHING CORP.
http://www.kensingtonbooks.com

BRAVA BOOKS are published by

Kensington Publishing Corp.
850 Third Avenue
New York, NY 10022

All Kensington titles, imprints and distributed lines are available at special quantity discounts for bulk purchases for sales promotion, premiums, fund-raising, educational or institutional use.

Special book excerpts or customized printings can also be created to fit specific needs. For details, write or phone the office of the Kensington Special Sales Manager: Kensington Publishing Corp., 850 Third Avenue, New York, NY 10022. Attn. Special Sales Department. Phone: 1-800-221-2647.

Brava and the B logo Reg. U.S. Pat. & TM Off.

ISBN 0-7582-1083-3

First Kensington Trade Paperback Printing: July 2006
10 9 8 7 6 5 4 3 2 1

Printed in the United States of America

EX,
Why,
and Me

Prologue

It was difficult going all the way with a guy when you were required to wear a tiara, but Michelle Nelson managed it. Barely.

She just never thought it would occur in the middle of the night behind the pinsetters at Pins & Pints, Carbon Hill's bowling alley and the only source of entertainment one could have standing up.

Michelle shifted, her knees aching against the hard, cold floor. The alley was closed, the lanes silent, but she was bumping up against ancient, oily machinery. The location hadn't been her first choice for her first time with her first love.

It didn't seem to hold the right ambiance for Ryan Slater, either. "Let's go back to my place," he suggested in a husky tone that made her skin tingle.

She glanced down at him, but the shadows made it difficult to read his expression. Michelle felt exposed as she straddled him, the weak overhead lights almost reaching her. Her evening dress from the JC Penney catalog bunched up against her thighs, the pink polyester rubbing her bare, flushed skin.

"No," she whispered, her heart pounding in her ears. She pressed her hands against his shoulders, pulling at his T-shirt with desperate fingers. "I can't wait that long."

2 / *Susanna Carr*

It had to be now. She was leaving for Europe in the morning. Her bags were packed, she'd said goodbye to her friends, but there was this one last thing to do.

It had taken her all summer to get Ryan Slater. She could have pursued another local guy in a lot less time, but she wanted Ryan and no one else would do. It had been that way ever since she could remember, so at least twenty years. Unfortunately, all the prettier, bolder girls wanted him, too.

No matter what she had done in the past, it wasn't enough to compete for Ryan's attention. He'd never seemed to notice her. Not even when she'd worn the tiara and the Miss Horseradish sash for the past year. And God knew those were hard to miss.

He noticed her now. Had stared at her in awe. Or maybe he was staring at her tiara, which had a tendency to catch the light and blind people. That was probably it, but she couldn't do anything about it now. The crown was pinned and shellacked to her updo.

The glittery distraction would serve her well, Michelle decided as she glided the condom onto Ryan. She didn't want him to feel her hands fumble and shake. Rolling the latex down was not as easy as her best friend Vanessa had led her to believe.

The tip of Ryan's cock nudged against Michelle's flesh. The intimate contact made her feel hot. Tight. She grasped him at the base and lowered down.

Michelle jerked, startled, when Ryan clamped his fingers against her bare hips. "We'll take it slow," he said roughly, almost as if he said it through clenched teeth.

Her heart raced as he guided her. White heat crackled just under her skin when he gently filled her.

She closed her eyes, her breath hitching, as she relished every sensation. Michelle had been expecting pain. Nothing major, but something unpleasant. Nothing like the delicious heavy ache that flooded her muscles.

Michelle rocked against him, smiling as the pleasure heated her blood with a shower of sparks. She flexed her hips. *Ooh . . .* She swayed the other way. *Mmm . . .*

"Michelle, slow down," Ryan said hoarsely, his fingers tightening, sinking into her hips.

She wanted his hands elsewhere. Everywhere. Cupping her breasts. No, squeezing them. Pinching her nipples until she begged him to take them into his mouth.

She wanted him to thrust. Grind. Drive into her.

Maybe that wasn't possible in this position. But she didn't want to change sides. Here she felt alive. Bold. Free. She was wild. Sexy. Powerful.

She moved against Ryan, each move fierce and unchecked. Her world centered where they joined. He bucked against her, his moves shallow and hesitant.

Michelle countered with a deep roll of her hips, but his cock didn't stretch or fill her to the hilt. She frowned and wiggled.

"Not like that," Ryan said, his voice bouncing off the machines. He tensed. "Damn."

He lay motionless underneath her. No thrusting, no rocking. Nothing. *This is it?* Michelle thought. *You have got to be kidding me!*

She felt his cock softening, drooping—

Michelle froze. *Oh, no . . .*

—as it slipped out.

I killed it.

Chapter 1

Five years later

"There's been a change of plans."

Michelle froze and her tired, aching muscles seized up. She pressed her cell phone against her ear and stepped out of the restaurant's back door and into the gray, empty alley. The cold nip in the October evening felt good after being in the hot, steamy kitchen.

"You guys don't need me to come home?" She should be relieved. Really. She'd rather save that vacation time to catch up on her sleep. Or clean her rinky-dink apartment. Get audited by the IRS. Anything but participate in another Horseradish Festival.

So that didn't explain the disappointment flooding her. It was thick and heavy, pulling down until her knees were about to buckle.

"No," her brother Danny replied. "We need you here more than ever."

That didn't sound good. "What happened? Is the festival still on?"

"Yeah, and the scavenger hunt is still on, too. We're getting a lot of buzz on that event."

Yay. Michelle rolled her eyes. She would never have agreed to take part in it, but Vanessa was responsible for breathing new life into Carbon Hill's main celebration. Michelle had said she would do whatever she could to help, and she meant it. She wasn't thrilled about taking part in the hunt, but she'd do it and keep her complaints to herself.

"But now it's couples only."

Michelle frowned, staring at the faded graffiti on the wall in front of her. "I don't understand. It was originally two people for each team."

"How can I put this?" Danny paused and Michelle could imagine him rubbing his forehead. "Did you know that horseradish is considered an aphrodisiac?"

"Are you for real?" Her brother had to be kidding. Horseradish *stank*, it was ugly, and not the least bit sexy.

But, considering how she avoided putting the root in any of her recipes—let alone eating it—that could explain her lack of love life.

"Seriously, Vanessa did some research on it and found this out."

Vanessa, who'd recently started dating Danny, was researching aphrodisiacs. Michelle really didn't want to know. "So what does this have to do with me?"

"Well, as you probably heard, the festival hasn't been doing so well. It's lost money for the past two years."

"Uh-huh." She hunched her shoulders, blocking out the city noises. "And I repeat, what does this have to do with me?"

"Everyone knows that sex sells, so Vanessa decided to put the two together."

"Sex and horseradish?" In a word, *Ew.*

"The scavenger hunt now has a theme," Danny said, his voice cracking. "A sexier theme."

Michelle was afraid to ask.

"The contestants have to find things that relate to Homer and Ida Wirt."

Michelle scrunched up her nose in disbelief. "The horse-radish farmers turned train robbers?"

"The *alleged* train robbers," Danny corrected her. "They were never brought to trial."

Michelle tossed her arm up with impatience. "Because when the authorities were chasing them, Homer and Ida fell off the bluffs and plunged to their deaths in the icy river."

"Allegedly."

Michelle placed her hand on her hip. "And how is an event that happened almost one hundred years ago and resulted in *death* considered sexy?"

"Okay, it's sexy Carbon Hill style," Danny admitted.

Michelle pressed her lips together. She wasn't going to say it. Wasn't going to say a thing—not one thing—about Carbon Hill style being an oxymoron.

"The contestants have to follow Homer and Ida's trail and find the treasure at the end."

"Is that the only change? No problem," she said with a shrug. That would actually make the hunt simpler.

"And," her brother continued in a suspiciously bright tone, "the winners are declared Carbon Hill's Sexiest Couple."

Michelle paused as the words sank in. "Excuse me?"

"So you and I are not allowed to participate as a team," Danny said in a rush.

Sexiest Couple? The words flashed before her eyes like neon lights.

"Despite what the other towns in the county say, Carbon Hill doesn't promote inbreeding."

"Sexiest Couple?" Michelle screeched. Her voice bounced off the brick walls.

"Only romantically linked couples are eligible. Which probably explains why nearly every team dropped out."

"Uh-huh. Ya think?"

Danny ignored that. "When that happened, Vanessa was

ready to reinstate the previous eligibility requirements, but the local media had latched on to the sexy element."

"And since media coverage will bring more visitors, she has to stick to it," Michelle guessed and she paced the alley, dodging the overflowing garbage cans.

"Exactly. The hunt needs at least three teams and the organizers need you to stay in the hunt."

"Me?" She stopped walking. That didn't make sense. She was no longer a resident of Carbon Hill. "Why not you?"

"I'm not a former Miss Horseradish."

Michelle's eyes narrowed at her brother's gloating tone. She knew that title would come back to haunt her. She just didn't think it would haunt her *so often*.

But this was for Vanessa. Who was obviously too much of a scaredy-cat to tell her about the change personally. Because Vanessa was smart.

Yet her friend shouldn't have to hide behind Danny. Vanessa should have known that she would accept the challenge, just as Michelle knew Vanessa would do the same for her. Although Michelle would never subject her best friend to this special brand of aggravation and potential humiliation.

"Fine." Michelle slapped her palm against her thigh in defeat, causing a cloud of white flour to billow from her apron. "I'll stay in. But how am I going to find a partner with this short notice?"

"I'll help you find someone."

Her big brother was going to find her a man. Scary thought. "Hey, what about Brett Shue?" Michelle asked. The guy was not the brightest crayon in the box, but he was cute and athletic.

"He's married to one of the Weiss girls, making him ineligible as your partner."

Well, that narrowed the field considerably. People married early in Carbon Hill. No idea why, but there were some unexplained traditions in that town. "How about Vance?"

"Vance? From next door?" Danny's stunned pause piqued her curiosity. "Uh, he's in prison."

Michelle's mouth dropped open. *"Really?"* The kid next door was now doing time. She couldn't say she was all that surprised.

"Don't you read Mom's e-mails?"

"Yeah," she said defensively. No need to mention that it was only when she wanted to go to sleep. Her mom always sent the longest, newsiest e-mails about people Michelle didn't remember.

"Who would be single and living a clean and wholesome life?" Michelle mused out loud. "There's Clayton." He was about as hot and sexy as horseradish, but he might be helpful when it came to the scavenger hunt.

"He's on one of the other teams," Danny informed her.

Michelle tsked with annoyance. *Figures.* Someone knew to snap him up quick. "Well, who can I get?"

"Don't worry. I'll find someone," her brother promised.

Michelle started to pace again. "Where are you going to find an eligible male whom I'm not related to and who is not over the age of forty-five?"

"There's no age requirement."

"That's my requirement." Michelle thumped her palm against her chest. "No way am I going to be hooked up with a guy almost as old as Dad." She shuddered at the possibility.

"Any other requirements I should know about?"

A memory resurfaced, rushing to the front of her mind like a rolling thundercloud. She recalled Ryan Slater in vivid detail. The first thing she always remembered was his hair. Short and wavy, the dark blond tufts were streaked from the sun. Ryan always raked it back from his forehead, leaving a tousled, almost fall-out-of-bed style.

Creases and grooves lined his tanned face, but she'd never thought they diminished his good looks. Rather, they added even more interest to his angular features because the man was always smiling. His teasing grins, knowing smirks, and wide full-wattage smiles made her heart race every time.

But it was his eyes that made her stop in her tracks. They were bright, stunningly blue, and almost uncomfortably direct. Ryan had the uncanny ability to make her lose her balance with a sideways glance, pierce her soul with a long gaze, or make her forget to breathe, like when she saw the agony flicker through his eyes that time . . .

Michelle dipped her head, her shoulders curling inward as she pushed the image back into the shadowy recesses of her memories. Her lungs squeezed tight, just as the words bubbled and pressed against her throat. *Anyone but Ryan Slater.*

No! She couldn't say those words out loud. It was safer not to say anything. Michelle took a deep, hitching breath, inhaling the sugar-laced aroma from the kitchen that mingled with the rotting fruit in the alley.

"Michelle?"

The chances of Ryan volunteering were so slim—so nonexistent—it wasn't worth singling him out. "He has to be male," she said in a husky voice, "unrelated, and under forty-five."

"That might take some time," Danny confessed. "Why don't you bring someone down from Chicago?"

Oh, sure. There were lots of guys hanging around the restaurant who would sacrifice vacation time for her. Mm-hmm. Right.

"No way, Danny. You offered to do this for me and I'm holding you to it. Call in favors. Bribe someone. Beg if you have to. Do whatever it takes and just find me a guy."

* * *

Pins & Pints was crowded as usual, but Ryan didn't pay attention to the noise or the people milling around. He was on a break and he was going to make the most of it. Focusing on his lane, Ryan released the ball. He knew his aim was good and smiled way before it smashed through the pyramid of pins.

The edge of his mouth dipped when he turned around and saw his bowling partner's sulking expression. "What's that face for?" Ryan asked Larry.

Larry set the beer bottles on the table and plopped down on the hard, plastic seat. "I am not doing the scavenger hunt, no matter who asks me."

Ryan didn't blame him. "Callie wants to do the hunt? Maybe she wants you guys to be known as the Sexiest Couple." He waggled his eyebrows and picked up his bowling ball, preparing for his second try.

"Callie?" Larry looked up as if he'd forgotten the name of his latest girlfriend. "Naw, man. Danny just asked me."

"Huh?" Ryan abruptly straightened his arm, the heavy ball hitting him in the leg.

"Danny Nelson." Larry belatedly realized how that sounded and scowled. "And before you get any wise ideas, it's his sister who needs a partner."

Ryan sharply curled his fingers before he dropped the ball. "Michelle?"

"Yeah." Larry took a long sip of his beer. "Seems she got roped into the hunt, but she doesn't have a partner."

His bowling buddy had to be wrong. Michelle didn't live here anymore. Rarely visited. Larry had probably misunderstood. Pins & Pints was usually so loud at night you had to yell over the noise. "The festival starts tomorrow."

"Yeah. So?"

Ryan scanned the hall. No sign of Michelle's brother anywhere. "Who does she think she'll get?"

"Danny says she'll take any guy under forty-five."

Yeah, any guy but him. Ryan flinched from that fact. He didn't know why that bothered him. It shouldn't.

"Hey." Larry had that glint in his eye. "Danny hasn't asked you yet."

"Send him this way and I'll stuff this bowling ball down your throat," Ryan threatened and made a show of focusing his attention on his lane.

But what Larry had said was true. He hadn't been asked. Which meant Danny had been given express instructions not to approach him.

He couldn't blame Michelle on that score, Ryan thought as he stared at the pins. But the pins were a white blur as he saw disjointed images of rhinestones and Michelle's amazing breasts spilling out of that pink dress.

The ancient pinsetters might have been replaced with modern technology a while back, but it couldn't erase the memory of that one night.

Ryan had been aware of Michelle Nelson long before that. She'd been one of those classy girls in school. She hadn't been the most popular student, or even the smartest, but there was something about her. Everyone knew she was going to go places.

Unlike him.

When the spotlight had finally been directed on Michelle during her reign as Miss Horseradish, the quiet beauty turned into a stunning knockout. She turned heads and tested her allure. She grew brazen and became irresistible.

He liked the bold way she had pursued him. Liked it? It had made him hot. Made him sweat. She had made his head spin and put his body on edge. It had been a mind-blowing turn-on knowing that someone like Michelle wanted him, and wanted him immediately.

So, of course he had to mess it up. And just to make it worse, his first reaction was to put the blame on Michelle.

As if that was going to hide the fact that he was a total loser.

Ryan grimaced, warding off that particular memory. He had been a jerk, and right in front of the one person he had wanted to impress most of all.

"Any day now, Slater."

"Huh?" Ryan looked over his shoulder.

Larry gestured at the pins. "Bowl."

Ryan walked to the red line and tossed the ball down the lane. It spun into the gutter before he could turn around and walk back to his seat.

Larry stared at the untouched pins. "What was that all about?"

"Nothing." Ryan sat down and sprawled his legs in front of him.

"Were you meditating up there or something?"

"More or less."

"Doesn't work for you," Larry decided as he rose to take his turn.

"Hey, Ryan." Danny tapped him on the arm. "You got a minute?"

"Uh"—Ryan and Larry exchanged a look—"sure."

Larry shook his head, obviously wondering why Ryan didn't make an excuse to avoid Danny. Ryan was tempted to let his friend know that it wasn't what he was thinking. Michelle Nelson wouldn't go anywhere near him.

"What's up?" Ryan asked Danny when they stood by the racks of bowling balls. Danny had the same dark hair as his sister, but other than that, they didn't look alike. Which made Ryan's life easier.

Danny looked him straight in the eye. There were no signs of awkwardness. Maybe some desperation, but that was about it. "I need a favor. A big one."

Ryan frowned. "What kind of favor?" It couldn't be

what Danny was asking from every other guy. Maybe he needed help in recruiting a partner for his sister.

"Vanessa needs Michelle to participate in the scavenger hunt, but Michelle needs a partner. Will you do it?"

"Me?"

"Yeah, you."

Ryan slid his jaw to the side as he tried to figure out what the hell was going on. "Me?"

Danny looked from the corner of his eye and back at Ryan's face. "Yeah."

"*Why* me?"

Danny sighed. "Okay, I'll be honest. No one else will do it. Andrews says it's against his religion."

Ryan cast an amused glance at Larry, who guiltily looked away. Ryan was going to torture him about that lame excuse.

"And Bryant doesn't want to piss off his ex-girlfriend now that there's a chance they'll get back together."

He had actually tried Bryant? How desperate was this guy? Well, that was obvious. Danny was talking to *him*. "And I'm your last resort?"

"No, no. Nothing like that." Danny paused and started nodding. "Okay, you're the last person I asked, but that's because I haven't seen you around."

"It's been busy around here." Ryan gestured at the Pins & Pints. His family's bowling alley was located in an old Turner hall that the first German settlers had constructed over one hundred fifty years ago. While it still served its purpose as a community center, Ryan worked constantly to keep the alley making money and prevent the building from crumbling down around them.

"Yeah, I know." Danny rubbed his forehead. "Everyone is busy. I get that. Most of the guys I asked can't get the time off."

Ryan knew he could use the same excuse. He didn't want

to have anything to do with the scavenger hunt. He didn't like puzzles and he wasn't a festival kind of guy.

But if he worked during the celebration, that wouldn't give him the chance to see Michelle face-to-face. He wouldn't find a way to keep that disastrous night from hanging over his head. It didn't happen too much anymore, but when it did, it was always at the worst moment.

On the other hand, accepting Danny's offer would give him a lot of opportunity to humiliate himself. Again. Compound the disaster instead of erasing it.

It was a toss-up, either way.

"I know it's a lot to ask for," Danny continued, "but I would owe you big. Vanessa and Michelle would, too."

Owe him. The deafening noise faded into the distance. That was a new take. Would that mean Michelle would owe him a chance to say he was sorry? To forgive and forget?

Probably not. And why was he even thinking about that? That was four or five years ago. He had moved on. So had Michelle. Why try to correct something that they both felt was better left ignored?

He knew the answer to that. Because it was Michelle Nelson. The one woman he had never thought he could get and the one who couldn't get away from him fast enough.

"But it's just a couple of events a day, right?" Ryan asked, the surroundings roaring back at him, brighter and louder than ever.

"No." Danny winced as if this might be the deal breaker. "The contestants are working together on the hunt the entire time."

She wouldn't be able to get away. Then again, neither would he. "I would have to get the time off . . ." That wasn't going to go over well. His parents relied on him more and more these days.

Danny's eyes widened. "You'll do it?"

He wanted to. Strange as it sounded, he'd find a way to make it work. "Count me in." Ryan gave Danny a firm handshake.

Danny kept pumping his arm. "Michelle is going to be relieved."

Not the word Ryan would have used. "You want me to tell her? Is she in town already?" Without warning, anticipation sparked right underneath his ribs.

Danny looked at his watch. "No, not yet. She's flying in. I'll tell her tomorrow before the hunt begins."

Yeah, that was one display of fireworks Ryan didn't want to miss.

Michelle strode into her parents' small but tidy kitchen Friday morning. She was bone tired and would have rather stretched out on the linoleum floor and slept for another hour. But she was determined to snap out of this pervasive fatigue. Being home would energize her. It always did. And if she didn't feel it immediately, she'd fake it until the energy came roaring back.

Her mother paused from dabbing a napkin to the corner of her mouth, watching her sit down at the table. "You're not leaving the house like that, are you, Michelle?"

"Good morning to you, too, Mom." Even to her ears, Michelle's voice sounded rough and lined with exhaustion. She had to work on that.

She had thought that returning to her childhood home would perk her up. Why she had thought that, she had no idea. Even going to bed in her old room didn't make her feel rested. Quite the opposite. Probably because it wasn't her room anymore. Nope, now it was Dad's dream media room.

She didn't begrudge the man his electronic toys. After all, he had saved up and waited for such a room ever since he had been unceremoniously laid off six years ago.

Anyway, it had been a long time since she'd been back

home, so it wasn't like they had to keep everything as it had been. They didn't need to create a shrine. She got that. But did all evidence of her existence need to be wiped out of that room?

Some things, unfortunately, never changed. The train still chugged by at 7:05 in the morning. Since her childhood home was a mere two blocks away from the tracks, Michelle's hide-away bed rocked insistently, and the windows rattled until what felt like a hundred cars passed.

Any chance of rolling over and going back to sleep was long gone five minutes later when the McKinley Express came screeching down the street, rocking her bed even more.

Oh, yeah. Good to be home.

"Michelle, you need to wear something else."

She looked down at her denim jacket, T-shirt, faded jeans, and worn sneakers. "What's wrong with it?" Oops, Michelle thought. She knew better than to ask. The question was going to give the woman too much ammunition.

Her mother took a dainty sip from her teacup, her thumb automatically covering the slight chip on the handle. "They aren't befitting to your station."

O . . . kay, she wasn't expecting that answer. "I have a station?"

"As a former Miss Horseradish."

"Uh, sorry, Mom. I gave my elbow-length gloves to charity." Although the tiara and sash were still here. Uh-oh. Michelle gnawed on her bottom lip and prayed that her royal accessories were sealed tight in a memory box.

Her mother pressed her hand to her throat as if she was clutching an imaginary strand of pearls. "All I'm saying is that you are the face of the local horseradish industry."

Gee, thanks.

"And you need to present yourself without your hair looking like a rat's nest."

Oh, yeah. Some things never changed. Obviously, breakfast wasn't going to give her a boost of energy. More like indigestion. Michelle stood up. "Mom, I don't have time for this. I have to be down at the square by ten."

Her mother glanced down and tsked. "At least change your shoes."

"These are the only pair I brought." She studied her favorite pair of running shoes. Sure, they were old and worn, but they hugged her feet like clouds.

"They are shabby," her mother announced, always the voice of authority on such matters. "You can borrow a pair of my flats."

Great. Why did her mother feel the need to dress her up in her style? "I'm sure all the other contestants will be wearing tennis shoes," Michelle assured her.

"But you're not like everyone else. And one of these days everyone will realize this and follow your sense of style."

It was happening. Already. First day back at home and she was getting a taste of the we-always-knew-you-were-going-to-do-something-special-but-we're-getting-tired-of-waiting-for-it-to-happen. Michelle couldn't remember offhand why she had been feeling homesick.

It was time to call in reinforcements. She looked at the other end of the table. "Dad?"

Her father didn't look away from the small TV set on the kitchen counter. "Wear the shoes."

Michelle looked up at the ceiling and counted to ten. Next trip home, no matter how much it would horrify her mother, she was booking a room at the Mark Twain Motel.

She heard her cell phone ring. "That's mine," Michelle announced, dashing to the front door where her purse sat.

"I'll get you those shoes," her mother called after her.

Michelle grabbed her phone as if it were a lifeline. "Hello?"

"Michelle? Is this little Michelle Nelson?" the woman

asked with such high-pitch excitement that it went straight to the filling in Michelle's back molar.

"Uh . . ." Michelle winced. "Yes."

"My, you sound all grown up."

Michelle hoped so, since she was already twenty-five. But for some reason, the woman spoke to her as if she were a toddler.

"This is Mrs. White. Of White Motors," the woman said. "Your mother gave me this number."

"Oh?" Michelle glared at her mother, who was approaching her with navy blue, boring, flat shoes.

"Yes, because I need to ask for a favor. As you know, there's a horseradish recipe competition at the fairgrounds. It's the highlight of the festival."

It was? Since when? Michelle had lived here for most of her life and couldn't remember that.

"The committee thought it would be perfect to have a former Miss Horseradish—who is also a world-class baker— as the final judge."

"Oh." Michelle almost lost her balance as she kicked off her sneakers and yanked off her socks.

"The rule is that the baker or cook has to use horseradish in the recipe. Isn't that great?"

"Uh, yeah." She shoved her feet into the shoes and discovered they were snug, especially around the toes.

"So when can we expect you?"

"For what?" She jerked back when her mom started in on her hair, fluffing Michelle's sleek style with her manicured nails. Michelle ducked for cover.

"To judge the finalists."

"Oh, you know, Mrs. White"—she dodged her mom's fingers that were descending on her like a scene from Alfred Hitchcock's *The Birds*—"I'm very honored that you are asking me. But . . . I'm going to have to decline your invitation."

She heard her mom gasp. The attacking fingers stopped. Michelle turned around just as her mom made a failed attempt to grab the phone.

"Oh," Mrs. White said, the warmth in her voice dropping to arctic temperatures. "I see."

"I'm taking part in the scavenger hunt, which I'm told goes on during the entire time of the festival."

"Oh! Not to worry!" The woman's tone skyrocketed back into the friendly zone. "The blue ribbon ceremony is after the scavenger hunt. Rightfully so. Don't worry about that. Vanessa said you can do it."

Thank you, Vanessa. "Well, in that case." Michelle shrugged in defeat. "I guess I can do both."

Mrs. White squealed with delight. "Wonderful. I can't wait to tell the girls. Bye now."

"I can't believe you almost did that," her mom said in a scandalized whisper.

"Did what?" Michelle put her cell phone in her denim jacket.

"Say no to Mrs. White. Do you know how much money their car dealership put into your Miss Horseradish scholarship fund?"

Michelle raised her hand to stop her. "No, and don't tell me," she pleaded. "I don't want to know."

"And now they're not doing so well." Her mother clucked her tongue.

Nothing like getting your daily dose of guilt first thing in the morning. "I have to go. Bye, Dad!"

"Good luck," her father called from the kitchen.

She was definitely going to need it, Michelle decided as she hurried across the street and headed for the square. She walked a block, retrieved her phone from her jacket, and hit speed dial before ruffling her hair back into the intended style.

"Hello?" Vanessa answered breathlessly.

"Hey—"

"Michelle! Tell me you are on your way to the square."

"I am. Did you—"

"Great. I can't talk right now, but I can't wait to see you." *Click.*

Michelle faltered and stared at the phone. Okay. She pocketed the electronic, knowing that her horseradish recipe competition gripe was nowhere as important as Vanessa getting this festival running smoothly.

And if it was required for her to eat horseradish and smile, then she'd do it. After all, she didn't just owe it to Vanessa, but to Carbon Hill.

That Miss Horseradish scholarship had come at a time when she needed it the most. Her dad had lost his job and there was no way her family could afford her education. While she hunted down every opportunity, it was Carbon Hill that delivered. She got the best culinary training she could get because of her hometown.

But that stroke of good luck also brought along high expectations. The shopkeepers and businessmen got it into their heads that they were investing in the next celebrity chef. A person who would create an empire and give back to the community.

Michelle was all for giving back. She wasn't against having stardom and an empire, either, but somewhere along the way she had lost the drive that was going to get her that. No matter how hard she tried, she couldn't get back the mojo, that legendary stamina which used to be a major part of who she was.

The sound of the high school marching band distracted her as she got closer to downtown. The buildings looked so much smaller than she remembered. The sidewalks began to get crowded as everyone faced the two-lane main street.

Schools were closed for the day and kids waited impatiently for the parade that traditionally kicked off the Horseradish Festival.

Michelle moved behind the people and made her way to the square. She saw the baton tossed high and heard the townspeople gasp with awe. But when she saw the glimmer of rhinestone, Michelle halted and unwillingly turned to face the street.

The reigning Miss Horseradish was perched on the back of a gleaming red convertible, courtesy of White Motors, and waved to the crowd, her white satin elbow-length gloves shiny and bright. The young woman was probably no more than five years younger than she, but Michelle felt there had to be decades yawning between them.

The beauty queen's enthusiasm and spirit was almost tangible. Her long blond hair streamed behind her as she eagerly waved to the townspeople. Michelle realized that the girl wasn't pretty as much as she was cute. And for some reason, the young woman's wide-eyed innocence and beaming smile made Michelle feel as old and worn as her running shoes.

She turned away from the parade and hurried to the square with a little bit more determination, but the comparison lingered like an ache. Michelle gratefully pushed away the troubling thoughts as she spotted her brother at the starting line for the scavenger hunt. "Danny!"

Her older brother's face lit up and he greeted her with a fierce hug. "Hey, Michelle. I didn't know if you were going to make it."

"I escaped Mom before she pulled out her makeup kit," she told him. "Did you find a partner for me?"

"Yeah. Where is—?" Danny looked over her head. "Oh, he's there talking to Vanessa."

Michelle turned, looking for her friend. *Please, just be under forty-five. That's all I ask . . .*

"Slater! Michelle's here."

Slater? Goose bumps blanketed her skin as she went from hot to cold. Ryan Slater? Her lungs shriveled up as her protest died in her throat.

Okay, let me revise that wish . . .

Chapter 2

Hearing his name was a jolt to her system. Michelle's heart shuddered from the impact as she stood motionless, watching Ryan Slater stroll toward her.

Her brain went on the fritz, filtering his approach in a dizzying collage of stop-motion images. Ryan's slow, casual gait didn't fool her. One look at those long, powerful legs and she knew he could catch her.

That thought did little to calm her nerves. Michelle's gaze seemed to gravitate to his soft, faded jeans. His body was as lean and tapered as when she last saw him. Maybe even more so.

It took some effort, but she managed to yank her attention upward. The autumn breeze tugged at his pale blue shirt, hinting at the sleek contours of his flat stomach and sculpted muscles.

Her stomach clenched as the old embers of desire stirred. No, no, no. She wasn't going to make that mistake again. No matter how hot and sexy Ryan looked, she knew from experience it was all false advertising.

That piece of knowledge was the only thing that gave Michelle the courage to look him in the eye. She was startled to see Ryan meeting her gaze head-on. She instinctively looked away, but his imprint remained.

If she had to, Michelle could turn around and describe

him easily. Sexy. Tousled. And had that *knowing* glint in his brilliant blue eyes.

He stopped in front of her. It was as if a live wire had suddenly dropped between them, right there on the crowded sidewalk. The currents darted wildly in the air, but she was almost afraid to move, not sure which action would take her to safety.

She felt his gaze on her face and her skin tingled. She could only imagine what he was thinking. The guy was a pro at teasing. A master flirt. She wouldn't put it past him to say something shocking, just to get a response out of her.

The heat rose into her face and she fought the urge to cover the blush with her hands. If anything, she should brazen her way out of this. Make the first move. Say something before Ryan did.

She gave a sharp, jerky nod. "Ryan." The word got stuck somewhere in her throat. She struggled to make eye contact and barely made it.

His smile crooked to one side, revealing two deep dimples. "Michelle."

She shivered at the way he drew out her name. There was no rush, like pouring a bowl of melted chocolate. The anticipation was building inside her, and she knew it was going to be worth the wait but was impatient for a lick.

Michelle didn't realize she drew on her bottom lip until her tongue swept along the tender flesh. She blinked in surprise and pursed her lips. She had forgotten about the mesmerizing effect of his voice. Combine it with those gorgeous blue eyes and she was a goner every time.

She darted her gaze away, unsure where would be the safest place to look. Even closing her eyes would be dangerous with Ryan Slater standing right beside her. "How have you been?" she asked briskly, studying his scuffed sneakers.

"Great. You?"

"Can't complain." But that vein in her neck was threatening to pulse right out of her skin. That might be a problem.

Michelle opened her mouth and her mind froze. As though it got stuck and the gears were grinding for something more to say. What? What had she been about to say?

The panic flashed inside her, hot and destructive. She frantically tried to calm down. Whatever she had to say couldn't have been important. It was probably routine and safe. Nothing memorable. Nothing at all like, *Hey, you know when we did it my last night here? That was my first time. What's your excuse?*

But that was probably why her mind skipped and paused. That good ol' self-preservation instinct kicking in. So she wouldn't say it.

Think it? Absolutely. Frequently, often, like the ticker tape headlines on the bottom of the TV news. Send ESP waves Ryan's way? No doubt about it. Maybe fit into the conversation that she'd had lots of practice since then, and too bad he'd never find out what she had learned.

Damn if she couldn't remember right now what one of those other guys looked like, let alone what they had taught her. But she did want Ryan to know one thing she had discovered. That she wasn't solely responsible for their disastrous night.

Yeah, the moment that came up in conversation, she'd mention that.

"Are you my partner for the scavenger hunt?" Michelle blurted out. *Please say no . . . Please say no . . .*

"Yep." His smile grew impossibly wider.

Her stomach twisted with dread. There went her last hope. She looked up at his face, wondering what possessed him to agree to this.

And was it possible that Ryan got taller since she last saw him? She didn't remember him towering over her. Making her feel small and delicate.

Michelle shook the thought away. "How did you get roped into the job?"

The lines creasing his forehead deepened as he frowned. "Sorry?"

"Was it bribery, blackmail, or just plain bullying?" Once she found out, she could pay whatever outstanding debt Ryan had and get him far, far away.

"Nothing like that." Ryan folded his arms across his chest and braced his legs. "I volunteered."

Michelle's eyes widened until they burned. "You did what?" She felt as if she was spluttering. "Why?"

"Michelle! You're here!"

Michelle heard her best friend's squeal before she saw Vanessa launching at her. One minute there was a blur of blond hair and long arms and the next she was smack dab in a rib-crushing hug.

"I can't believe it!" Vanessa said. "I've missed you so much!"

Can we say overkill? "It's good to see you, too," Michelle replied cautiously, certain that her words were muffled. She wondered what was going on with Vanessa. She had just seen her best friend a couple of months ago up in Chicago.

"Oh!" Vanessa pulled away, but held Michelle's shoulders in a death grip. "You wouldn't believe what happened— excuse us for a minute, guys. Girl talk."

"We'll be here," Danny said with his hands up as Ryan took a prudent step back.

Danny? Michelle whirled around, putting a crick in her neck as Vanessa dragged her out of earshot. She had completely forgotten her big brother had been standing beside her all this time.

"I am really, really sorry, Michelle," Vanessa said, turning her back on the guys so they wouldn't see what she was saying. Unfortunately, it gave Michelle an eagle-eye view of Ryan.

"You have nothing to be sorry about."

Vanessa spread her arms out wide. "I didn't know who your partner was until he signed up five minutes ago."

"I know." Her friend would have called her the second she found out. In fact, Vanessa would have gotten rid of Ryan. At the very least, she would have talked Danny into finding someone else.

"Now listen." Vanessa leaned forward and spoke softly without moving her mouth. "I know the two of you did it on your last night here, and only you and I know it was simply a matter of ticking an item off your to-do list."

Michelle flinched. Her summer with Ryan had been much more than that. "That's not—"

"And now that makes things awkward. I get that." Vanessa folded her hands across her heart.

"I'm fine," Michelle lied.

"I'll give it to you straight. You know that deer-caught-in-the-headlights look? You are so beyond that level. It's more like you've already been hit and tied onto the roof of the car."

Michelle instinctively looked over Vanessa's shoulder. Her gaze collided with Ryan's. Her ribs pushed into her lungs. She couldn't breathe. Couldn't move. Couldn't think.

Damn, Vanessa was right. How was she going to deal with Ryan 24/7? It was impossible!

"If you want to dump him and get a new partner in the next five minutes," Vanessa suggested, "or if you want to drop out altogether, that's fine with me."

That got Michelle's attention. She looked back at her friend. "But then—"

"Don't worry about me, or about the hunt, or even about what your mom is going to say."

Wow. Vanessa was giving her permission to duck out of the festival and hightail it back to Chicago. Michelle knew she could take the offer, walk away, and her friend wouldn't hold it against her.

It was a tempting offer, but she immediately knew she wasn't going to back out. Michelle straightened her shoulders. She wasn't going to run for cover because of one insignificant yet embarrassing episode in the past. No guy, not even Ryan Slater, was going to prevent her from fulfilling a promise.

"No, I'll be fine," Michelle said, very proud of her calm, strong voice. "I can handle Ryan."

Vanessa tilted her head to the side. "Are you sure?" she asked, unconvinced.

"Positive," Michelle said with more gusto than she felt. "After all, being in a contest for the Sexiest Couple title doesn't mean sexual contact is involved." She froze as she realized her assumption. "Does it?"

"Uh . . ." Vanessa's eyes drifted up as she recalled the events planned. "No."

"Positive?"

"Oh, puhleeze." Vanessa rolled her eyes. "This is Carbon Hill, remember?"

Michelle breathed a little easier and wrapped her arm around her friend's. "Then let's do this."

Vanessa sighed with relief. "Good." She dragged Michelle back toward the men. "There's something else I needed to tell you, but I can't remember what it is." She motioned at her mouth. "It's on the tip of my tongue."

"You have a lot going on." Michelle patted her friend's arm. "Don't worry about it."

"I don't mind telling you that the festival planning has been stressful," Vanessa admitted under her breath. "I can't wait until this celebration is over."

I know how you feel . . .

Ryan couldn't take his eyes off of Michelle. He had always thought she was beautiful, and that one night he caught a glimpse of how breathtaking she would become.

It turned out he had been wrong. She was even more extraordinary than he had imagined.

He didn't know what did it, what made her so beautiful that it caused something deep inside him to shift when he looked at her. All he knew was that he had better find out before he did something like fall to his knees. Serenade her. Let his tongue hang out and pant.

Ryan pulled his attention up and away from her face. It couldn't be her hair that threw him into a tailspin. He wasn't even sure if he liked the short cut. He was pissed off for the loss of all that long, silky black hair. Not that he had a say in the decision, but he remembered how much he had enjoyed finding any excuse to sink his hands into the waves of her hair.

Although there was something to be said about the new style. It was flirty, chic, and it emphasized her gentle features. He was tempted to rub his fingertips along the feathery ends to see if it was as soft as it looked.

Her brown eyes seemed bigger. Wiser. Yet he still saw the innocence lurking in the shadows. There was something about her face that made him think she had braved through a lot of life in just the past couple of years.

Even the informal clothes had a cosmopolitan edge. The jeans hung low on the graceful slope of her hips, offering a glimpse of silky skin. The simple T-shirt screamed designer, but he was more interested in how the expensive cotton skimmed her curves. The denim jacket she wore looked trendy and aggressive. Very big city.

Maybe that was the problem. No matter how hard he had tried to hide it in the past, Ryan had felt uncivilized with the previous version of Michelle. God knew what he was going to do around this sophisticated incarnation.

And as much as he wanted to prove to himself that that one night wasn't going to get the better of him, that he could erase his mistake, he had a bad feeling he was about to make it worse.

He didn't know why he was making that prediction. It didn't make sense. He had dated a lot. Even the most beautiful and sexiest women around. So why did Michelle Nelson have the power to tie him up in knots?

Now wasn't the time to find out. Not in front of the watching town and definitely not in front of the local newspaper reporter. It was time to admit his error in judgment and get the hell out before it was too late.

"Sorry about that," Michelle said, not quite looking him in the eye as she stuffed her fists into her jean jacket.

"Good luck, you guys," Danny said as he curled his arm around Vanessa's waist. "And, Michelle? You owe me. You owe me big."

Michelle's smile was wry as she watched her brother and friend walk away. "Oh, yeah, Danny. Don't worry. I won't forget this for a long, long time."

Yep. She's not happy at all. Ryan didn't blame her, but that was the point of why he had volunteered to do this stupid hunt. He had never gotten the chance to do or say anything about that one night because she had left the next morning. This scavenger hunt was supposed to be his chance.

But his chance for what? He didn't know. Now that he thought about it, when he had said he'd do this, he'd had a vague idea of a plan.

Okay, he had no plan. No strategy. Nothing.

Which was mistake number one. Maybe mistake number two or three, because why did he think he had the power to change the past. To erase it? To make Michelle forgive and forget?

While he was often accused of being too optimistic, Ryan never strove for the impossible. He might have gone over the edge this time. What he wanted to accomplish was unrealistic. He got that now. If he really wanted that episode to be forgotten, wouldn't it be more effective—not to mention easier—if he avoided Michelle for the next fifty or sixty years?

Anyway, did he really want to spend all this time with a woman who refused to look at him?

Ryan turned toward her. "Michelle, maybe this was a bad idea."

Her head jerked up. The bare look in her eyes made his gut twist. As though he had betrayed her. Let her down.

"I can tell the organizers I can't do it. Family obligations"—which wouldn't be far from the truth—"and they can find you another partner."

Her mouth dropped open. "You're bailing out on me?"

Ryan couldn't stop staring at her soft, parted lips. It took him a minute to realize what she was saying. "No! I'm not doing that at all."

She gestured at the scavenger hunt starting point. "This thing starts any second now and you're leaving?"

"I'm trying to give you a—"

"Typical." Michelle tossed her hands up in the air with frustration. "If this isn't just like a man."

Ryan held up his hands. "Hey!" He was trying to do her a favor. Couldn't she see that?

"I should have known." She shoved her fingers in her hair. "Just when you're ready to go all out for it, the man will leave you high and dry."

Heh. Ryan rocked back on his foot. That almost sounded as if she was complaining about that night. Which couldn't be, because Michelle would never bring it up. Never.

"I'm here at the starting gate and you're ready to withdraw." She jerked her thumb back.

Although she might hint to that night.

Michelle planted her hands on her hips. "Just goes to show that men can't stick it out," she said to no one in particular.

And be sneaky about it. Ryan frowned as the slow, rare anger simmered inside him. He hadn't expected this response. He had imagined undying gratitude, not thinly veiled comments. "Now wait a minute."

"Men have no staying power," she announced and gave a shrug, as if she should have known this all along.

"*What?*" He gave a quick look around, but no one on the crowded sidewalk was paying attention.

"None whatsoever." She shook her head. "If I could go solo, I would."

"Michelle," he said with a bite of warning, but she didn't hear it.

"I could get the job done on my own, and in about half the time," she bragged.

That gave him a wild image. Michelle naked, legs parted, her hand dipping . . . "I'm staying," he said through clenched teeth.

"No, no." She gave him a dismissive wave. "Don't stick around for me."

"I'm not." He grabbed her wrist. Heat sparked under his palm when he touched her. His thumb pressed against her thudding pulse point. "I'm sticking around to prove you wrong."

She warily watched him bring her hand to his chest. "About what?" she asked, curling her fingers closed.

"I am more than willing to show you just how much"— he paused until she looked at him straight in the eye— "*staying power* I have."

Michelle squeezed her eyes shut. Why wasn't the ground opening up and swallowing her whole? "R-Ryan." She knew her face was beet red. "I wasn't suggesting—"

"Oh, of course not."

She wasn't! It just came out that way, but she didn't mean it *like that*. "Seriously. I was talking about the hunt."

"Uh-huh." His thumb brushed back and forth against

her wrist. The teasing touch was turning her quick responses into sludge.

She yanked her arm away from him. "I was."

"Michelle, after this hunt is over, you'll forget all about that one night."

She folded her arms across her chest and glared at him. "What's that supposed to mean?"

The left side of his mouth hitched up. "Exactly what it sounds like."

Michelle shifted her bottom jaw. "You do realize that Sexiest Couple is in name only, right?"

Ryan didn't answer, but the two sly dimples appeared next to his devious smile.

"Ryan," she said in a growl. She was about to lay down the ground rules when the high-pitch screech of a microphone interrupted her.

"Ladies and gentlemen," Vanessa said, front and center on a makeshift stage. "Welcome to Carbon Hill's first scavenger hunt."

Michelle studied the audience as they applauded. They looked curious. Some showed interest while others appeared doubtful. The town as a whole didn't embrace new ideas easily.

"Before I introduce the teams," Vanessa continued with a bright smile, "let's go over the rules. Each team is comprised of Carbon Hill's natives and residents. One man and one woman who are romantic partners. They are battling with their competitors for the title of Carbon Hill's Sexiest Couple."

"Battling?" Michelle said under her breath. "I wouldn't say that."

"Oh, c'mon, Michelle." He nudged her arm with his elbow. "You know you want the title. Tell the truth. It would go so well with your Miss Horseradish tiara."

She was tempted to threaten one of his body parts with

her tiara, but decided he'd take that as a sexual proposition. Instead she ignored him, realizing that tactic would probably get her through the scavenger hunt with her sanity intact.

"The hunt follows the lives of Carbon Hill's most famous romantic couple, Homer and Ida Wirt," Vanessa explained to the crowd. "Legend has it that the married couple were horseradish farmers by day and train robbers by night."

So much for the overuse of "allegedly," Michelle noted. She wondered about that. As far as she knew, the Wirts didn't have any descendants. So who would have been kicking up a fuss?

"With only their beloved dog as their sidekick," Vanessa went on, reading from an index card, "Homer and Ida became the most successful train robbers of their time. No one quite knows how much they acquired, or where it was stored, but the Wirts became two of the most wanted thieves in the country during the Depression until their untimely death in nineteen thirty-two."

Michelle questioned the buried treasure idea. It was a nice fairy tale, but she bet whatever Homer and Ida stole, they cashed it in as fast as possible.

"Our contestants will follow the lives and some of the exploits of Homer and Ida Wirt during this hunt."

"We're going to rob a train?" Ryan asked from the side of his mouth.

"And meet our untimely death?" Michelle added. She glanced at Ryan, smiling, before she remembered she was supposed to be ignoring the guy. She straightened her mouth into a firm line and looked away.

"At the end of the trail, the winning team will find this." Vanessa whipped off the cover with a flourish and revealed a large treasure chest.

Everyone oohed and ahhed. Michelle stood on her tiptoes, wondering what she was missing. From what she could see, the chest was filled with a lot of fancy paper, knickknacks, and what looked like glittery gold grass that usually was used to line Easter baskets.

"Our shops and businesses have donated to this prize, bringing the value up to ten thousand dollars."

The growing crowd gasped with surprise and a healthy dose of envy.

"Not including the one carat ring displayed in the window of Duguay's Diamonds on Main Street," Vanessa said over the increasing chatter of the townspeople. "It has an estimated value of five thousand dollars."

Wow. Michelle joined in with the crowd's enthusiastic applause. Vanessa had managed to get the chamber of commerce members to donate fifteen thousand dollars. Michelle was very impressed with her friend's achievement.

Too bad she couldn't win. Because no way was she going to add another couple of thousand dollars to her hometown's expectations. Or the ring. Michelle sure would like diamonds. Not going to go for it, though.

But this would definitely explain why Vanessa had been stressed about pulling off this event. Get the media coverage and get the whole town involved in the dying Horseradish Festival, and Vanessa would find smooth sailing to her dream of becoming Carbon Hill's next mayor.

Michelle always thought Vanessa was aiming low when it came to her dream of mayor, an odd goal at that. And this event was an example of her friend's strength that could take her places. But that was an ongoing argument she wouldn't pursue this trip. Right now, Michelle was glad she could help her friend in her own small way.

"There are a few rules for this hunt," Vanessa said as she pulled out another index card. "If any townspeople see a contestant violating the rules, and have the proof, the couple will be disqualified."

"No pressure there," Ryan muttered.

"The couple must stay together at all times. They can't go separate ways to fulfill a task."

Together at all times? She felt the crowd closing in. Ryan's height seemed to really tower over her. Michelle swallowed the lump of dread forming in her throat.

"The couple can get help when it comes to gathering information, such as asking for directions or research, but they can't have another person join or assist them in completing a task."

Michelle pressed her lips together. This was sounding more difficult than she had anticipated.

"And finally, the couples can't use their cars or any type of transportation other than walking to get from one point to the next. The scavenger hunt committee will provide transportation when necessary."

In other words, lots of walking. Michelle looked down at her impractical, boring flats. *Thanks, Mom.*

"Now it's time to introduce our contestants. Our first couple is Dennis and Margaret Aschenbrenner. Mr. and Mrs. Aschenbrenner? Come on up."

Michelle applauded with the crowd as she saw the couple take the stage. They were short, stout, and in their sixties. And, if Michelle remembered correctly, they were *the* house to go to for Halloween. Not only did they make their home a haunted house maze, but they gave the intrepid trick-or-treaters the good candy at the end of the game.

"Our second couple is Ryan Slater and Michelle Nelson."

Oh, jeez. Already? Michelle tried not to grimace. Despite what she said to Ryan, she wasn't ready for this.

Her spine went rigid when she felt Ryan's hand on the small of her back, under the short hem of her jacket. The span of his fingers was much wider than she remembered. She tried to discreetly move away, but it didn't work. Instead, the hem of her T-shirt bunched and Ryan's palm pressed against her skin.

That was enough to make Michelle bolt up the stage. Her beauty queen smile and wave kicked in. She was sure it was a bit rusty, but it was either that or go catatonic.

"And our final couple," Vanessa announced as Michelle quietly greeted the Aschenbrenners, "is Clayton Byers and Brandy Rasmussen."

Shit. Michelle's eyes went wide and she slowly turned around. That must have been what Vanessa couldn't remember. Michelle zeroed in on the beautiful redhead making her way through the crowd, pulling Clayton behind her.

Brandy hurried up the stage and blew a few air kisses to the crowd as Clayton obediently stood a few steps back. When they made their way to where the other contestants stood, she bestowed a perfunctory smile on everyone except Michelle.

Just like old times, Michelle decided. She felt Ryan lean toward her and inhaled his scent that made her blood rush through her veins.

"Why is Brandy glaring at you?" he whispered in her ear. His warm breath teased the wisps of her hair.

Where did she begin? No, she wasn't going to give the full history starting with the instant animosity on the first day of kindergarten. "She was runner-up the year I was Miss Horseradish."

"Ah," Ryan said as he straightened to his full height.

That wasn't even half of it. Brandy lied and cheated throughout the pageant and didn't take being second place very well. In fact, she found the "and if for any reason Miss Horseradish can't fulfill her duties" clause as a challenge. A mission.

And now they were competing for another title. As far as Michelle was concerned, Brandy could have the Sexiest

Couple title. She would gladly give it to her on a silver platter. But she knew she wouldn't get off that easy. Brandy was going to use this hunt as payback time.

Terrific. Wasn't it bad enough that she was doing a scavenger hunt, which had never been her thing, in front of onlookers? Nope, she was also stuck with Brandy, who was going to make her miserable as she took revenge, and Ryan, who had given her the worst night ever and seemed interested in repeating it.

Michelle wondered if there were any rules against being heavily medicated during the scavenger hunt . . .

Chapter 3

"Now, contestants," Vanessa said, turning to face the scavenger hunt participants, "would you please join together for the official photo?"

As the teams huddled together for the photographer, Brandy slid toward the center of the group. Ryan felt rather than saw Michelle's violent hop before she slammed against his arm. Ryan stretched his arm around her shoulders and held her before they both fell into a heap.

"Sorry!" Michelle winced.

"Are you okay?" When she nodded he asked, "What was that about?"

"Trust me," she said through her picture-perfect smile aimed at the camera, "you don't want to know."

Ryan had a feeling Brandy stomped on Michelle's foot, but he couldn't say if it was an accident. Whatever happened, he benefited from it. There was something deeply satisfying having Michelle tucked against his side.

"Give us a kiss!" someone yelled from the crowd.

But that might be short-lived, Ryan decided as other onlookers found that a great idea and demanded the same.

He chose to ignore the "kiss . . . kiss . . . kiss" chant. Sure, he had nothing against kissing Michelle. Okay, it was in the back of his mind every time he looked at her mouth.

He wanted to see if that magic he had felt that summer five years ago was still there. If it was better. He bet it was.

But now would be the worst time to find out. If he was going to make up for that night, strategy and timing were everything. He wasn't going to test his luck.

Vanessa approached the contestants. "The *Carbon Hill Herald* would like to take pictures of each team separately."

"Smooching?" Margaret asked with a chuckle.

Vanessa scrunched up her nose by way of apology. "If you don't mind," she said and quickly flashed a worried glance at Michelle.

Ryan couldn't see Michelle's expression, but there was something about Vanessa's look that rubbed at him. Did she know what went on between him and Michelle? *All* the details?

A cold chill swept down his spine. It was likely. Women shared everything with their friends, didn't they? He didn't like the possibility of Vanessa knowing what had happened, but it was more than that.

That night didn't bring him closer to Michelle, but it did create a bond, whether she liked it or not. It went past sharing a secret. He wasn't sure how he would describe it other than being war buddies, but Michelle might take offense to that comparison.

From the corner of his eye, he saw Brandy whisper something to Clayton. Ryan was surprised to see the guy's ears turn bright pink. Just when he was beginning to wonder if Clayton's glasses were going to melt, Clayton grabbed Brandy and dipped her over his arm.

The crowd broke out into a cheer as Clayton planted a big kiss on Brandy. Ryan had never thought that guy had any showmanship, but that stunt was worthy of a movie star.

When he saw the Aschenbrenners go in for a more sedate peck, even though the newspaper reporter was still snapping away at Brandy and Clayton, Ryan knew there was no graceful way Michelle could avoid his kiss. To be honest, he didn't want to help her find a way out.

She slowly turned toward him, as if she knew what was required of her and was resigned to the fact.

"We don't have to," Ryan said quietly. The last thing he wanted to do was kiss an unwilling partner. Despite his playboy reputation, his mouth was going to slide off of her if she didn't respond. He kind of wanted her to express a degree of enthusiasm.

"It's no big deal."

Kissing him was no big deal? Ouch. No time like the present to convince her otherwise. But he wasn't going to swoop in and grab this opportunity.

He reached up and cradled her face. His hands seemed dark and huge against her exquisite beauty. Ryan gently swept the side of his thumb against her soft cheek, watching her eyelashes flutter down as she looked away.

The noise from the crowd spiraled into a faint buzz as Ryan stroked her mouth with his thumb. He drew slow, lazy circles against her lips. His thumb prickled with heat as anticipation coiled tight against his ribs.

His patience was rewarded when Michelle parted her lips. Triumph roared through Ryan, but he ruthlessly reined in his impulses and gently brushed his mouth over hers. He heard her gasp at the first touch. He knew how she felt.

The magic was still there.

His first instinct was to capture the magic before it vanished. His fingers flexed against her jaw, just as he was about to deepen the kiss. He stopped himself in the nick of time.

Instead, he outlined the edge of her lip with his mouth. Tasting, savoring. The hunger inside him grew fierce and powerful, but his shaky restraint wouldn't allow him to indulge. No matter how much he wanted to.

Especially when Michelle kissed him back. Hot need leapt through him, unleashed, as her tongue swept his bottom lip. His muscles clenched, his fingers shook against her skin as he pulled back. He was not going to devour her. Not yet.

And he wasn't going to cave as she darted her tongue between his lips. His breath hitched in his lungs as she explored. He was trying not to capture the tip of her tongue and suck hard when he heard the insistent whir of a digital camera next to his ear.

Michelle jumped back, clearly startled. She looked as if she was ready to bolt. Ryan wrapped his arm around her waist, feeling clumsy and disoriented, and held her against his side.

"And now," Vanessa said to the rowdy audience, "to start our scavenger hunt, the couples will be given their first clue."

An assistant, who looked as if she had to be related to the Mueller family on C Street, gave a sealed envelope to each female contestant.

"Are you guys ready?" Vanessa asked.

Everyone said yes, but Michelle seemed to give more of a shrug. Ryan looked away, his heart still pounding from the kiss, when he noticed Brandy discreetly running her fingernail along the envelope flap. Some people were taking this challenge way too seriously.

"What about you guys?" Vanessa asked the crowd, who cheered loudly. "All right, then. On your mark . . . get set . . . go!"

While Margaret and Brandy tore open the envelope, Michelle neatly sliced open the flap and removed the card. Ryan read over her shoulder. "Experience keeps a dear school, but fools will learn in no other."

O . . . kay . . .

Michelle looked up at him, her eyes wide and anxious. "I have no idea what this means."

"That makes two of us." Ryan glanced at the other contestants. "How much you want to bet no one else gets this
riddle?"

Michelle looked at the paper again and frowned. "I
think it's a quote."

"What does it say?" someone with a deep, masculine
voice yelled from the crowd.

"Yeah, tell us what it says!"

Vanessa plucked the card from Michelle's hand. "I'll
read it out loud, but no one yell out the answer, okay?"

After she received a cacophony of consent, Vanessa read
the quote. The townspeople stared back at her, their expressions mirroring Ryan's own confusion. No chance of them
spilling the beans.

Ryan bet they didn't envy him right about now. He should
have known the chance for a big money prize wouldn't have
been as easy as "go here" and "go there."

Not that he was doing it for the big bucks. It would have
been a nice bonus. But, hey, he had just as much of a chance
as the other contestants.

"The first couple to get there will have a head start on
the next task. Good luck!" Vanessa said and walked off the
stage, heading for the next scheduled festival event.

"Great," Michelle said as she stuffed the first clue into
her jacket pocket. "Might as well give up now."

Ryan pumped his fist in the air. "That's the spirit." He
moved to get off the stage, but another team blocked their
way.

Brandy stared down Michelle. "I didn't know you were
in town," she said, bristling with such anger that Ryan was
ready to step between the two women.

"Just for the festival," Michelle replied and turned to
Brandy's partner. "Clayton! It's good to see you."

Ryan watched Michelle hug the other man and jealousy
flashed through him. It had been a while since he felt any-

thing like that and he wasn't prepared for it. All he knew was that he wished Michelle greeted him that way. Hell, the dazzling smile would have been enough.

Clayton caught Ryan's eye and immediately backed off. Ryan had no idea what his expression gave away, but it made the other man move fast.

"Michelle and I go way back," Clayton said, readjusting his glasses.

Ryan felt his eyebrow go up. The jealousy flashed hotter and it took some effort to remain still.

Clayton turned pale. "I—I was her history tutor all through high school."

"Oh, come on. You were more than that to me," Michelle said in a chiding tone, oblivious to Clayton's panicked look. "Remember when—"

"We have to go," Brandy interrupted. She grabbed Clayton's arm and hauled him away. "Good luck," she said over her shoulder. "You're going to need it."

"She's right, you know," Michelle said as she watched the competitors walk away. "As much as I hate to admit it."

"Everyone needs luck," Ryan said. "There's nothing wrong with that."

Michelle rolled her eyes. "Right," she muttered as she sat down on the stage step.

"We have just as much of a chance to win this scavenger hunt as they do."

"Uh-uh." She pulled out her cell phone from her jacket. "I believe that as much as I believe the Wirts really did hide millions of dollars in one of those river bluff caves."

Ryan frowned. "Huh?"

Michelle looked up from her phone and groaned. "Don't tell me you believe there really is hidden treasure in Carbon Hill."

Ryan shrugged. "Sure, why not?" Obviously Michelle thought in terms of probability. He viewed it from a different angle. To his way of thinking, why *shouldn't* there be buried treasure?

Anyway, it was fun knowing there was something important and wonderful waiting to be found. He liked the idea of possibilities. Of hidden opportunities waiting to be revealed.

Michelle muttered something he couldn't catch. "What was that?" he asked.

"Never mind," Michelle said and continued pushing buttons on her cell phone.

"You know, when I said we had a chance of winning, I wasn't saying it's going to be easy," Ryan admitted. "I'll be honest with you. I have no idea what that clue is about or how to approach it."

"Join the club," Michelle said, staring intently at her cell phone.

"But we can figure it out. We will."

"Yeah, eventually." Michelle's fingers flew over the phone buttons. "Like after everyone else."

"Our opponents are not that good. We are just as smart and just as capable as they are."

"Clayton is a genius and the Aschenbrenners are into puzzles, games, and trivia," Michelle said, still tapping away at her phone. "Not to mention that all three are also members of the Historical Society."

Ryan did a double take. "Carbon Hill has a Historical Society?"

Michelle looked up. "See? You didn't even know that." She went back to her phone. "We are going to be left in the dust," she muttered her prediction.

"No, we're not," he said with a hint of steel in his voice. "Once you get off that phone, we can go hit this Historical Society and ask—"

"Benjamin Franklin."

Okay. The stress from competition had already affected her brain. "What about him?"

"He made that quote."

"How do you know that?"

"I looked it up." She waved the phone under his nose.

He stared at the slim electronic unit with suspicion. "Just like that?"

"I'm addicted to my cell phone," Michelle admitted as she pocketed the device, "and can navigate around it faster than Brandy can come up with a devious plan."

"Can that phone tell us what Benjamin Franklin has to do with Homer and Ida?"

"Technology isn't that advanced. Okay, let's look at what we have." She held her hands up as if she could make the world stop while she studied the puzzle. "Benjamin Franklin, Homer, and Ida."

Ryan thought about it. What could one of the leaders of the American Revolution and horseradish farmers have in common? "I got nothing."

"Me, either." She looked out onto the square, watching the last of the curiosity seekers walk away from the stage.

"Benjamin Franklin and horseradish," Ryan said.

Michelle gave him a strange look.

He shrugged. "Benjamin Franklin and trains? Train robbers? Train tracks?"

Michelle suddenly perked up. He hoped she wasn't going to pursue the train track idea. He was going to have to keep his mouth shut on the brainstorming sessions.

"Franklin is on the one-hundred-dollar bill," Michelle said. "Train robbers steal one-hundred-dollar bills."

"Yeah . . ." Ryan drew out the word. "But that doesn't tell us where to go."

"A bank? Probably Cedar Hill's First National." She jumped up and walked down the steps. "Let's go."

"No, the clue would have said something about bills or national or something along those lines. Give me the paper again."

Michelle handed him the clue and Ryan reread the quote. "Hey, wait a minute." He looked around the square, trying to get his bearings. "Isn't there a Benjamin Franklin Public School around here? I think it's an elementary school."

"Sounds vaguely familiar, but I couldn't say for sure. I went to Alexander Hamilton myself."

Ryan tapped the paper against his chin. "Do you think the Benjamin Franklin School has any connection to Homer and Ida?"

She made a face. "The school can't be that old."

Ryan wasn't so sure. "How would we find out?"

Michelle grabbed her phone again and punched a few buttons. She pressed it on her ear and held her finger up, indicating for him to wait.

"Hi, Dad," Michelle said. "Quick question. How old is the Benjamin Franklin Public School? Uh-huh . . . uh-huh . . ." She shifted from one foot to the other. "Uh-huh . . . Really?" Her face brightened.

Heat seeped inside Ryan as he watched Michelle's face. She didn't usually show her emotions, but when the hope flickered across her face, it was a breathtaking sight.

"So that means it would have been around in the early nineteen-hundreds?" She gave Ryan a thumbs-up.

Ryan felt a sense of relief flooding his chest. He had been right. They did have a chance. Maybe this scavenger hunt wouldn't be so bad after all.

Michelle had no idea this scavenger hunt was going to be so hard! She ignored the navy blue leather rubbing against her big toe and shuffled down the sidewalk. She knew the difficulty wasn't going to be from solving the clues, or the walking trek from one edge of the city limits to the other.

It was the long, uncomfortable stretches of silence that were freaking her out. Michelle snuck another look at Ryan from under her lashes. She had to do something—say something—before it drove her insane.

But it had to be a safe topic. They had already discussed the people they both knew. That hadn't lasted long since they didn't have the same circle of friends.

"So . . ." Michelle reached for another discussion thread. "What have you been doing since I saw you last?" *Naked and pissed off underneath me.*

"This and that. Nothing much." His smile dimmed. "Still working at the bowling alley."

"Oh." She did not want to discuss the bowling alley at all, under any circumstances. "And you took time off because Danny asked for a favor?" What did her brother have over Ryan? It must be something really good.

The corner of his mouth twitched. "I didn't do it for Danny."

Michelle frowned. What did that mean? "Then—"

"*Voila,*" Ryan said as they turned the corner, gesturing to the big, brick building. "Benjamin Franklin Public School."

Oh, yeah. She remembered seeing this building from time to time while growing up. There was nothing memorable about the architecture. It was just another tall brick building in a town created by bricklayers.

Ryan tilted his head to one side. "Are you sure it was around that long? I mean, it looks old, but not that old."

"Dad says Carbon Hill did a lot of renovating and additions to meet safety standards." All that work must have been done on the inside. At least she hoped so.

Ryan seemed to have trouble believing it, too. "Sure, okay." He headed for the front door. It swung open, a good sign that they had found the right location. "After you."

"Where do you think we're supposed to go?" Michelle asked, her voice echoing in the cavernous hallway. The high ceilings and detailed woodwork made her feel as though she had stepped back in time. "Should we search every room?"

Ryan sighed. "If we do that and find out we're in the wrong location, we will have lost a lot of time."

The door down the hall opened abruptly. "Hello?"

Michelle shrieked and jumped. She reeled back, colliding against Ryan's chest.

An older woman with tightly permed gray hair peeked around the door. "Oh, I apologize. I hadn't expected anyone so soon. You're with the scavenger hunt, correct?"

"Yes," Michelle said, stepping away from Ryan. She'd had no idea the guy was that solid and buff. Now wished she didn't have that type of information. "And we're the first ones here?" she asked the woman.

"That's right. Now hurry along with me. You don't want to squander your lead." She motioned them to approach the door which led them to the steps of the basement.

"I'm Dr. Doris Fielding, the principal of this school," the older woman introduced herself.

"I'm Michelle, and this is Ryan."

"What does the school have to do with Homer and Ida Wirt?" Ryan asked as they walked down the steps.

"It's where they first met," Dr. Fielding said. "Homer was from the farming community and Ida's father worked at the railroad. They both graduated eighth grade, but didn't attend any more schooling, which was common in those days."

At the foot of the stairs, Michelle saw two older women standing by a long wooden table. Photos, plastic trays, and what looked like toys littered the tabletop. Dr. Fielding escorted them to the far end.

"Now listen closely," the woman said. "Your task involves some construction and engineering."

Construction? Engineering? Dread flooded through

Michelle. Those weren't her strong points. Especially when it came to creating anything multitiered. Like cakes. Construction took time. Steady hands. Nerves of steel.

"This picture"—the principal held up a faded, black-and-white photograph of a building—"is what the Benjamin Franklin Public School looked like when Homer and Ida attended."

"I don't like the sounds of this," Michelle muttered.

"No talking, Michelle," Dr. Fielding said sternly as she picked up a color photo of building blocks. "And this picture is what you're supposed to build using the materials we are providing."

Michelle stared at the pile of miniature building material until the primary colors blurred. She was in trouble. Big trouble.

"I'm giving you three minutes to look over the picture before I take it away. No constructing at this time. Understood?"

Michelle nodded automatically. Dr. Fielding didn't have to worry about her. She wasn't going to attempt constructing any time soon.

"You may begin"—the principal looked at her watch—"now."

Michelle grabbed the picture and studied it closely. As if her life depended on it. Her fingers pinched the photo, creasing the paper.

She stared at the picture and then looked at the building pieces laid out. As far as she was concerned, none of it matched. Had they given her the right picture?

The panic began to rise. She didn't know what was wrong with her. Whenever a challenge was thrown her way, she rose to the occasion. Every time. But records were made to be broken and this scavenger hunt might be her downfall. "We are screwed."

"Ssh. If Doris hears you, she'll put you in the corner," Ryan whispered. "And since I'm supposed to go where you go, guess where that puts me. In the corner."

"I'm serious," Michelle said in a hiss. "I suck at this kind of thing."

"Then it's good you brought me along."

"You can do this?" The picture rattled in her hand.

"Definitely. Blindfolded and with one arm tied behind my back."

Michelle rolled her eyes. "You don't need to rub it in," she said as the relief coursed through her.

They heard the clatter of footsteps. Michelle looked up and saw Brandy and Clayton hurrying down the basement stairs. It was a struggle, but Michelle contained her surprise. "How did they get here so fast?" she whispered fiercely to Ryan.

He shrugged. "You said yourself that Clayton is a genius."

True, but having Brandy as his partner should have negated the intelligence factor. "I think they followed us."

"Which would be a genius move."

The principal appeared before them and snatched the picture out of Michelle's hand. "Time's up. Follow me." She scooped the building pieces in a plastic tray and motioned them to another door.

"Take this. You have to go into this room and build the replica of the Benjamin Franklin Public School." She ushered them inside the dank, windowless room. Michelle looked around and decided it had to be a custodian's office. It was small, cramped, with nothing but a rickety desk and chair.

"When you think you have done it properly, knock on the door and we will view your work," Dr. Fielding instructed. "If it's not done exactly as the picture, then you will return to this room until it's done."

Okay, fine. Michelle was more than happy to hand this assignment over to Ryan. Let him be in charge. She would hand him the pieces. She could do that.

"I forgot one thing," the older woman said. "Are either of you afraid of the dark?"

Warning trickled down her spine. "No," Michelle said. She looked at Ryan, who slowly shook his head. "Why?"

"Because the scavenger hunt organizers want you to build the replica in the dark, so we took out the lightbulb." Dr. Fielding flipped the switches, but the lights didn't go on.

Michelle's jaw dropped. "Are you kidding me?"

"No, I never kid." The principal grasped the doorknob. "Best of luck."

Michelle stared as the woman closed the door with a firm click. She watched, disbelieving, as the door snuffed out the last beam of light. She was stuck in a tiny, pitch-black room. With Ryan.

Chapter 4

Ryan blinked hard, but he couldn't see anything in the room except for the pale light outlining the door. He tried to recall how the room was situated. The desk was immediately behind him and the chair to the right. Had there been a file cabinet? He didn't want to jog his memory by walking into it.

"I don't believe this!" Michelle's indignation echoed in the small room.

"Why would they make us do this in the dark?" he asked. This assignment didn't make sense to him.

"Sexy, Carbon Hill style."

Ryan's hands clenched the tray and the pieces rattled. "What?" he asked hoarsely.

"I said it was se—" Michelle stopped abruptly. Ryan could imagine her pressing her lips together. The cold air twanged around him and goose bumps blanketed his skin.

This was not good. It was bad enough being alone in a small room with Michelle, but after that kiss, it was bad timing. Especially since the kiss was all he could think about. That, and wondering when he could kiss her again. He might not be able to see anything right now, but he had a clear memory of her soft mouth.

Yeah, he was in trouble. Big trouble.

"They wanted to make the assignment more difficult," she finished saying, her voice trailing off.

"They've succeeded." When he had suggested he could build the replica blindfolded, he had been exaggerating. Okay, he had been lying.

And why? To look good in front of Michelle. He obviously hadn't matured much since she last saw him. Was that what he wanted her to know? No. He wanted to prove that while he hadn't gone to some fancy French school, he had skills. That she was going to need him to complete this scavenger hunt.

He needed to come up with a new plan.

"I'm sure they'll have an excuse," Michelle said, her voice wrapping around him. He froze, wondering if she had moved. If she was closer.

"Yeah, probably," Ryan agreed. To what, he didn't have a clue. Nor did he have any idea about Michelle's perfume. Maybe it was her soap or shampoo. Whatever it was, the faint scent made him think of cinnamon. It smelled good. Smelled expensive.

"They'll say that the Wirts had to do all their clandestine work in the dark, but you know what? That's not why they're doing this. They are doing this to make us suffer."

"Way to face the day." He was suffering. Could feel the blood rushing from his head and pumping through his veins. He needed to leave. Now. Ryan made a cautious step toward the door.

"What they're asking for is impossible!" Michelle announced just as something like a hand glanced off Ryan's cheekbone. He flinched back and saw a spattering of stars.

Michelle's gasp ricocheted off the walls. "I'm so sorry!" Her hands fluttered against his face. "Are you okay?"

"Yeah, it's no big deal," Ryan assured her as the heel of her hand pressed against his nose. Did she really think that was his cheekbone?

To his disappointment, she pulled her hands away. "But don't you agree?" Michelle asked. "That the scavenger hunt organizers are being unreasonable?"

"Yeah, I do. So let's quit."

"What?" She said it so low and quick that he almost missed it.

"You said it yourself. It's impossible." He took another step to the door, this time holding his arm out, but his hand didn't brush up against anything. "Why knock ourselves out trying to do it?"

"We can't just quit!" Her voice rose and fell with each word.

"Sure we can. Hey, are you hungry? There's this great new restaurant on Main—"

"We are not quitting," Michelle said with surprising force.

Ryan stopped and turned toward where he heard Michelle. "Why not?"

She hesitated before replying. "Lots of reasons . . . but we're not going to get into that right now. We need to build this thing."

Ryan shook his head, even though he knew Michelle couldn't see him. "That is not gonna happen until we get some light in here."

She exhaled sharply. "It's not *that* dark."

"Oh, really?" A few minutes ago it was unreasonably dark. Amazing. "How many fingers do I have up?"

"The middle one?"

"Funny." He shuffled his feet toward the door, but Michelle snagged his shirtsleeve and quickly grasped his arm before he moved away.

"We need to try."

Ryan sighed. It sounded old and weary and he could feel it deep in his chest. He wanted to find the right time to apologize to Michelle, but that shouldn't require him to do this. It should mean sharing a cold beer at the corner bar, a couple of laughs, and a really hot kiss that ended in another kiss and another . . .

"Please, Ryan."

Aw, hell. That did it. He wasn't sure if it was the tiny catch in her voice or that she had said please. He couldn't ignore her request.

"Okay, fine," he said gruffly. "I'm stepping toward the desk. Where are you—oomph!"

He collided into her and dropped the tray. The sound of the container clanging against the floor was nothing compared to the rainfall of wood and metal pieces.

Michelle didn't say a word, even after the last metal nut spun to a standstill. The silence pulsed around them. Ryan stood frozen as a statue. *A little too late for that strategy*, Michelle decided.

She wanted to move, but she knew the way her luck was going, she'd step on a piece and it would shatter. "Which direction did they go?" she whispered.

"I'm going to guess . . . down."

"Hey!" Michelle bristled at Ryan's sarcasm. "I don't need this attitude coming from you. I'm not the one who dropped the tray."

"Get on your hands and knees."

Michelle gasped. She reared back as heat shot through her blood. The back of her knees tickled. *"Why?"*

"Because we are going to cover every inch of this floor," Ryan said, his voice sounding closer to the ground, "and find the damn tray."

A blush scorched her skin. She could feel it sizzling. Michelle decided it was better not to say a word and slowly lowered herself. There was no need to give Ryan any idea of how her imagination ran wild. Or how his command caused jitters low in her stomach.

Reaching out, she planted her hand against the floor, only to find one of the pieces. One of the *sharp* pieces, of course. "Found one," she said as she scooped it up and held it in a loose fist.

"Good," Ryan said, his voice low and husky. He sounded close. Too close. Michelle raised her head, scenting trouble. Where was he? In front of her? Behind her?

The not knowing was agony. She had to keep on her guard with Ryan. It had always been that way, even when they were casual acquaintances. Michelle looked around wildly, but she saw nothing. The beat of her heart echoed in her ears and she couldn't tell which direction the sound of clothes brushing against skin came from.

Michelle gritted her teeth as her nipples strained against her bra. She felt vulnerable, crawling around the floor with Ryan in the dark. Defenseless . . . and, much to her embarrassment, intrigued.

She had to move. Now, before he pounced. Or worse, before she went after him. "Where could they—"

She slammed against metal—that had about a million corners. This really wasn't her day. "Ouch," she said as she rubbed the sore spot on the side of her head.

"Are you okay?"

"I see dancing spots." And now that she thought about it, she preferred the darkness. "What did I hit?"

"Probably the desk."

She jerked in surprise when she felt his large hand on her thigh. "That would be my leg."

Ryan flattened his hand and skimmed up. She went rigid under his touch.

"Hip," she told him, her voice high. What was he doing? Couldn't he tell the difference between a woman's body and a piece of office furniture?

His hand cupped her side and Michelle fought the urge

to curl into him. "Waist." It came out as a warning. If he moved his hand up, he was going to find out how turned on she was. She'd rather he didn't know.

She felt Ryan lifting his palm and her choppy breath caught in her lungs. She grabbed his hand, wishing she had nails to use as a threat. Her fingers shook as she kept a tight hold on him. "What are you looking for?" she asked in a hiss.

"Your phone."

She dropped his hand in surprise. "You need to call someone? Now?"

"Turn it on," he told her. She could hear his smile in his voice. "We'll use the light."

She gave a start, her head bumping against the metal again. "We can't do that!" she said as she rubbed the sore spot again.

"Why not?"

Was he being deliberately obtuse? Wait, he had been a rule breaker growing up. She had been fascinated by that side of him. Before she knew better. "That would be cheating."

Ryan made a scoffing sound. "No, it isn't."

"Dr. Fielding said no lights." And that woman was the type with eyes in the back of her head. She'd catch them for sure.

"They didn't say anything about bringing our own lights to the party."

"It's cheating," she repeated. And she'd keep on repeating it until he got it into his head.

"No, it's not."

"Yes," she said through clenched teeth, wishing she sounded as patient as Ryan, "it is."

She heard him take a deep breath right before he changed tactics. "Do you really want to spend more time in this room?"

Good point. She stuffed her hands into her pockets, by-passing the hard candy and paper she seemed to accumulate every time she wore the jean jacket. "Here's the phone."

"You keep it."

Oh, sure. Have her handle the incriminating piece of evidence. "But we're going to get caught and then we're going to be disqualified."

"Explain why that would be a bad thing."

Well, he had her there. Michelle turned on the phone. The eerie green light didn't go far. She held it to the floor and moved it around. "Found the tray."

Ryan grabbed the tray. "Okay, now the pieces."

"How many are there?"

"I don't know, but I'm sure we'll find them all. The room isn't that big."

The room wasn't that large, but neither was her phone. By the time they collected all the pieces, her knees and elbows were sore, and she really wished the custodian swept the floor once in a while.

"Aim the light at the tray and I'll put the pieces together," Ryan said. "We'll be done in no time."

Michelle shifted her bottom jaw to the side. "Your optimism is beginning to annoy me."

"We have just as much chance as everyone else."

"Right." She aimed the light at the tray.

"And of all people to be pessimistic," he muttered as he swiftly put the pieces together.

"Huh?" She had been distracted by his hands. They were large and lean. Just like someone who worked with their hands a lot and knew how to use them. "What was that?"

His hands stilled. "Never mind," he said and worked faster. His fingers were a blur.

"What's that supposed to mean?" She wasn't allowed to be cynical? Well, she had news for him.

"Nothing." His hands didn't skip a beat as the replica grew. It was mesmerizing.

"You better tell me."

"Or what?" he asked, his voice laced with amusement.

"Or . . . or . . ." Okay, she had nothing. "I'm serious. Why did you say that?"

"Someone who has the Midas touch shouldn't be pessimistic."

Michelle almost dropped the phone. The light zigzagged as she held it steady. "Midas touch?"

"You are Carbon Hill's golden girl."

And therefore everything came easy for her? She wished! "You don't know what you're talking about. I have worked hard—"

Michelle stopped and pulled back. Her fingers tightened around the phone. Now was not the time to discuss this. She quickly changed the subject. "Are you sure that matches the picture exactly?"

He paused and Michelle assumed he was studying the replica one last time. "No, I'm not positive."

She waited, but he had nothing to add. That was it? That was all he had to say? Was there anything else they could do? "Then?" Michelle said, hoping to prompt him.

She sensed Ryan's shrug. "We'll do it again and we will eventually get it right."

Michelle clucked her tongue. "There's that optimism again."

Ryan chose to ignore her comment. "Guide me to the door," he said as he took the tray, "and then hide your phone."

"Why would I have to hide it if it's not cheating?" she asked as they slowly made their way to the door. She pocketed the electronic device before pounding her fist against the solid door.

It swung open, the sudden light blinding as the shadowy figure of Dr. Fielding stood before them. Michelle winced and blinked until she could see the older woman's features.

"Well," Dr. Fielding said in a haughty tone that made Michelle feel sorry for any schoolkid who dared to be tardy. "We were beginning to worry about you two."

Ryan flashed a crooked smile and presented the replica with a flourish. "Here you are."

"I have to inspect and compare it with the photo, so please put it on the table next to the others."

"Others?" Michelle and Ryan parroted. She looked at the table and saw two replicas of the Benjamin Franklin School.

"The other teams are on to the next assignment," Dr. Fielding explained as she escorted them to the table. Ryan slid their project onto the table, silently staring at the competition's handiwork.

Michelle's mouth dropped open. "No. Way."

"It's true." Dr. Fielding tipped her eyeglasses as she leaned down to study their offerings.

"By how many minutes?" Michelle wasn't sure if she wanted the answer, but it would be a special brand of torture if she didn't know how close or far away they were with their competitors.

Dr. Fielding paused from her inspection and looked over the rim of her glasses. "I don't believe I'm allowed to give out that kind of information."

Translation: a lot. Michelle struggled not to show her disappointment.

Ryan shifted impatiently as Dr. Fielding studied every minute detail of their assignment. The urgency to run and catch up with the others started to build inside Michelle. Couldn't this woman work any faster?

But what if the replica wasn't exact? Michelle didn't even want to think about it. She would go back in the dark room and try again, but she wouldn't be sweet about it. And it was going to take more to convince Ryan to do the same. That would be harder than reconstructing the damn thing.

Dr. Fielding straightened and looked at them. "The replica is exact to the photo. You have passed this level and may proceed to the playground, where you will be given instructions for your next assignment."

Michelle didn't have time to sag with relief. Ryan startled her when he grabbed her by the wrist. She was even more surprised that she didn't yank away. The sight of his large hand curling around her made her feel fizzy inside.

"C'mon," he said, tugging her toward the stairs. They hurried to the main floor, the metal steps clattering under their feet.

Once they got to the hallway, Ryan headed for the back of the building. Michelle tried to keep up, but was all too aware of how her shoes rubbed against her feet.

"You do realize that the other teams cheated?" Michelle asked in a hissing whisper. "No way could they have finished so quickly."

"You don't know that for sure."

"I don't know what the Aschenbrenners did, but Clayton probably used his watch. I saw it this morning and it was sweet. It definitely had a powerful light."

"If that's cheating," Ryan said as he peered down one hallway before taking another route, "then you need to remember that we cheated, too."

That didn't make her feel better. "Yeah, well . . . they cheated first."

"No, they cheated better."

"What is the rush?" Michelle asked, wincing as Ryan made a hard right turn when she wasn't expecting it. Her feet were killing her. "It's not like we're going to win this thing."

"You keep saying that." Ryan looked over his shoulder. "Is there something you know that I don't?"

Now, there's a leading question . . . "You really want that treasure chest, huh?"

"I really want to be able to walk around town with my head held high," he muttered.

Must not have had to handle many disastrous one-night stands. Michelle scrunched up her face when she realized how snarky she was being. God, she was making up for lost time. She hadn't given it too much thought all these years, and then, bam! It was constantly on her mind.

She really had to stop holding it against him. Most of the women she knew didn't have a good first time, and if they had the chance, they would have done things differently. Like made the guy work harder for it, or gone for a different guy completely.

She didn't want anything like that. It wasn't as if Ryan had cheated her out of anything. Although, now that she thought about it, he could have been nicer on the way home. He didn't have to make her feel as though she did something horribly wrong. The way he went on about it, she had started to wonder if she caused him permanent damage. And he definitely didn't need to make her think that there was something wrong with her.

Nope, Michelle thought as she glared at Ryan's back. She changed her mind. She had every right to be snarky. In fact, she should be snarkier.

An older man dressed in faded overalls and a baseball cap so worn she couldn't make out the advertisement greeted them at the playground door. "You guys the final team?"

"I guess so," Michelle answered reluctantly. She couldn't believe they had lost their lead. She hoped they could make up for it on this task.

"Good. Here is your next assignment." He handed the envelope to Michelle. Ryan dropped his hold so she could rip it open. She frowned as she read the card.

"Tell me it's not another riddle," Ryan said.

"Homer and Ida had several friends living in Carbon Hill," Michelle read out loud. "While it was never proven that they assisted the Wirts, people around here called them the Butcher, the Baker, and the Candlestick Maker." She looked up from the paper. "Well, they don't get extra bonus points for originality. Why were they called these names?"

The old man hooked his thumbs behind his overall straps. "Dunno. All you need to do is find out who these people were. Then visit what had been their homes and you'll get a piece of a map."

Michelle closed her eyes and tried not to whimper. Did they have to make everything so freaking difficult? Couldn't they just give her the address and be satisfied?

"Once you put the map together," the old man continued, "you'll find your final destination for the night."

"Great." The word dragged from her throat.

"At least it's not a riddle," Ryan pointed out.

Michelle turned and looked at him. Could he spare her? She didn't want to see the brighter side right now. "We have to walk all over town. This could take us until tomorrow."

"You don't have to walk," the man told her. "The organizers offered transportation on this leg of the hunt."

"Oh, thank goodness." Michelle thwacked her palm against her forehead and sighed with relief.

"Meet Lucifer." The old man gestured to the side of the school. When she spotted the horse—the big, black, snorting horse—she went rigid.

Ryan seemed to pick up on her attitude change immediately. "What's wrong?" he asked, for her ears only.

Michelle started to back away. "I can't ride that thing." She couldn't take her eyes off of the animal. There was no telling what the creature would do if she turned her back.

Ryan placed his arm around her shoulders and held her firmly. As if he knew she was going to bolt. "It'll be fine," he assured her.

She shook her head side to side. "No, I don't think you understand. I would rather eat a bucket of raw horseradish than get on"—she pointed a shaky finger at the horse—"that thing."

"Michelle."

"No. No. No." She folded her arms tightly across her chest and ground her heels into the playground's trampled grass. "I can't do it and you can't make me. You know what? I quit!"

Chapter 5

"You're quitting over a horse?"

Ryan's disbelief rang in Michelle's ears. It probably did seem strange since she had told him that they weren't quitting. And had sounded as though she wouldn't budge on her position.

And she had meant it, too. But he didn't realize that there were special circumstances. Like horses. Big ones that looked as if they could knock you down with the flick of their tails. "I can't ride it."

He stroked her upper arm. "Sure, you can."

Michelle was already shaking her head. "No, you don't understand."

"It's going to be okay." His voice was kind and gentle. Ryan was being very patient. And that was making her very suspicious. He was probably figuring out the best way to throw her onto the horse like a burlap sack.

"Have you ridden before?" Ryan asked.

"Yes," she answered with false brightness, "and I have fallen before, too."

His hands curled around her shoulders. "The rule is to get right back on the horse."

"I did that," she said as she hunched. "I rode it all the way back to the stable, got off, and never looked back. It's amazing how easy one can get through life without riding a horse."

"Guess what?" He stepped behind Michelle and propelled her toward the horse. "You're going to break that streak today."

"If I do that, I'll break more than a streak," Michelle predicted as she dug her heels in, feeling the dirt spraying behind her.

She noticed that they were getting closer to the horse. Her strength was no match for Ryan's. She hooked her legs around his knees.

Ryan halted before he fell. "Michelle," he warned. She responded by hooking her elbows with his. "This is ridiculous."

"Easy for you to say." She looked at the old man who was watching her as if he saw panicked women every day. "Am I required to ride that horse?"

He adjusted the dingy brim of his hat and he pondered the question. "Probably."

You're a big help, mister. "Well, unless the organizers officially demand it, to my face, I will walk beside Satan here."

"Lucifer," the man corrected.

"Same thing." It was a nice compromise. They would use the horse and she wasn't quitting. A very mature handling of a crisis if she did say so herself.

Ryan disentangled himself from Michelle. "You can't keep up with this horse."

"Excuse me? Are you saying I can't hold my own with a horse?" She glanced at the old man. "No offense. I'm sure it's a fine animal."

"Uh . . . none taken."

"Yeah," Ryan said. "That's what I'm saying."

"You're wrong." Michelle folded her arms across her

chest and looked at Ryan in the eye. He really did have gorgeous eyes. It was unfair.

"You really want to crisscross town on foot in those shoes?" He gestured at her feet.

Michelle remained still although her toe started to throb harder from all the attention. "Yes. More than I want to ride that horse."

He held his hand up. "Enough arguing. You're wasting time. Get up on this horse. I'll help you."

Michelle held her ground when she really wanted to make a run for it. She had a feeling he could catch up with her easily. "The other teams couldn't have gone far on their horses."

"They don't have horses," the old man said.

Michelle's and Ryan's heads swiveled. "*What?*" they asked in unison.

"First team out got first pick of transportation," he explained. "I thought you guys knew that."

Michelle closed her eyes and pinched the bridge of her nose, warding off a hell of a headache. "What were the other choices?" she asked with unnatural calm.

"Well"—the man rubbed his stubbly chin with his hand as he remembered—"the Aschenbrenners came out first. They picked the bikes."

"They got bikes?" Michelle cried out. She turned to Ryan. "I could have ridden a bike!"

"You never fell off of one of those before?"

Michelle closed her mouth with a snap. She glared at him, but his smile only grew bigger. The man had no idea that falling off a horse was a completely different thing than taking a tumble from a bike.

"Then the Rasmussen girl and the quiet guy came out right after the Aschenbrenners," the old man said. "They took the car."

"Car?" Michelle blinked and she tilted her head closer, to hear better. "I'm sorry. I thought I heard you say the word 'car'?"

"I sure did. Don't know what kind it was. An old, beaten-up jalopy, just like the one the Wirts had."

"Wait a second," Ryan said. "I don't understand. If the Aschenbrenners came out first, why didn't they take the car?"

The old man gave him a sly look. "Have you ever drove a car built in the nineteen-twenties?"

"No."

"I had a feeling. Because you're asking me that question."

Michelle and Ryan looked at each other and shrugged. Just what she needed. A guy talking in code.

"Come on, Michelle." Ryan wrapped his hand around her arm. "We've wasted enough time. Get on the horse."

She removed his hand. "I'm walking." She headed for the street. Her feet were going to pay the price for the brisk pace, but she had a point to make.

She sensed Ryan following her on horseback. Michelle sighed with relief. He had backed off. For now.

"Fine," Ryan said. "Then you can clean up after the horse. Now, do you have any idea of where we're going?"

"No," she admitted. She was probably walking in the wrong direction.

"The butcher, the baker, the candlestick maker," Ryan mused out loud.

"Knaves all three," Michelle finished. She never did like that nursery rhyme.

"What is a knave?"

Michelle shrugged. "No clue." She looked over and noticed that Ryan seemed very comfortable on the big, black horse. The big, black horse that was too close to her. Michelle moved to the far end of the sidewalk.

"One option," Ryan said, "is that we find out who are the current butcher and baker and—"

"Candlestick maker? Does Carbon Hill still have one?" Did they ever have one?

"There's a fancy candle shop off Church Street."

"Hmm . . ." Michelle thought about it and shook her head. "No. That's way too easy."

"Do you remember anything Mother Goose around here?" Ryan asked. "A nursery school or a shop?"

"We are not going to get off that lucky." Michelle reached for her phone. "I'm going to call the local library. They might know who the Wirts' friends were."

Michelle searched for the phone number and dialed it, trying really hard not to notice every sound and smell of the horse. She hoped they weren't required to use it for the rest of the hunt.

"Carbon Hill Library," a young woman answered. "Elizabeth Finch speaking."

"Hi, Elizabeth. This is Michelle Nelson—"

"Oh!" the librarian squealed. "Michelle Nelson! You're the celebrity chef."

Michelle's eyes widened. What had her mother been saying about her? "No! I'm a pastry chef for a restaurant in Chicago." Pastry. Celebrity. They sounded similar . . . ish. "I'm participating in the scavenger hunt—"

"And judging the horseradish recipes," Elizabeth added. "Everyone is very excited about that."

How did she know that already? "I'm looking forward to judging," Michelle lied. "But about the hunt . . ."

"Yes?"

"I need some background on the Wirts' cronies. Particularly the ones that were called the Butcher, the Baker, and the Candlestick Maker. Do you know where we could get that information?"

"Let me look that up," the librarian offered. "I can call you right back."

"That would be great." Michelle gave her the number, so thankful she didn't have to walk any more than necessary.

"By the way," Elizabeth said, "how do you feel about gelatin molds?"

Michelle pressed the phone harder against her ear. "Excuse me?"

"Gelatin molds."

What was she asking? Did she like them? Have a gelatin philosophy? "I'm . . . not . . . against them."

"I entered my family's recipe in the horseradish contest."

"Oh . . ." Michelle felt increasingly lost in the conversation. "Did you now?"

"Lemon-lime gelatin with cottage cheese, pineapple chunks, and horseradish. Lots of horseradish," Elizabeth added proudly.

Michelle swallowed roughly. "Mmm. Tasty." There was a pause and she wasn't sure what the librarian expected from her. "I'll keep an eye out for it."

"Wonderful! I'll get right back to you."

Michelle ended the connection and slowly put the phone in her jacket pocket.

"Anything wrong?"

She glanced in Ryan's direction, but saw the horse looking at her. She turned to face straight ahead. "I think I was just bribed."

She heard Ryan's chuckle and imagined his smile. Crooked with a faint dimple. "Did you accept?" he asked.

Michelle halted and clapped her hand over her mouth. Oh, God. Did she? "I'm not sure."

Ryan leaned against the white picket fence and glanced up when he heard the old-fashioned streetlight buzzing to life. It was going to get dark fast and they hadn't started on the last leg of the assignment.

Worse, they hadn't seen the other teams for a while. The Aschenbrenners had zipped by them on their bicycles two hours ago. Earlier, he and Michelle had passed the other team undetected. Clayton and Brandy had been too busy cursing over their stalled car.

"Whoo-hoo!"

Ryan paused. Was that Michelle? Could it be that she was having some fun with this hunt? Perish the thought. He turned to look at the small brick house and saw Michelle wave a fragment of paper as if it were a flag.

"We got the final piece of the map!" she called out to him, limping her way down the brick path. She raised her arms in victory. "Yes!"

Ryan smiled as her jubilant expression tugged at his heart. That was the old Michelle Nelson. Ready to take the world by storm.

"Okay," she said as she approached him. "Give me the other papers and then we will be on our way."

After he gave her the map fragments they had acquired, she knelt down on the sidewalk and arranged the papers. Then rearranged them. Again and again, her movements growing impatient. "Shoot. Why isn't this working? This should be simple."

"Because it's not a traditional map." Ryan crouched down. "Let me do it."

"Thanks." She leaned back and frowned. Glancing over his shoulder, she asked, "Where's Beelzebub?"

"If you're talking about the horse," Ryan said as he concentrated on putting the map together, "I tied Lucifer to the hitching post down there."

Michelle made a little huff. "Only Carbon Hill would have hitching posts."

Ryan pointed at the small sign on the corner. "It's here because this is the historic district."

He had noticed Michelle's disparaging comments about Carbon Hill as they went from one corner of town to the other. He had heard plenty about how tiny and suffocating the town was. The many empty storefronts and the all-around shabbiness.

He could have pointed out the strong sense of community, the pride of heritage, and a bunch of other things, but she'd just accuse him of being optimistic. Like it was a bad thing.

He fitted the last map piece and studied the markings. "There we are." He tapped at the symbol and then slid his finger down an artistic interpretation of a country road. "And this is where we need to go."

"Where, exactly, is 'this'?" She moved closer to see. "How far away do you think it is?"

"Past the cemetery." The autumn breeze pulled at them and he caught the faintest whiff of expensive cinnamon.

"*Way* past the cemetery."

"Looks like farmland." Ryan picked up the pieces and stood up. "The Wirts' farm, I bet."

"That would make sense." Michelle rose to her full height. He couldn't believe that she only reached to his shoulder. She had always seemed taller. Larger than life.

"Do you know where it is?" she asked as they headed for the horse, who was snacking on some weeds.

"Yep. The Wirts' only living relative turned the home into a bed and breakfast."

"Really? Why would someone come to Carbon Hill for a bed and breakfast?"

Ryan ignored that. He was getting the feeling that Michelle was trying to convince herself of something. "We have to go across town and pass the city limits. You're going to need to ride the horse."

Michelle squeezed her eyes shut. It appeared she wanted to whimper. Stomp her foot. He bet the only thing stopping her was a big blister on her heel.

"I'll hold on to you," he promised. He knew he was asking a lot from her and he would do whatever was necessary to make it easier.

Her eyelids flew open in surprise. "You're riding the horse, too?"

Ryan frowned. He thought that was a given. "The horse can take the both of us."

"But . . ."

"I'm not walking." He needed to make that point clear. "And it will take too long."

Michelle stared at the horse and Ryan could feel her wavering. He was not going to let her walk anymore. She had taken her stance too far. He needed to step in and he was angry with himself for not doing it sooner.

"C'mon." He stood behind her and placed his hands on her waist. She felt small and delicate. A wave of protectiveness crashed through him. "I won't let anything happen to you."

She looked over her shoulder at him, the move sharp and swift. She immediately looked back at the horse, but it was too late. He had seen her eyes. He knew that what he said got to her.

But he didn't know why it did. Because no one ever told her that? Or was it because no one ever had to?

She grabbed the saddle horn and clambered onto Lucifer. Her mount wasn't going to be the envy of any equestrian, but it got her up.

The horse shied and backed up. Ryan saw Michelle's knuckles whiten as she gripped the horn. He quickly untied the reins from the hitching post and gave them to Michelle so he could mount.

He saw how her hands trembled. Something inside him twisted at the sight. He got on the horse as quickly as he could and took the reins.

Michelle dropped them gratefully. Her hands slapped against the pummel and he bet they weren't going to leave the spot for the remainder of the ride.

Ryan wrapped his arm around her, holding her firmly. She felt good in his arms, nestled against him. But he wasn't sure how she would react. He hadn't realized he'd been holding his breath until he felt Michelle slightly relax against him.

He slowly exhaled as his body tightened. It was going to be a long ride.

Michelle didn't think she could take much more of this. She had thought the fear would subside after a few minutes, but no such luck. Her heart felt as if it was going to burst from her skin. Her mouth was dry with panic as her stomach twisted in knots.

She wanted off the horse so badly. Michelle knew that once she got off, she'd kiss the ground or faint dead away. And she would never, ever get on a horse again, even if it meant she couldn't complete the scavenger hunt.

The horse paused at the crest of the hill. The sun was setting, the streaks of orange and red reminding her of the fallen leaves. For one brief moment, Michelle forgot all about the horse as she drank in the sight. She sighed with pleasure as she saw the miles of wide-open space.

It was as though she could breathe again. Get some elbow room. Off and on during the day, it had felt as if Carbon Hill was closing in on her.

"Been a while since you've been back," Ryan said. He

hadn't said much during the ride, which suited her perfectly. It was as if he knew exactly what she needed.

"Yep."

He clicked his tongue and the horse moved. Downhill. Michelle closed her eyes and burrowed closer to Ryan, where it was safe, warm, but far from comfortable.

"What kept you?" he asked.

Michelle frowned at the question. Kept her? As if she had been expected to come back. That had never been the plan. "After I trained in France, I started my apprenticeship. I couldn't get that here."

"Where'd you go?"

The names of towns and restaurants flickered through her mind at warp speed. "Everywhere." It seemed that way. Just when she got used to the routine, something would happen and another restaurant would bite the dust. It didn't matter how hard they worked, or how many hours they put in, or how tightly they wrung the passion right out of their bones; nothing was guaranteed in this business.

"Doesn't sound like you had a lot of fun."

"I did. I mean, I do." Even to her ears she sounded defensive. It was exciting, inspiring, nerve-wracking, and stressful. She had left home and everything familiar to find out what she had in her and what she could accomplish.

It was the hardest thing she had ever done and she had been so proud that she survived. But now she knew that the hard part of her career was only beginning.

"Is that why you're back now?"

Why did he think her career had anything to do with her visit? It wasn't as though every waking moment and decision was based on her job.

Okay, maybe it was. But he didn't need to know that. "I'm here because Vanessa asked me."

"Uh-huh." Ryan wasn't taking that answer at face value. "And she didn't ask you before?"

"This is different. She needs me here." Michelle didn't know why she felt compelled to explain it to Ryan. He wouldn't understand. Hell, she didn't understand it herself.

"And you now have the time to come home?" he asked. "Just like that?"

Ha! She'd had a lot of difficulty taking the time off. "What point are you driving at?"

"I think there's more to it. To you being home," he clarified. "I know you're here to help Vanessa, but I think it's only one part of the puzzle."

"What are you saying? That I'm homesick?" He was digging too close to the truth. "Feeling nostalgic? You're way off the mark, Ryan. I'm immune to stuff like that."

"No, it's not nostalgia. Close, but not quite. But I'll figure it out."

"Oh, joy. I can't wait." *And when you figure it out, tell me the answer.* "Hey, that farmhouse has a sign out front. I bet it's the Wirts' place."

"Or maybe your cynicism is meant to hide your deepest, darkest secret. That you really want to win the scavenger hunt," Ryan teased.

Michelle chuckled, inhaling the smoky scent of autumn. "Yeah. You got me. I'll do anything for that gift certificate at the Knitting Korner."

"Thought so."

"What about you?"

"I don't knit."

"No," Michelle said with a smile as she tried to imagine that. "Why did you agree to do the scavenger hunt?"

"Ah, well, that's a simple answer. I heard you needed a partner."

"And you volunteered? Just like that?" Why would he do a favor for her? She would have thought he'd keep his distance.

"Well . . ." He drew the word out, as if he didn't know how to broach the subject. "You see, I do have an ulterior motive."

Michelle tensed, all flirty feelings and smiles vanished. "I should have known. You tell me this *now* when I'm in the middle of *nowhere* on top of a *horse*."

"Yeah, it's called strategy." His hand spanned against her stomach. "Stop tensing up or you'll scare Lucifer."

If only she could. And if only she could slap him away. But that would mean letting go of the saddle. "What do you want?"

"First to say I'm sorry."

"About what?"

Ryan hesitated. "About that night."

Aw, man. Of all the times to bring up that subject! "I don't want to talk about it." Her hands gripped the saddle horn tightly. Her palms burned and she vaguely wondered if she would find welts on her skin later.

"But then," Ryan continued, his voice low and seductive, "after kissing you, I got to thinking . . ."

"That's always a bad sign." She knew kissing him had been a mistake. Bad things always happened when you caved in to peer pressure.

"What we had five years ago is still between us. Stronger than ever." His thumb slipped under her shirt hem. She gasped when his cold skin touched her warm stomach. "And I want that."

"Oh?" She stretched the word into long syllables. She should shut him up. Quiet him before he said something that he couldn't take back.

"I want a second chance."

A thousand possibilities bombarded her mind. Each one required them to get naked. She was making assumptions. She knew she was. The guy had to be more specific. "A second chance on what?"

"You and me."

"Are you insane?" her voice rang out. Lucifer's ears perked up but he kept plodding on.

"No," he answered. His mouth was next to her ear and his warm breath tickled her skin. It would tickle even more if he darted his tongue in her ear and then blew against it. Not that she wanted him to do that.

"What's insane is this hunt," Ryan said. "We had to show up and we've kept our promise. There is no reason to keep going."

He had a point. Of course, he made it *after* she got on the horse.

Ryan's thumb stroked her stomach. She knew he could feel her muscles bunching under his soft touch.

"I say let's bail," he whispered, "head back to my place, and start where we left off."

Michelle's eyes were wide with disbelief. Start where they left off *five years ago?* After that disaster? Was he serious? She wasn't going to jump at his offer.

Then again . . . Michelle swallowed hard as she became acutely aware of every slope and angle of Ryan as he sat behind her. She vividly remembered his sleek muscles and inquisitive mouth.

They could start where they left off and erase that night. See how good they could have been together. Would it be as good as she had hoped for?

But what if it turned out to be just as bad? Or worse? Well, for one thing, she wouldn't be as devastated. But was she ready to take that risk?

Ryan was right about one thing. There was something still there between them. It was stronger and ignoring that wasn't going to make it go away.

"So," Ryan said, his mouth pressed against her ear. "What do you say?"

Chapter 6

Michelle pulled away. "Stop the horse!"

"Uh . . . that wasn't a choice."

"Right now, or . . . or . . ." Her spine was ramrod straight, but she was still too close to him. Every breath she took was short and shallow.

Oh, jeez. What had she been thinking? She was tempted to raise a shaky hand to her forehead and see if there was a dew of cold sweat. The kind a person got after a close call. She needed to be on the defense. She had almost caved!

All to sleep with Ryan Slater? After all that had happened? It was laughable. And here she was, considering his offer!

Why? Just because his kiss made her turn to mush like it always did. Or that he had the most amazing tongue and he was really too hot and sexy for his own good? And . . . why was she saying no, again?

"Or?" Ryan prompted her.

Or what? Oh, right. My God, the guy managed to rattle her so fast and furious, she couldn't think straight. "Or . . . I'll jump." She cautiously looked down. It was pretty far. It wasn't going to be pretty.

Ryan snorted with laughter. "Yeah, right."

"I mean it," she said in a growl and watched with horror as the horse's ears twitched.

"I'm sure you do." He patted his hand against her stomach before sliding it out from under her shirt hem. "Not going to happen when you have a death grip on the saddle."

It was true. She tried to let go, to show that she meant business, but the way the horse was swaying side to side, it was not a good idea.

"But since you're prepared to take a nosedive because of my offer," he said as he took the reins with both hands, "I'm going to assume you're refusing."

"There is no way—no freaking way—we are ever going to sleep together again." She couldn't believe she was telling it to him bluntly. Was it because she didn't have to look at him? She wasn't going to question it further, but rather go with it. "And you want to know why?"

"I have a few ideas," he answered dryly.

"Because after the last time, you put all the blame on me." The emotions, dormant for so long, began to swirl inside her. "And, you know what? I believed you back then. Because I figured you knew what you were talking about. Why shouldn't I? Every girl you dated raved about you."

"I'm—"

"And it took me a while to get over that. It's a good thing I did." She regretted not getting over it faster than she had. "I should have been living it up in France. France, for goodness sakes! The place where romance and love and sex were created."

"I wouldn't go that far," Ryan muttered.

"I should have treated the place like a kid in the candy store. But no. I didn't. More like a kid with an allergy to sugar. Because there I was, thinking something was seriously wrong with me."

"Okay, okay. I got it."

"No, you don't." He had no concept. He had no idea

what it was like. "That was my first time, Ryan. Did you know that?"

He was silent for a moment. "It occurred to me. But by that time, it was too late to say anything because you were long gone."

Michelle cringed. She didn't want to know what had tipped him off. What other mistake had she made? No. She wasn't revisiting the past in any way, shape, or form.

"It was a first for me, too," Ryan said. "The first time I couldn't . . . the first time something went wrong and I didn't know what to do about it."

Michelle rolled her eyes. Yeah, it didn't take a rocket scientist to have figured that one out. He had handled it badly. And it had shocked her. The Ryan she had loved and wanted was charming and a gentleman. Thoughtful and had a sense of humor. The way he had acted went against everything she knew about him.

"And," Ryan continued, "I would like to point out that it hasn't happened since."

Just like a man to make that point. Michelle shifted in the saddle as her back ached. She would have to take his word on it.

But it would be interesting to see how he would cope with mishaps and mistakes in the bedroom these days. She wanted to believe he'd handle it with a sexy grin and improvisation. Rise to the occasion, so to speak, Michelle thought with a sly smile.

"Not that you are the common denominator or whatever," Ryan quickly backtracked. "But I got to tell you, it freaked me out."

"No kidding." She had seen the panic in his blue eyes when he couldn't maintain his erection. She had taken it to heart.

"I don't remember every detail when I took you home,"

he admitted with reluctance. "But I know some of the things I said weren't nice."

"*Weren't nice?*" The sulky silence hadn't been *nice*. The comments, on the other hand, had been sharp and cold, chipping away until all that was left of her was a throbbing sore.

The only silver lining in that situation was that she had been leaving town the next morning. Gratitude wouldn't cover how she felt, knowing that she would never have to see him again.

But his words had stuck with her until finally she started to wonder if he was wrong. Was she going to take one man's opinion as the truth? Hell, no!

The second time she got lucky. Jean-Albert had been a persistent and patient lover. They never fell in love, but he had a special place in her heart because he had revealed the truth to her.

"Okay, okay," Ryan said, breaking into her reverie. "I was an ass."

"Much better." Although she would have been more creative on the name-calling.

"And I've felt bad about it ever since," Ryan said, his voice wobbling. "I'm not proud of how I handled the situation. It was all my fault, and I blamed you. I hurt you and I never had the chance to say I was sorry."

She wanted to accept the apology and wipe the slate clean. The words were dancing on her tongue, but a part of her wanted to say "too little, too late."

Sorry didn't make up for the way she had walked around with no confidence. Sorry didn't make up for how jumpy she had been about sex. And sorry wasn't going to make her jump back into being with him to see if it was an aberration.

"And that's why I volunteered to help you out."

"Gee, thanks. But if you think being a Good Samaritan is going to get me into your bed, think again."

Ryan sighed with annoyance. "First of all, that wasn't why I said I'm doing this. Michelle, haven't you been listening?"

Yes, unfortunately. "You're saying now that we're here, together, and you've apologized, we should kiss and make up. Especially considering how well we were up until that night . . ."

"Exactly."

Heh. Right. She knew *exactly* how his mind worked. "Hmm . . ." she said and smacked her lips as if she were giving it some thought. "No."

"You're going to base your decisions on one night?"

"Pretty much, yeah. Oh, don't get me wrong. I know all about your reputation in bed." It had been one of the reasons why she had taken the failure so personally. "But I'm not interested."

"Really?" His voice took on an edge. "Because five years ago that was the only reason you wanted me."

"That is not true!" Why were people thinking that? First Vanessa and now Ryan.

She hadn't gone after him because of his alleged legendary lovemaking skills. She had pursued him because she was tired of waiting for him to wake up and notice her. After years of wanting only him, it had seemed to make perfect sense that she would make sure he was her first!

"Yeah, it is. You only wanted me for one thing," Ryan said. "Not that I'm complaining."

"It's not! I was hopelessly in love with you for about forever." It had been the most pathetic case of unrequited love. What a waste of time that turned out to be.

"You *were?*"

How could he not know? It felt as though everyone

knew, even though she tried to hide it with feigned cool elegance. Apparently teenagers didn't have a good grasp on the concept of cool elegance. "But those days are long gone. You might still be hot and have those amazing baby blues—"

"You think I'm—"

"But too much has passed between us. I've learned my lesson. And, you know what that was?"

"Uh . . ."

"I'm just too sexy for you."

Ohhhhh. Michelle closed her eyes. She felt her stomach flip. She couldn't believe she just said that. She should have stopped while she was ahead.

Ryan Slater wasn't too sure about the sanity of the scavenger hunt organizers, but they had done one thing right. He knew it the moment he walked into the warm and sunny bed and breakfast. He didn't want to leave.

Annie Lang was the proprietor and, if he heard it correctly, was also the great-grandniece of Ida Wirt. He could have gotten that wrong. His memory usually went blank after the first hyphen.

Even more amazing, Annie seemed to know how to handle all types of guests. Especially the treasure hunter kind. One look at them and she ushered everyone into the dining room for a home-cooked dinner.

As he tried not to shovel the food into his mouth like a starving man, Ryan glanced at the old framed pictures cluttering the large dining room walls. Homer and Ida Wirt didn't look like anything he imagined. They looked . . . well, normal.

In one picture, Homer and Ida were dressed for a drive in the country. They posed beside their car and their dog sat at their feet. The Wirts looked as though they were ready to relax with some friends, not thinking about another crime spree.

EX, WHY, AND ME / 91

And now he was following their footsteps, minus the re-
laxing. For money? No, something even more pathetic. For
a woman who didn't want to have anything to do with him.

Ryan slid another glance down the long table and caught
Michelle's gaze. She really was a stunner. Just looking at her
made his heart pinch, the ache lingering as Michelle turned
abruptly and spoke to Clayton sitting next to her.

Clayton. The bitter taste of jealousy filled his mouth. He
wondered how friendly Michelle had been to her former
history tutor.

Ryan shook his head in self-disgust. Well, not that friendly
since he had been Michelle's first.

Damn, he wished he had known that back then. It made
his behavior even worse. And it was another example that
what Michelle said was true.

She had been too sexy for him. He had been in awe of
her beauty, her sensuality, and all the while, she had been
inexperienced.

Michelle might exude bold sensuality, but he still couldn't
believe she had said she was too sexy for him. From how
quiet she had been afterward, he got the sense she was equally
stunned.

But he didn't argue. He doubted that she noticed.

"So, Ryan, what about you?" Dennis Aschenbrenner
said, sitting at the head of the table. The overhead chande-
lier cast a glow on his bald head. "What competitions have
you been in?"

"This is my first one," Ryan said as he took a drink from
the crystal glass. He didn't realize how hungry and thirsty
he had been until he walked into the house and sniffed the
heady aroma of a roast beef dinner.

"Your first scavenger hunt?" Dennis asked, his eyeglasses slipping down his nose as he frowned.

"My first competition. Ever."

Dennis paused, his fork hovering above the plate. He

looked at his wife, who sat at the other end of the table. Margaret shrugged and then they both stared at Ryan as if they didn't quite understand.

"You can't mean that," Brandy said with a smile. "What about sports?"

"Nope. I worked at the bowling alley after school." He had never developed an interest in after-school events, probably because he knew his parents would never give him permission to try out for them. He was needed at work.

"The lottery?" she asked.

"Um, no." He pulled his leg back when Brandy determinedly brushed her toes against him. Again. Since she sat right next to him, he knew it wasn't an accident. And he didn't think it was a coincidence that she suddenly developed an interest in him.

"Spelling bee?" Clayton asked, joining in. "Math Olympics?"

That sounded like torture. "Not a chance. Why?" He looked at the others. "Is previous experience mandatory?"

"Well, no," Dennis said as he pushed up his glasses. "But it might prove helpful. Margaret and I are sweepers."

"Excuse me?"

"Contest sweepers," Dennis repeated, dabbing his mouth with a napkin. "Whenever a business has a contest, we enter it. Sometimes we have to write a poem, or maybe it's calling in at the radio station for a prize."

"We've won lots of great prizes," Margaret said as she daintily ate her dinner.

"And this is what you do for . . . fun?" He couldn't wrap his head around the idea. But these guys probably thought bowling would be a waste of time unless there was a prize attached to it.

"Yes, and it helps make ends meet," Dennis admitted as he lowered his eyes to his plate. "Don't you think this scavenger hunt is fun?"

"It's had its moments." Like when he kissed Michelle. Ryan glanced at her and watched the blush stain her cheeks. Yeah, they were on the same wavelength. That knowledge gave him more pleasure than it should.

"No offense, but if you're not doing it for fun, why are you in this hunt?" Dennis asked.

"I'm doing it for Michelle," Ryan said. Everyone looked at her and he smiled when he saw Michelle's blush deepen. She refused to lift her head as she pushed the food around her plate.

"I enter beauty pageants all the time," Brandy announced unexpectedly. "You should see my talent. It's with the hula hoop, but I bring in rhythmic gymnastics moves."

"I remember that," Annie said as she entered the dining room, ready to serve dessert. Ryan's mouth watered at the aroma of baked apples. "It was when you competed for Miss Horseradish a couple years back."

"Yes-s-s." Brandy paused and slid a look Michelle's way. "But that pageant is minor league compared to the others in the area. Most serious beauty queens treat it as a warm-up. This year I finally reached my goal and was crowned Miss Beefalo."

Michelle gagged on her water and put the crystal goblet down quickly.

"Beefalo?" Ryan asked. "Don't you mean buffalo?"

"Beefalo is a cross breed of cattle and bison," Clayton answered. "Bison, as you know, is frequently mistaken as buffalo."

Clayton was beginning to really annoy him. Ryan returned his attention to Brandy. "And beefalo is a step up from horseradish?"

"Duh." She tossed her head, her red hair floating around her face as she giggled. "Livestock is way more important than a root vegetable."

"It's a food chain thing?"

"No, silly." Brandy leaned forward. "Livestock pageantries usually offer a bigger crown."

Michelle slapped her napkin against her mouth.

"It's the least they could do," Brandy confided, placing her hand on Ryan's wrist. "When I was competing for Junior Miss Swine—"

Michelle choked and coughed. Hard coughs that made her eyes water. Or maybe she was coughing to hide the fact that her eyes were already watering.

"They made us do the one-hundred-yard dash riding a pig. Can you believe it?"

Ryan didn't glance in Michelle's direction when he heard her chair legs scraping the floor. "Is that right?"

"I won that race."

"I have no doubt." Otherwise she wouldn't have mentioned it.

The redhead leaned forward, giving him a front-row view of her ample cleavage. "Do you know how hard it is to ride a pig bareback?"

He was at a loss. "I'm guessing not as hard as getting a saddle on them."

Michelle bolted up. "Excuse me," she said, her mouth against her hand as if she was covering a yawn. "I didn't realize how tired I am. All the events really wore me out. I think I better turn in."

"The hunt organizers picked up your overnight bag from your mom's house and brought it here," Annie said as she headed back to the kitchen. "I put it in the first room to the right."

"Thank you. Good night everyone."

"And, Ryan," Annie added, "I put your backpack in the second room to the left."

Ryan looked at Michelle and she couldn't quite hide her smile. Separate bedrooms? Did Homer and Ida sleep in separate rooms? Was this any way to conduct a romantic legend? Weren't they going for the Sexiest Couple title?

What was he thinking? He should have known better. It was sexy, Carbon Hill style. These organizers needed to cut him some slack.

He froze when he felt Brandy's toe creeping up his leg again. Ryan sighed. It was going to be a long night.

Michelle had expected the knock on the door. Soft but firm, as she predicted. She had lain on her bed, desperate to go to sleep, but couldn't. All because she knew Ryan was going to pay a visit.

She sighed and got out of bed. Michelle tiptoed to the door, wincing at the pain in her feet. She wasn't listening to her mother's fashion advice ever again.

She leaned against the door. "Who's there?"

"Who are you expecting?" Ryan asked. The gruff tone should have made him sound grumpy, but she found it very seductive.

"I already gave at the office." She pushed off the door, wondering why she got up in the first place. Or why her heart did that crazy flip-flop thing. She hated that. Really, she did.

"Come on, open up."

She watched the doorknob twist as he tried to open the door. "Whatever you are selling, I'm not buying."

"Michelle."

"Unless you are under five feet and selling cookies."

"I can pick locks, you know."

She didn't know, but she believed it. Michelle swung the door open. "Don't you dare!"

Whoa, he looked good. Michelle stared at him, taking in everything. He had recently taken a shower and his wet hair was dark and slicked back.

But what really got her attention was that Ryan wasn't wearing a shirt. His damp skin gleamed under the hallway lights. She itched to rake her fingers down the lean, compact muscles.

Her gaze dragged down the arrow of dark blond hair that dipped past his drawstring pants. The very pants that hung dangerously low on his narrow hips. One pull of that string and . . .

Be strong. He was good-looking, but he was false advertising. Remember that.

"What do you want?" she asked.

Ryan's smile hitched to one side. As though he knew what she was thinking. Feeling. Wanting. "To look at your feet."

She curled her toes against the hardwood floor. Her feet suddenly felt cold. Naked. Vulnerable. "Why?"

He revealed a first-aid kit and rattled it. "I asked Annie for it, so you might as well use it for your blisters."

Michelle took a step back. Okay. She hadn't expected this from him. It was sweet. Thoughtful.

She narrowed her eyes with suspicion. There had to be a catch. "Thank you." Michelle didn't reach for the box, wondering if there were strings attached.

"You need any help?" he asked, his bright blue eyes dancing with hope.

"I can manage on my own."

His eyebrow arched. "Even the hard-to-reach places?"

One hard-to-reach place was flaring to life. "I'll be fine. Thank you." She reached for the kit and tried to do a quick grab and go, but Ryan proved quicker. His hand encircled her wrist before she could close the door.

His grip was gentle, but insistent. His thumb rubbed against the jumping pulse at her wrist. She knew it was a matter of moments before he drew her against him.

Michelle reluctantly looked up. She saw those dimples and her knees weakened. Okay, one kiss, but that was all she could allow.

"Sweet dreams," Ryan murmured and dropped his hold before turning away.

Michelle stared at him, openmouthed. What was that all about? He could have gone in for the kiss, press her against him, but he didn't. All he did was get her a little hot and bothered and walk away.

Michelle stiffened and her jaw snapped shut. She was tempted to aim the first-aid kit at the really defined muscles in his broad back.

Stop looking at him. Michelle swung the door shut and locked it with the flick of her wrist. He *had* gotten her interested. With incredible ease. After all that vowing that she would never sleep with him.

Rat bastard. At least he knew to carry Band-Aids.

Michelle hobbled back to her bed and perched herself on the mattress. She had put on the last of the Band-Aids when she heard a soft knock on one of the doors outside.

"Hey, Ryan."

Brandy? Michelle's head bolted up. What was Brandy doing visiting Ryan?

Well, duh. Michelle rolled her eyes on that one.

She heard Ryan's voice, low and murmuring, but she couldn't make out the words. Michelle craned her head in the direction of her door, hating the fact that she was considering peering through the keyhole.

Not her business, Michelle reminded herself as she heard Brandy whisper. She had no intention of sleeping with Ryan, so it really didn't matter what was going on there.

But why were they still standing at his door? Were they going to talk all night?

She didn't care. Michelle snapped the first-aid kit closed,

set it down by her bedside table, and resolutely turned the lamp off. She slid underneath the bedsheets and pounded her pillow a few times.

She really, truly didn't care. It had nothing to do with her. She didn't feel the need to interrupt them. Or stop them. Or pull Brandy by her red hair and drag her far, far away.

She heard Ryan's door close.

Michelle's heart stopped. At least, she thought it was Ryan's. Her breath hitched painfully in her throat.

And then she heard the indignant stomp of Brandy's bare feet.

Michelle slowly released her breath as her pulse pounded in her ears. She really shouldn't care. She didn't want Ryan anymore.

No, that wasn't true. Michelle curled the pillow tightly under her head as she thought about it. She didn't *want* to want Ryan. And it was more than just that one night.

Or was it? Was she refusing him a second chance based solely on that disaster? She'd been telling herself it was because of how he had destroyed her confidence. It had taken her a while to rebuild, so why give him a second chance to destroy her again?

Could the truth be something more . . . shallow? Michelle turned onto her back and stared at the ceiling. She didn't like that possibility. She wanted to be someone smart. Admirable.

But was she holding a grudge against Ryan simply because her first time was the worst time?

And she couldn't hold him fully responsible. She had been too eager, thinking only of herself and her rite of passage. She knew that now.

Well, what was done was done. There was nothing else she could do about it. Even if she had the opportunity, she didn't know what she would do differently for her first time.

Okay, probably a different setting, Michelle decided as she closed her eyes. But at the time she had wanted somewhere private and memorable. Something different so she would have a story to tell.

Maybe that was where she went wrong. She should have let Ryan take her to his bed. She should have done something common. Normal. Like the missionary position, or the backseat of a car. Or do the ultimate cliché and join the Mile High Club.

Michelle smiled sleepily over that idea. Her first time would have been infinitely worse if she had tried to have sex in a bathroom that could barely fit one person.

She imagined there would be a lot of fumbling and interesting bruises afterward. It would be a tight fit, pressed against the shallow sink and Ryan. Or maybe against the accordion-style door, praying it wouldn't burst open as he drove his cock into her.

The encounter would be clumsy but wild. Daring. Her imagination took hold and wouldn't let go. They wouldn't have room to do anything but mate. No fondling, no suckling. Just . . .

Well, she would expect something more. There was plenty of room to give Ryan pleasure. She vividly imagined all the ways she could make him go wild. But while she could make his eyes roll backward one hundred and one ways in a room the size of a postage stamp, she couldn't imagine finding much satisfaction with very little movement.

But what if she'd promise to be extremely still as he dipped his fingers inside her? He would know her response by watching her face closely. Watching her pupils dilate, her lips part, her skin turning pink.

She wouldn't be able to part her legs too wide, though. And she couldn't bump too hard against the wall when she came. Although, the way the planes bounced and rocked, maybe the passengers would think it was turbulence.

She'd have to be very, very quiet. That was nearly impossible for her when it came to sex. But only whispers and stifled moans for the Mile High Club. People walked past the lavatory. Call bells chimed and the flight attendants were everywhere. She would easily be found out.

But she would give it a try with Ryan. There would be nothing to hold on to as he drove into her. Nothing but him. She'd hold on tight and burrow her head into his shoulder, muffling her moans as—

Michelle jerked awake and lifted her face from the pillow. Her heart raced. Her breasts felt heavy and tight. She rested on her elbows and looked around the unfamiliar bedroom. Where was she? She stared at the morning sunlight peeking through the curtains.

Bed and breakfast. Treasure hunt. Morning. Phone!

Michelle cricked her neck as she whirled around and saw her cell phone lighting up on the bedside table. She grabbed for it, almost dropped it, but caught it before it hit the ground.

Her head dangled inches from the floor as her feet were flailing in the air. Michelle punched the talk button.

"Hello?" she said in a raspy voice. She realized she held the phone upside down and righted it.

"You are on the front page of the *Carbon Hill Herald,* but I'm not cutting it out for the scrapbook. First of all, it's not your best side, and it gives you a double chin."

"Mom?" She bolted up.

"But no one will notice that because the picture shows you kissing Ryan Slater!"

"Uh-oh." Michelle scooted away from the edge of the mattress.

"In color."

"Mom, it was part of the hunt." Okay, technically it wasn't, but how would her mother find out the truth?

"You are slipping him tongue."

Michelle winced. She didn't want to have this conversation with her mother first thing in the morning.

"What are you doing with this Slater boy?"

"Ask Danny. He's the one who got him for me." When cornered, always blame the older brother. The technique had worked well in the past.

"Now listen to me, Michelle Louise Nelson. You keep your eye on the prize."

"The treasure chest?" Since when did her mom care about this scavenger hunt?

"No." Her mother's voice dipped low. Michelle knew the woman was about to blow. "Your career."

"Oh, that." How did they get on this topic? What was she thinking? They *always* got around to discussing her career plan and goals.

"This Slater boy is a charmer. He will distract you. You don't want a guy to slow you down."

Michelle nodded and slowly moved into a sitting position. "Okay, Mom."

"That's what happened to me. I was going to travel the world and—"

"Then you met Dad on your first stop and that was that. I know." She knew all about her mom's grand dreams dashed by an unexpected pregnancy. "I have to go."

"Did you listen to a thing I said?"

She had been listening for years. She was sure some of it stuck and was embedded into her DNA. "Yeah, I got it. Bye!" She hung up and flopped back onto her pillow.

But some of the things her mom said did make sense. Should she start listening to the woman? Michelle glanced at her swollen feet. *Nah . . .*

Chapter 7

Michelle strolled around the backyard of the bed and breakfast as everyone else ate their morning meal. She hoped she didn't appear rude, but she was unwilling to handle conversation with Brandy. About Brandy. Brandy all the time. It was enough to give her indigestion.

She noted that the weather was warmer and took that as a good omen. She had already found something unexpected this morning. Walking around the Wirts' farmhouse, Michelle got a better sense of Homer and Ida.

The grounds were unkempt, but with her untrained eye, she could tell that the enormous garden had been lovingly planned. The landscaping was much more formal than she expected from a Midwestern farmhouse, complete with sculptures and a rather ornate birdbath.

It was as if the struggle of their double life played out in the garden. Common household plants wrapped around a broken Grecian urn. The herb garden by the kitchen was designed in artistic geometric shapes, but impractical.

Instead of thick hedges or intimidating fences, the Wirts had chosen to border the garden with twisted, gnarled apple trees. She didn't understand the choice and wondered if it was once again the struggle between their fantasy world and reality.

Michelle zigzagged between the trees, dodging the rotten

apples. As she jumped over a decomposed fruit, she accidentally stubbed her toe on something hard. Michelle hopped back and swallowed a colorful curse.

She looked to see what she hit, kicking down the overgrown weeds, and discovered a marker. It looked as if it was made out of marble. She looked on the other side which faced the garden and noticed the word "Golden" engraved on it.

"That can't be right," she muttered to herself as she picked up one of the scrawny apples on the ground. She studied it before glancing up at the marked tree.

"The trees are in bad condition," Ryan said, causing Michelle to turn around and watch him approach her. "I'm surprised they're still standing."

"I wasn't looking at that. I was wondering about this marker." She pointed at the small slab of marble.

"What about it?"

"Why is it marking this tree as a Golden Delicious?"

Ryan shrugged. "What is it?"

"I don't know. Probably an heirloom variety." She tossed him the apple in her hand and looked around the trees. "I don't think any of these trees are goldens."

"Maybe it's marking where a tree used to be," Ryan guessed.

"Why would they do that?" Michelle dismissed the idea. "They could have planted another tree in its place."

"That tree could have been important to them. Like it was where they first did it." He waggled his eyebrows.

Michelle made a face. "Tell me, do you have a plaque next to the pinsetters?"

His smile was slow and wicked. "I'll get right on it, if it makes you feel better."

"No, that's okay." An idea popped into her head. "Hey!" She nudged Ryan with her elbow. "Maybe this is where they stowed the treasure. Golden. Get it?"

Ryan scoffed at the possibility. "They wouldn't be that obvious."

"Unless they were playing mind games. Hide it in plain sight. Or make us think that we know they would hide it plain sight so—"

"Stop!" Ryan held up his hand. "What would be the point of putting it there in the first place?"

"There is a point," Annie said as she came up from behind them. "But not the kind you're thinking. That's a grave marker."

"Ew!" Michelle scurried away from the marker. Who had she been stepping on?

"For a pet," Annie added.

"Are you kidding me? That marker had to cost a lot, even back then."

"You never had a pet, did you?" the proprietor decided. "Homer and Ida adored their dog. I don't know what kind it was. I think it was a mixed breed."

"I saw pictures of the dog in the dining room," Ryan said. "It looked like your average mutt."

"That would be Golden. Or Goldie. They called her that as well."

"So much for our buried treasure theory," Ryan told Michelle.

"We really do suck at this, don't we?" she admitted.

"Come on." Annie gestured them to the house. "Everyone needs to get into the van for your next destination."

"Let me go get my cell phone before we leave." Michelle hurried ahead of them and ran inside.

"You know, if there was any treasure, it's not around here," Annie said. "I went through every nook and cranny when renovating the house. The yard is next, but treasure hunters have been here off and on through the years. They never found anything."

"Michelle doesn't believe there was a treasure," Ryan

said. "I disagree. I think it's still around here somewhere, waiting to be found."

"Huh. I'm with you on that, Ryan. It's probably in one of those river bluff caves."

"Why do you say that?"

"When Homer and Ida died, they didn't have a lot of money in the bank. It has to be somewhere, right?"

"Unless they weren't train robbers." Hmm . . . Michelle was definitely rubbing off on him.

"They were. Ida bragged about it constantly to her sister, who happened to be my grandmother. Grandma considered calling the authorities just to stop hearing about the stories."

Ryan smiled. Sibling rivalry at its best.

"But I know Ida was proud of her double life," Annie continued, "so I don't feel guilty about advertising it. I'm going to use the romantic legend to get some business for this place."

"Good idea."

"I hope it will bring in a profit soon. It's not easy operating a B&B in the middle of nowhere. Come to think of it, it's not easy doing any kind of business in Carbon Hill."

"You guys." Michelle hurried down the steps and went directly to the phone sitting on the hall table. She rapidly punched in the numbers, but didn't put the phone to her ear. "Do you hear a phone ringing?"

Ryan and Annie listened. "No," Ryan said, shaking his head. "What's going on?"

"Have either of you seen my cell phone? It was on the bedside table and it's not there."

"I'll go ask the others," Annie offered, "but we have to leave in five minutes with or without the cell phone."

"I'll come help you." Ryan ran up the steps. They needed that phone. It was the only way they got through yesterday. "When was the last time you used it?"

"This morning. My mom called me." She tossed back the bedcovers and looked under the pillow. Michelle lifted the mattress. "Anything?"

"No." He looked under the bed, but it was completely empty. "You didn't take it outside?"

"Nope."

"Jacket?"

She patted down her pockets. "Nothing. Let's check the other rooms—starting with Brandy's."

Ryan grabbed her arm before she stepped out of the room. "You think Brandy took it? Why would she do such a thing?"

"Oh," she said with a sad smile and patted his cheek. "What it must be like to live in RyanWorld."

"You're calling her a thief."

"Now you're catching on."

"But you have no proof!" Ryan pointed out.

Michelle looked up at the ceiling and closed her eyes. "I don't need proof. I know she's behind this."

"Ryan? Michelle?" Annie called up the stairs. "No one has seen the phone. I'm sorry, but we have to get going."

Michelle sighed. Ryan rubbed her back, noticing every swell and dip his hand glided over. "It's going to be okay," he said. It wasn't true, but she didn't need to know that.

"We can't use my cell phone anymore. How is that going to be okay?" She looked up at him, her brown eyes holding a weak glimmer of hope. "Do you have one?"

Ryan shook his head, feeling very unsophisticated. But he didn't need a cell phone since he spent most of his time at Pins & Pints. Anyone who needed to reach him called the bowling alley.

"I should have known Brandy would do something like this," she said, her voice a low growl as she hurried down the steps. "I should have kept my guard up."

"If I find the phone, I'll meet up with you and give it to you," Annie said.

"Thank you," Michelle said with a tense smile. "Here's the number. I tried calling it, but I didn't hear it ring. The ringer might be off, which"—she cast a dark look at Ryan—"is something I never do."

"We don't know if it was stolen," he pointed out. "Or if Brandy is behind it. For all you know, the batteries could be dead."

"Just keep her away from me," Michelle said as she strode out of the house.

"Oh, sure thing," Ryan called after her. "But who is going to keep her away from *me?*"

"Where are we going?" Margaret asked as the bed and breakfast's van turned into the downtown area.

"Back to the square," Annie said, slamming on the brakes as the light turned red. The brakes squeaked and hissed ominously. Ryan was beginning to miss Lucifer.

"The square?" Clayton asked, clutching the shoulder seat belt as the van shook. "That doesn't make sense."

Annie glanced in the rearview mirror. "I'm sure you'll figure it all out once I drop you off and give you your next clue."

Annie screeched to a stop in front of the makeshift stage where they had first started the hunt. She hit the emergency lights and turned around to face the teams. "Okay, everybody out."

Ryan helped everyone out of the van, but he noticed Michelle was very quiet. She hadn't said one word about maniac drivers. Nothing about starting at square one. He hated to say it, but he could really use a snarky word or two. It was as though her head was not in the game.

"Okay, everyone. Here is your next clue," Annie said as she handed the sealed envelopes to the men. "Do not open until I give the go-ahead. Ready . . . set . . . go!"

Ryan ripped the envelope open and pulled out the card. "Track the Knights' warnings to the Graveyard."

He stared at the message. No moment of recognition. No lightbulb moment. Nothing.

"What?" Clayton asked, his voice sounding more like a squawk. "This can't be it. You seriously can't expect us to figure this out from"—he looked down and counted quickly—"seven words."

Good, Ryan decided. If a genius didn't understand the message, it made him feel better.

Annie pressed her hand against her chest. "Hey, I didn't come up with the clue. I just hand them out. Okay? Good luck!" She gave a jaunty wave, got back into her van, and swerved into the heavy traffic, eliciting a symphony of car horns and screeched tires.

"Track the Knights' warnings to the Graveyard," Ryan said in a whisper before turning to Michelle. He showed her the card. "Any ideas?"

She didn't look at the message. "Nope. Not a one."

Her lack of curiosity boggled his mind. "Are you planning to come up with one? Say . . . in the next few minutes?"

Michelle shrugged and dragged the toe of her tennis shoe against the sidewalk. "I got nothing."

"You know," Ryan said as he folded his arms across his chest, "you can do this without the help of technology."

"How about if you come up with an idea?"

He came up with the one idea she would balk at. That should jump-start her brain. "I say we follow one of the other teams."

She glanced over at them. "They look about as lost as we do. It'll be the blind leading the blind."

She didn't reject it out of hand. He should use this to his favor. Ryan dipped his hand in his pocket to find a coin.

"Okay, heads the. Aschenbrenners, or tails, Clayton and Brandy."

He stopped when he noticed Michelle was off in her own world. "Oh, look. We get to follow Brandy."

Michelle didn't respond.

"Okay, what's wrong?" Ryan asked. "This isn't about the phone, is it?"

"I'm fine," she said as she walked toward the park bench and plopped down, sprawling her legs in front of her. "Where should we go? You can lead this time."

He felt his eyebrows shoot up. "Oh, can I? Gee, thanks. What do you mean, this time?"

She looked at him. Her eyes didn't appear confused or dazed. They looked blank.

"Don't you remember yesterday?" he asked. "You wanted to go to the bank. You wanted to put together the replica without the benefit of light, and you wanted to get to the farmhouse without using the horse."

"What's your point?" she asked, each word and gesture dripping with fatigue. "That you come up with all the ideas?"

"No, that we are a team," Ryan said. Why was he fighting this? She wanted to quit. No one needed to twist his arm to quit.

But he sensed it would be a mistake. He couldn't give in. Not yet. Not until he figured out what was going on with Michelle. "We come up with the answers together. And we need to get the answer to this clue. Now."

She sighed and leaned her head back against the bench. "Ryan, what is the point? We're never going to win."

She'd been saying that since the moment the hunt started. What had changed since then? "I vote for trailing the Aschenbrenners."

"We're just going to go through the motions," Michelle went on as if he hadn't spoken.

He studied her face, void of any expression, and wondered what caused this. Was it because of his proposition? No, she would have called it quits. Was it something bigger, like coming back home? Or was it smaller, like the hunt not going their way?

That had to be it. Everything always went her way. Michelle Nelson wasn't familiar with failure. Now she was getting a taste of how the other half lived. It was good for her. "I get it now," Ryan said, not caring that his voice took on a cold edge.

She frowned with disbelief. "The clue?"

"No. I get *you* now." He sat down on the bench next to her. "This hunt has gotten too hard for you, hasn't it?"

"What?" She sat up straight.

He gestured at the square. "You thought you could breeze in here, win this thing, and walk away without breaking a sweat."

Michelle scoffed at the idea. "No."

"And now it's getting too hard. It's requiring Carbon Hill's golden girl to break a sweat."

Her mouth sagged open. "Are you sniffing glue?"

"This hunt is making you work, and you can't handle it. Don't worry, I'll walk you through it."

Michelle pointed her finger in his face. "Don't tell me about work," she warned him. "I know all about work. When every hour, every minute is focused on—"

He swatted her hand away. "Then you should be enjoying this. The hunt is a break from work."

"It's a distraction," she muttered.

Ryan pinned her with a look. "It's meant to be."

She rubbed her face with her hands. "You're right. I'm sorry. I . . ." She sighed. "Okay, let's get back into the game. I don't want to be anywhere near Brandy, so I vote for trailing the Aschenbrenners."

"Good, it's unanimous." Ryan looked around, searching

for their prey. "Let's not make it too obvious." He stood up and looked around the square. "We can . . . Okay, we need a new plan."

"Why? Don't tell me it's because it's cheating."

"No, because Dennis and Margaret are already gone. So are Clayton and Brandy."

Michelle growled in the back of her throat. "Give me that clue." She studied it, put it down, and then looked at it again. "Track the Knights' warnings to the Graveyard."

"There aren't that many graveyards in town," Ryan said. The problem was that they were scattered around the area.

"Graveyard is capitalized," Michelle pointed out, "so I'm not going to take the word literally."

"Great. That means it could be anything. Let's look at another word. How about Knights? There aren't too many around here."

"Okay, what kind of knights?" Michelle stared at the traffic as she came up with some possibilities. "White Knights? Knights of the Round Table? Knights of Columbus?"

Ryan froze. Round table. The picture was clear in his mind. He started to pace, tossing around other possibilities, but his mind kept going back to the picture. But it couldn't be right. He would have heard about it.

"You have an idea?" Michelle asked, walking in tandem with him. "Tell me."

He shook his head. "No, I'm wrong." He had to come up with another idea. But all he could see was the picture.

Michelle stopped and looked at him. "How do you know you're wrong?"

"Just a feeling." He shrugged and lowered his head, staring at the sidewalk as he paced.

"We should investigate it."

"No." Knights . . . knights . . . There had to be other knights.

Michelle placed her hands on her hips. "Do you have any other ideas?"

He sighed. Long and hard. "No," he admitted.

She motioned at the street. "Then lead the way."

Michelle stood at the street corner and put her hands on her hips. "Pins & Pints?"

Ryan rubbed the back of his neck and stared at the hundred-year-old building. "Yeah."

She pursed her lips, stared at the brick structure, and considered her options. Okay, there were no options. She had to go in there and act as if it didn't matter. And it didn't. Not at all. She had even forgotten this place existed.

It was just a surprise to see it after all this time. It looked smaller. Quiet. Just another brick building.

When she came back home, she didn't entertain any thoughts of this place. She had no reasons to visit the bowling alley. Even during her fly-by visits to her parents, Michelle never drove past this side of town.

Michelle cleared her throat. "You think there are knights at the Pins & Pints?"

"Keep an open mind," Ryan suggested as they crossed the street.

Michelle's eyebrows shot up. Who was he to make that suggestion? "I'm very open-minded."

"Uh-huh." He held one of the wooden doors open and escorted her inside the building.

"Whoa." Michelle skidded to a stop. The entryway was no longer the grayish blue designed to hide the dirt and age. Instead, there was a bold and colorful mural stretching across the spacious room.

"What is this?" She twisted and swiveled her head when she noticed that the mural continued into every nook and cranny.

"The history of Carbon Hill." Ryan didn't move from the door. He didn't seem to show any interest in the artwork at all.

"Where does it start?"

Ryan pointed at the far right entrance door. Michelle slowly walked along the wall, instantly recognizing a few landmarks and forefathers. The exaggerated lines and shapes gave the subjects personality, she noticed as she peered closely at some of the hidden details.

She was surprised that the warm colors made her think of Carbon Hill. The patchwork farmland reminded her of the fields she saw the day before. Only this interpretation was brighter. Joyful. It was obvious that the artist loved this area, warts and all. Whoever drew this wanted the viewer to feel the same way.

Michelle's throat suddenly felt tight and dry. She swallowed hard. "Where are the Knights you were talking about?" she asked, her voice raspy. "Are they in this mural?"

"Over here." Ryan took the steps to the front counter and walked to the staircase that would take them to the top floor. He pointed at the gentlemen sitting at a round table. "These guys owned the breweries, but during Prohibition, they had to shut down their companies."

She looked at the men, then at Ryan. "How does that make them knights?"

"Believe me, they weren't. The owners went into more criminal activities."

Michelle's mouth sagged open. "Are you telling me Carbon Hill had a mob?"

Ryan laughed, the lines around his eyes deepening. "More like wannabe mobsters."

Michelle's smile stopped midway. The edges of her lips froze into place as her heart took a tumble. There was that laugh. That sound that would always make her day.

"The *Herald* kept tabs on these guys," Ryan continued,

studying the mural with a critical eye. "But they had to be careful. Instead of using their names, the reporters called them knights because they always met at this big round table at a local bar."

Michelle didn't realize she was staring at Ryan until he looked back at her. His brilliant blue eyes really did pack a wallop. She blinked as an unfamiliar sensation coiled around her chest.

"Butchers, bakers, candlestick makers and now knights," she said with a vague smile. "What's next? Princesses? Little Bo Peep?"

She made a show of studying the picture, but the aggressive lines blurred before her eyes. She found it difficult to concentrate as her heart raced wildly. "I see where you're going with this, Ryan, but where would the warnings be? The papers they are holding are *Carbon Hill Herald* editions."

"Ryan?" a female voice called from the room behind the front desk. "Is that you?"

Ryan's smile vanished as his hand dropped from the wall. "Damn," he muttered.

An older woman came to the front desk. There was something instantly friendly and comfortable about the casually dressed woman. Michelle immediately recognized her as Ryan's mother.

"Ryan!" Her relief was evident. "You're back. The hunt is over? Just in time, because—"

"Mom"—he waved his hands to interrupt her—"I'm still on the hunt."

"You didn't get voted off yet?" She winced when she realized her error. "Not that I don't think you could win, but it's never been your thing."

"It doesn't work that way, unfortunately." He approached the front desk. "Mom, you remember Michelle Nelson?"

"Oh, hi, Michelle!" The woman's smile was warm and genuine. "What have you been up to?"

"I'm a pastry chef in Chicago," she said as she clasped Mrs. Slater's hand with her own. "And how about you?"

"A chef? Really?" Her eyes brightened with interest. "Is it your own restaurant?"

She stopped short at the question. There was no way she could get her hands on the kind of money needed to establish her own restaurant. "No, not yet."

"Do you have a TV show?"

"No," Michelle answered with a hint of apology.

"A cookbook?"

Michelle shook her head. She didn't know how to explain that TV and book deals were hard to come by. It wasn't as if she was a slacker or anything. "Nothing like that. Sorry."

"Really? Well, don't worry, honey." Mrs. Slater patted Michelle's arm in a comforting gesture. "You'll get on the Food Network real soon."

"Mom, sorry to interrupt, but did the hunt organizers drop by here earlier this month? Did they want to use the mural as a clue?"

"No." She looked at her son as if he spoke a different language. "No one like that came around here. Why?"

"No reason." Ryan stepped away from the desk and looked at the mural one last time. "I thought there was a clue in here, but I guess I'm wrong."

"Are you going to be done tonight? You know the Kleins rented out the reception room." She motioned at the double doors next to the front desk.

"No, I won't be here tonight," he said patiently, like a man who had explained something several hundred times before. "I'll be back tomorrow night."

Michelle could feel Ryan's regret. It was as if he was torn. He didn't want to be in the hunt and he didn't want to be at the bowling alley. He was stuck disappointing someone and it didn't sit well with him. Michelle wondered where Ryan wanted to be.

Mrs. Slater silently studied him and then slowly looked at Michelle. Her mouth twitched with a smile as her gaze returned to her son. "I understand," she said, with a twinkle in her eye that must be a family trait. "Take your time. We'll be fine."

Ryan tilted his head to the side as if he didn't quite believe what he was hearing. "Are you sure?"

"Yes, absolutely. I don't want to see you until tomorrow night. No, make it Monday morning." She waved him off. "Now, go have fun."

"We'll try," he answered dryly and turned to Michelle. "Where should we try next?"

She shrugged. She was out of ideas and she couldn't imagine where a knight would hang out in town. "Do you know where the Historical Society is?"

"Carbon Hill has a historical society?" Ryan's mother asked in surprise.

"So we are told," Ryan said.

"Let me check." Mrs. Slater bent down and lifted the phone book from underneath the counter.

As she started thumbing through the thin pages, Michelle drifted to the wall she didn't get a chance to look at.

"You seem to like our mural, Michelle."

"Mom."

"It's wonderful," Michelle said, ignoring the hint of warning Ryan gave his mother. "I don't know much about art, but this reminds me a lot of what I've seen in Europe." She turned to the older woman. "I can picture this in a restaurant."

Mrs. Slater tilted her head and looked at her son. "Did you hear that, Ryan?"

"Yep," Ryan said as he skipped down the steps. "We gotta go."

Mrs. Slater gave Michelle one of those woman-to-woman looks. "I keep telling him he did as good a job as a professional."

"Ryan?" She cast a quick look at him. He had stopped on the middle step and his shoulders slowly slumped. Michelle looked at his mother. "*Ryan* did this?"

"Yes," the older woman said with a beaming smile. "My son is quite the artist, don't you think?"

Chapter 8

Michelle wasn't going to say a thing, she decided as she silently tapped her toe. She'd done pretty well for the past twenty minutes. She was even standing in the tiny Historical Society office right next to Ryan, acting as if she was listening to some local historian drone on about the town's railroad industry.

It helped to focus on the historian's odd hairstyle. The man unsuccessfully hid his bald spot by moving his part all the way to his ear. Distracting, to say the least, but she still felt tempted to interrupt.

She wanted to break her polite silence, present Ryan with a flourish, and announce, "Did you know that you have a talented local artist in your midst?"

She wasn't going to. She wasn't going to say a word. Because, first of all, Ryan would kill her. He didn't have to say anything for her to arrive at that conclusion. There were some unspoken rules that a person just knew.

Most of all, it would be a waste of breath. She had a feeling everyone already knew about Ryan's artistic ability. Everyone, that was, but her.

She, Michelle Nelson, had no clue. The girl who knew every freaking detail and statistic about Ryan Slater, right down to his class schedule in high school, didn't know he was an artist.

She was still reeling from it.

"You're telling me," Ryan asked the historian, "that a *hobo* was considered a knight?"

"Yes," the man said in his monotone voice that could put anyone to sleep. "Now they are known as transients or vagrants, but back then they were called hobos. They were also known as the Knights of the Road."

Ryan turned to Michelle. "I never would have figured that one out."

She tried not to smile at his bemused expression. "That makes two of us."

"They had their own communication system," the historian explained. "The hobos left markings and symbols along the way. This allowed other hobos to know what they could find. Things like a sympathetic lady who would give food, or a mean dog."

"Those must be the warnings." Michelle pulled the card from her jacket pocket and read it aloud. "Track the Knights' warnings to the Graveyard."

"Sounds right," Ryan said with a nod. "Where can we get the list of symbols?"

"They're available on the Internet, but I can get a print-out for you," the man said as he strode to the back office. "I'll be right back."

"Where do we go look for the symbols?" Michelle asked Ryan. "Start wandering down one street to the next?"

"No, the railroad tracks." He tapped the paper with his fingertip. "Track the Knights' warnings. Get it?"

Michelle nodded, feeling a little bit more hopeful than she had when they first got the clue. "And the Wirts might have used them when robbing trains."

"Where does the Graveyard fit in?" Ryan asked. "What could that be about?"

"Here you go," the historian said and gave the printout of symbols to Ryan.

"That was fast," Michelle said as she stuffed the clue back into her pocket.

"I made extra copies after the first request," the man explained.

Michelle paused. She sensed Ryan's head jerk up in surprise. "First?" she repeated.

"Who was here before us?" Ryan asked.

"Oh, it was Clayton, one of our most active members," the historian said, his monotone voice pulling at Michelle's eyelids so hard that she was ready to take a nap. "He was with a pretty girl I haven't seen in here before."

"One more thing," Ryan said as they walked to the door. "Did the hobos have anything called a Graveyard?"

The historian's eyes dipped as he frowned. "It doesn't sound familiar."

"Okay, thanks," Michelle said as they left the Historical Society. They stood at the doorway and surveyed Main Street, which was closed to traffic to make room for the Horseradish Festival's sidewalk sale.

"You know," Michelle said as she stuffed her hands into her jacket pockets. "I would like to come in first in something."

"We already did," Ryan reminded her. "It was on the first clue."

Michelle wrinkled her nose. "That doesn't count. How about come in first in something *today?*"

"Today's not over yet."

Michelle rolled her eyes toward the cloudless sky. "Which way should we go?"

"Let's find a train track. There aren't any laid down on Main Street, but I think the closest track is in that direction." He motioned to the left with the tilt of his head.

Might as well. "Okay, let's do it." She headed down the sidewalk with Ryan at her side. She noticed how he automatically moved to walk between her and the street. The protective gesture was pure Ryan, but the way her heart fluttered against her ribs was surprising. She abruptly looked away, uncertain if she liked the feeling or not.

A sparkle in the window caught her eye. "Ooh, wait!" she said as they passed Duguay's Diamonds.

"Michelle," he said with a long-suffering sigh and back-tracked to where she stood. "We've already lost a lot of ground. Now isn't the time to window-shop."

"I know," she said with her nose pressed against the tiny square display window. She cupped her hands around her temples, shielding the bright sunlight from her eyes. "I wanted to see the ring that's part of the prize. I guess that's it."

The large platinum ring consisted of three diamond rows. It looked thick and heavy nestled against the soft black velvet bedding. Michelle knew it would dominate any woman's hand.

Ryan leaned in closer and her senses erupted into life. She inhaled his clean scent and it hit her in the back of her throat. His body heat enveloped her and every layer of clothes felt too warm and tight. Michelle let out a slow, staggered breath, clouding the glass.

"It's big," he said.

"Yeah." She wiped the fog off the window, hoping he didn't notice her high-pitched voice.

"Do you like it?" Ryan asked. She heard the uncertainty in his voice, as if he couldn't imagine her wearing something like that. His insight pleased her.

"It's okay," she answered. "It isn't something I would wear. Oooh! Oooh!" She pressed her nose closer. "I like that pendant and chain behind it."

Ryan leaned in closer. His body surrounded her, but she didn't feel contained. She felt safe. She wanted to lean into him, gather his arms around her, and hold tight.

"That purple triangle thing?" he asked.

"That is gorgeous!" She tilted her head, wishing for a

better view. Whose bright idea was it to make miniscule store windows?

"I like it better," he decided, "but it's not as big."

"But it's prettier. And that chain you could wear by itself." Michelle sighed as she turned away from the display window. "One day."

"One day, what?" Ryan prompted when she showed no sign of finishing her thought.

Michelle reluctantly moved away from the window. "One day I'll have enough money to buy that necklace."

"Don't you celebrity chefs make millions?" he asked with a teasing grin.

"What is it with you guys?" She splayed her hands in the air. "I am not a celebrity chef. Everyone seems to think that they have the best idea for a cookbook and—snap!—they will be the next Julia Child."

"It worked for Julia Child," Ryan explained as he reached for her hand and guided her through a crowded part of the sidewalk.

"Life doesn't happen that way for most chefs. That's what makes it such a big deal when it does happen." She tried to come up with an example. "It's like the legend of Homer and Ida."

"I don't follow," he said as they turned the corner from Main and went down a side street.

"People have found buried treasure throughout time," Michelle said, slipping her hand out of Ryan's grasp. She tried to be sneaky about it, but had a feeling she failed spectacularly. "When everyone hears the rumor that there might be buried treasure, everyone thinks it's going to be their lucky day."

"Except for you," he said with a sidelong glance. "You're too busy telling everyone buried treasure doesn't exist."

"I never said that." Michelle shook her head. "Buried treasure exists."

Ryan stopped, turned, and put his hands on his hips. "Even in Carbon Hill?"

She shuffled to a stop. "It's . . ." She felt her nose flare as she took a deep breath. "Possible."

"Wow, what a jump!" he said, flinging his hands up to the sky. "You went from impossible to possible. Next stop, probable."

"Oh, that's not going to happen," she said, looking for cars before she dashed across the street.

"There's that cynicism again," he said as he jogged behind her. "But you know—"

"Railroad tracks!" She pointed at the tracks embedded in the street. She paused and checked for any oncoming traffic. "Which way do we follow?"

"Hmm." Ryan ruffled his hair with his fingers. "You choose."

Oh, right. And then she'd get the blame when they accidentally walked all the way to the next county. "What if I pick the wrong way?"

He flashed a knowing smile. "I won't hold it against you. Promise."

"You better not." She looked in both directions and pointed to the right. "This way."

"As I was saying," Ryan continued as they walked the tracks side by side, "if Ida herself rose from the dead and came to you, pointed where 'X' marks the spot, you wouldn't believe it."

"Well, probably because I'd be too busy wondering why a ghost was bothering me. Or if it was really a ghost, and how would I know the ghost was Ida? It's not like they carry I.D."

"But the weird thing is—"

Michelle gave him a look of disbelief. "And ghosts aren't considered weird?"

"You would dig," Ryan said, pointing at her, "but you wouldn't think you'd find anything."

Michelle considered what he said. "You're probably right. I didn't think I had a chance to win Miss Horseradish. My goal was to try for anything that would pay my tuition."

"See, there you go." He stopped as if something clicked in his memory. Ryan walked back to the railroad sign they passed and looked at the metal pole. "I think we're on the right path. Here's a symbol for 'Go This Way.' "

Michelle crossed her arms as she stared at the symbol, which was simply a circle with an arrow attached to it. "I'll take your word for it."

As they continued down the tracks, Michelle kept an eye on the ground, when a thought occurred to her. "But, Ryan, you would handle it the opposite way."

"I don't know what you're talking about."

"You'd believe the buried treasure was there. No Ida ghost necessary. If there was a chance that treasure was around, you would believe it."

"So?" Ryan said, sounding preoccupied as he looked around for the next hobo code.

"But you wouldn't hunt for it," she said as she jumped on the rail joiner and tried to keep her balance. "Even if you had details on where the treasure was located, you wouldn't go after it. You'd wait for it to fall in your lap."

"No, that's not true."

"Do you think Homer and Ida stashed their fortune somewhere in Carbon Hill?" she asked as her arms wheeled.

"Yeah."

She looked up, smiling with pride as she kept her balance. "Where have you dug for it?"

"Okay," he said with a reluctant smile. "You got me."

"The same when it came to me," she said as she looked down at the train tracks.

"And you lost me again."

"You said you were interested in me, but did you go after me?" she asked, putting one foot in front of the other. "No, I went after you."

"Now, that I kind of liked," he said with a slow smile that made her insides melt. "I wouldn't change that for a thing."

"And the same goes with your artwork," she said briskly as she jumped off the rail joiner and stood at his side.

Ryan froze. The expression on his face closed up and his jaw tightened. She knew he was mad at himself for not seeing where she was headed.

"You have talent that is waiting to be untapped." She poked her finger against his arm. "Plan on doing something about it?"

"I don't want to talk about it." He turned and continued down the tracks.

"Yep," she muttered under her breath, "that's what I thought."

Ryan walked down the tracks at a hard, fast pace. If he was lucky, it would knock the breath right out of Michelle. She'd be too busy gasping for air to think about wasting it on conversation.

His mouth tightened with anger. He knew she was going to bring up the mural, sooner or later, and he had bet on sooner. It had been a sure thing.

Squeezing his eyes with regret, Ryan knew he shouldn't have taken her back to the bowling alley. It had been a risk. There had been too strong of a possibility that he was wrong about the clue, but once the idea had grabbed hold, he couldn't shake it off.

And yet, he had a feeling he was lying to himself. He was looking for a reason to take her to the bowling alley. He wanted her to see what he had created.

Of course, he went mute the minute she saw it. He backed off, not wanting her to know the identity of the artist, but at the same time, wanting her to figure it out. He was undoubtedly going insane.

Even when he walked into Pins & Pints—hell, the minute they headed in that direction—he knew what would happen. He could predict what Michelle would do if she found out about his interest in art.

She would prod. Poke. Push. And keep pushing. It could be her greatest virtue, as well as her most annoying trait. And right now, he didn't want to be pushed.

Ryan saw the squiggly symbol clear ahead and had the printout ready before he reached it. Michelle was at his side sooner than he expected.

"What does it say?" she asked, looking over his arm. Each gasping breath she tried to control added to his guilt. He shouldn't have set a neck-breaking pace.

"It promises food." He placed his hand over his stomach when it growled in anticipation. "They wouldn't tease us about that, would they?"

"Maybe they got Annie to make lunch," she suggested. "She's a good cook. That bed and breakfast is going to be one of the best kept secrets around here."

"Annie has some good marketing plans," he said, wondering why he was bothering to come to the woman's defense. "Just wait and see."

"Yeah, Vanessa is the same way," Michelle said, huffing and puffing as she tried to regain the use of her lungs. "Big plans, small audience. She should go where it would be appreciated."

"You know"—he came to a sudden halt and swiveled to face Michelle—"you don't have to go to a big city to follow your dreams."

"But it helps."

"Just because you don't want to stay here doesn't mean everyone else is dying to get out of town."

Michelle took a step back and held her hands up in surrender. "Okay, okay."

"And maybe I don't feel the need to 'untap' my artistic ability. I'm fine the way things are," he told her and marched onward.

He heard her mumbling behind him. He decided to ignore it, but the mumblings grew louder. And louder. He could easily imagine her with exaggerated facial expressions and hand gestures. "What was that?" he asked, turning back.

She immediately stood to attention. "Nothing," she answered with injured pride.

Yeah, right. She had something to say and he wasn't going to be able to shut her up. *One . . . two . . . thr—*

"What's your favorite kind of art?" she asked. Her perky attitude was kind of scary. He almost preferred the negative Michelle.

"I don't have one." His cold tone should have quelled further questions, but this was Michelle he was dealing with.

"Is your medium paint?"

He wasn't going to look at her. Wasn't going to stop and chat. The sooner they got off this track, the sooner he could get away from this conversation. "Michelle, stop trying to make this into something it's not."

"Is your mural the only thing you've made? I have a feeling it's not."

He pictured his parents' basement filled with his attempts. Some of which no one had ever seen and he'd like to keep it that way. "I'm not talking about it."

"I would love to see what else you've done."

"You won't." He immediately realized his error. He

should have lied. Told her there wasn't anything else. Now she was going to pursue it until he begged for mercy.

"You know what?" Michelle's tone indicated she was swerving around topics and he had better keep on his toes. "You should see some of the museums in Chicago."

"I don't want to," he lied. He'd love to go there, with Michelle. He could see it clearly in his head and it grabbed at his heart.

"You need to explore your full potential."

The muscle bunched in his jaw. "Full potential meaning fame and fortune?"

"Not necessarily. Full potential means facing your fears, overcoming them, and becoming a better artist because of it."

"What are you talking about?" He slowed down and looked at her. "I'm not afraid."

"Yeah, you are." She nodded her head matter-of-factly. "About your art."

"Wait a second." There was that twinge again. He had to stop listening to her. She was getting into his head and that could be dangerous. "Do you honestly believe that not pursuing a hobby or interest means I'm afraid?"

"Bingo!" She raised her arms above her head. "We have a winner."

"I don't want to make art my career. My life. Has that occurred to you? Not everyone wants to make sacrifices to support a *hobby*." Great, he just admitted he had a hobby. She was going to catch him on every slip he made.

"I get what you're saying." She held her hand up, placating him. "But your case is different."

He knew better than to ask, but he really wanted to hear her opinion. "Why is that?"

"People who treat art as a hobby love what they do. You have a *passion*, and it showed in your work."

She was getting too close to a raw nerve. He wasn't ready to hear this. To do something about it. "And you have a passion for your work?" he asked as he continued walking the track.

"I sure do," she said, her stride matching his. "Sometimes it's the only thing that gets me through the low points. And there are plenty of those."

"Did you . . ." Aw, hell, he might as well ask, "Did you face your fears?"

"I do it *constantly*. The usual stuff. Am I good enough? Can I do better? Can I come up with a recipe that will cause a buzz? Do I have what it takes? I deal with those questions every day."

"Sounds exhausting." And familiar. There had been plenty of times when he struggled to face a blank canvas. He never told anyone, though. People would think he had a fear of paper.

"Not really. It's part of the process. Although . . ." Michelle's voice trailed off. "I'll tell you a secret," she continued in a low, confidential whisper.

He leaned closer, not liking how good it made him feel that she was sharing something private with him. Not liking it one bit, but not stopping it, either.

"You were right about why I came back to Carbon Hill," she confessed. "There was more to it than helping Vanessa."

"I'm shocked."

"Stop it." She playfully pushed his arm. "I was getting worried. I felt stalled. Running on empty. I thought I was losing my mojo."

"Mojo?"

"Uh . . ." She rotated her hands, trying to come up with a different word. "My energy. Verve? Zest for life."

"Okay. Mojo." Was it required for creative people to give bizarre names to their emotions? He hoped not.

"And I remembered that the last time I felt it strongly was here"—she gestured around her—"in Carbon Hill."

"Maybe it's something in the water."

"No, seriously. Back then I was pumped and ready to take on the world. All cylinders blasting. It felt good. Real good. I've never felt anything like that since."

"It's called youth."

"I don't think so. I felt it before. I'm feeling it right now while I'm here. Not as strong as I hoped for, but my mojo is coming back."

"Okay, first of all, what you are feeling is reduced stress from taking a vacation."

"Nope, this is something else entirely. Hey!" She ran ahead and pointed at a fence next to the tracks. "It's another hobo code."

He stopped beside her and looked at the sign. The broken fence was part of the train yard filled with rusted, abandoned boxcars.

"This is the Graveyard," Ryan said as he folded the printout and put it back in his pocket. "I'm sure of it."

"Might as well give it a look." They walked down the slope to the fence and entered the yard, when Michelle gasped.

"What?" Ryan looked to see if she was okay. "Did you get hurt? What is it?"

"Over there." She pointed at something in the yard. "On that orange boxcar. Is that . . . blood?"

He looked over his shoulder at where she indicated. A dark red splotch, right about at the height of his shoulder, had dripped down the rusted metal.

"No, that's not blood." Ryan walked over to the car and inspected it. "It's paint."

"Are you sure?"

"I'm the one with artistic capabilities, right?" He headed deeper into the yard and Michelle kept close to him. It wasn't long when they saw the paint blotches and drips staining the cars and ground.

"Weird graffiti," Michelle decided. "They really need to start teaching art classes in the schools."

"This must be where people play paintball. I heard about this place. It's new to the area."

"Paintball?"

"It's a sport where teams shoot paintballs at each other."

"Yeah, yeah, yeah. The name is self-explanatory. It's a messier, low-tech version of laser tag." She looked around. "I'm surprised this is here. I thought Pins & Pints was the only place in Carbon Hill you could have fun while standing up."

Ryan wasn't even going to try to hide his smile. "You can also have fun there lying down."

"Yoo-hoo!" Annie called out, partially hidden by a boxcar. She waved them over. When they got closer, Ryan could see that the woman was standing next to a picnic table that dipped under the weight of the food.

Ryan waved back, his stomach rumbling with impatience. "I see Clayton and Brandy sitting at the table, but I don't see the Aschenbrenners anywhere."

"Then it's a good thing we didn't follow them," Michelle said.

Ryan greeted Annie, who shyly offered them a large spread of food. It dawned on him that the woman was intimidated by feeding a professional chef. He could heap the compliments as fast as he heaped the food on his plate, but it seemed Michelle's opinion mattered more to Annie.

Michelle appeared to sense this and took the responsibility seriously. She managed to say just the right things to put Annie at ease. Ryan always knew Michelle was a class act.

"Oh, honey," Annie said, "I looked everywhere and I still can't find your cell phone."

"Thanks for looking," Michelle said, making a point not to look at Brandy. "I'm sure it will show up."

Ryan noticed Brandy's sly smile. Michelle was probably right that the woman had something to do with the disappearance of her cell phone.

Brandy and Clayton hadn't greeted them warmly, but he expected that. These guys were in it for themselves. He also noticed that there was some frost between Brandy and her team member, which didn't surprise him.

The only thing that surprised him was that Clayton had lasted this long with Brandy. Either the guy was head-over-heels in love with the woman, or . . . nope, that had to be the only thing that kept him going. Poor guy.

"What's the next assignment?" Michelle asked Annie as she filled a cup of ice-cold water and handed it to Ryan. The simple act threw him off. He liked being waited on, but that hadn't happened for quite some time.

"We still need to wait for Dennis and Margaret, but I don't see any harm in telling you that you guys will be in a paintball game."

"We figured that much out," Michelle said as she filled a cup of water for herself.

"And that you will be reenacting the shoot-out scene between the Wirts and the authorities."

Ryan's plastic fork stopped midway to his mouth. "Excuse me?"

"You're going to start from one end of the yard"—she pointed at where they came in—"and have to get to the other end without getting hit by the 'authorities.' "

"Who are the authorities?" Clayton asked hesitantly.

"Some paintball fanatics who volunteered," Annie said. "They'll be here soon."

Clayton closed his eyes with dread. Ryan suspected the guy hated sports of any kind.

"Once you get to the exit without getting hit, you're on to the next leg of the hunt."

"And what if you do get hit?" Brandy asked.

Annie grimaced. "Well, you'll still be in the game . . ."

"But?" Brandy prompted her.

"Trust me," Annie said. "You don't want to get hit."

Chapter 9

Michelle screamed and dove for the ground just as a paint-ball whizzed past her. She coughed as the dust billowed around her and she clenched her paintball gun as if it was her only ally. Her only hope. "We are never going to get out of here alive!"

"These guys are good," Ryan said, peeking over a cor-roded sheet of metal. The sunlight glinted off the sweat dripping from his lean cheekbone.

Not looking at the bright side of the situation right now, are we? Michelle noticed with grim satisfaction. That could mean only one thing. There wasn't a bright side. It was all bad.

They were so in trouble. Michelle wiped the dust that settled on her goggles. The goggles that looked mean and sleek on everyone else but made her look like an amphib-ian. Her mom would have a conniption fit if she saw her.

What would the consequence be if they just got caught right now? Annie wouldn't tell them, but it couldn't be that bad. Not as bad as being hunted down by guys who'd watched way too many dumb action movies.

Could it?

Ryan jumped up and zoomed past her. "Run!"

Michelle looked around her, her heart pounding fast and

furious, but she didn't see any immediate danger. "Where?" she yelled frantically after him.

"Follow me!"

Easier said than done. Michelle bolted after Ryan, but the guy was fast. She could barely keep up and her gun kept knocking against her leg. She felt clumsy and slow. She couldn't believe people did this for fun.

And there must be some sort of filter in her eye goggles, because Ryan looked really, *really* good wearing a thin, long-sleeved T-shirt and faded jeans. She'd seen him wear stuff like that all the time, but not like this. Not as the fabric strained against his muscles.

Even his expression looked sexy. The man was focused. Ready to defend his turf. To defend her. That sensation coiling in her chest tightened. What was she doing getting hot and bothered over a bunch of guys playing war? It was a *game*. Male fantasy. He wouldn't do the same in real life.

She caught up to him as he aimed and shot their attacker. The paintball clipped the guy, smearing red paint along the brown camouflage jacket.

"Yes! Bull's-eye!" Ryan crowed and pumped his fist in the air.

"You grazed him. It barely hit his arm," Michelle pointed out, watching the helmeted guy get called out by the referee who stood at the sidelines. "How is that a bull's-eye?"

Ryan's smile made her blood fizz and pop in her veins. "Maybe that's where I was aiming."

"Whatever." She heard the scurry of footsteps. "We've got company." Oh, great. Now *she* was sounding like a male action hero. "Hide."

Ryan grabbed her hand and ran a couple of boxcars down. There was a red one lying on its side in the weeds. "Get in," Ryan told her and she jumped into the opening, landing awkwardly on her hip. She was going to be bruised and battered by the end of the game.

Michelle pulled off her goggles, knowing it was against the safety rules, but at this point, she didn't care. It was too shadowy to see. She looked around when Ryan jumped in after her. And managed to land on his feet, unlike her, of course. "We're trapped," she informed him.

"Only if they find us." He pushed up his goggles and looked around. Ryan gulped in air, his chest rising and falling rapidly. Michelle was mesmerized by the sweat trickling down his neck.

"It's going to be like shooting fish in a barrel." She inched far away from the opening, but there wasn't much wiggle room in the small boxcar.

"Keep your voice down," he said in a whisper. "You don't want it to echo."

The guy had a point. She fell silent and listened for any noise in the train yard. Nothing alerted her. "How far do you think we are to the exit?"

"Very."

Oh, that was helpful. "We should be doing better than everyone else, don't you think? How far do you think are the other teams?"

"Dunno." He shrugged as he checked his paintball gun. "I haven't seen them. Which is kind of strange."

They had probably found a way out and were already on to the next level. "How is it that we aren't always last, but *dead* last?"

"It doesn't matter," Ryan said as he brushed away spiderwebs and settled into a corner of the car. "We don't have to be first or last to get to the exit. We have to get there without getting tagged."

"Great, let's do that," Michelle said. "What's the strategy?"

Ryan shrugged. "Watch my back and I'll watch yours."

"That's it?" Simple, but that could take all day. "Is there a way we can speed this up?"

"Do you have any ideas?"

"No, but we need to come up with something. Do we go on the offensive or defensive?"

"I pick defense."

She slumped back against the metal wall. "Shoot. I was going to say offensive." It sounded faster. Less nerve-wracking.

"Michelle, we can't outgun these guys."

"There are only six of them," she pointed out, "and they are trying to tag six of us. We already took out one of them. We're at an advantage, so let's make the most of it. What do you say?"

"But they only have to tag one person on a team for that team to get out."

"Okay . . ." Michelle leaned her head against the wall. "We're screwed." They might as well wait here until someone was smart enough to look inside. It would take longer, but she wouldn't have to move.

"Not necessarily."

Great. Now he was going to see the silver lining in the situation. Wasn't she suffering enough? Michelle's sigh rattled deep in her ribs. "I wish I had my cell phone."

Ryan frowned. "How would that help us?"

"It wouldn't." She winced as she tried to find a comfortable spot on the wall. There weren't any. "But I would call Vanessa and tell her I'm taking her off my Christmas list because she put me through this hell."

"Focus on getting through this level, and then you can tell her to her face."

Michelle tilted her head and looked at the opening above her. "Do you hear that?" she asked in the quietest of whispers.

"No." Ryan mouthed the words. "What?"

"That's just it." She moved away from the wall and gripped her gun tightly. "I don't hear anything."

He looked at the opening. "That can't be good."

"Oh, great. Now you're sounding like me." The end of the world must be near.

Ryan gestured at the open door above them. "Peek out and see if anyone is around."

"Me?" she asked in a squawk. So much for being her protector and defender. "Why not you?"

"I'm not the one with the mojo," he said with a crooked smile.

Michelle held up a finger. "Rule number one, don't mess with my mojo. Rule number two"—she held up another finger—"don't misuse the mojo."

"You just made that up."

"It's still true."

"Someone has to look outside. You do it, and I'll cover you," he promised.

Not good enough. She was going to be ambushed with paint the minute she peeked outside. That thought alone made her put her goggles back on. "How about you look outside and I'll cover you?"

Ryan held up his hand to stop the argument. "Okay, we're at a draw. This calls for one thing."

"Rock, paper, scissors?"

The fanning lines around his blue eyes deepened. "I was going to say we both go up at the same time."

"That works, too." Michelle crawled closer to the opening. Her heart pounded hard. She had never liked games like these. She always got caught.

"On the count of three," Ryan said as he readjusted his goggles.

"Oh, I am not falling for that." She crawled back, wincing as each move made the metal yawn and buck.

"Not falling for what?"

"Cut the innocent act," she whispered fiercely. "I know what's going to happen. You're going to say three, and I pop out alone like a jack-in-the-box."

Ryan's smile was slow and downright wicked.

"Uh-huh." She pointed an accusing finger at him. "I know what that smile means. I am on to you. I have an older brother, you know."

"Okay, fine. I'll be on the lookout."

"Good." It served him right. She didn't feel the least bit guilty about her cowardice.

"You come up with a strategy," he said as he slowly crept toward the opening.

No problem. "My strategy includes a really fast getaway car." There. Her job was done.

"Good luck finding that." Ryan peered out of the opening.

Michelle sighed with relief when he wasn't clobbered with paint. "It would have worked, too. The paint wouldn't hit us—hey! What if we used metal as a shield?"

"It's too heavy," he decided as he looked around.

"We'll get a small metal slab." She wasn't sure if there were any around here, or if she'd want to touch it . . .

"It'll make us too easy to spot."

"But we can block the paint."

"But it won't cover all of us. The paint could hit our shoes and then we're out."

Michelle folded her arms across her chest. "I think I like your optimistic side better," she muttered.

He looked down at her. "Are you coming up with a different strategy?"

She smiled sweetly. "How about if you walk in front and I walk behind you, facing backward."

Ryan pondered the idea and gave a nod. "That'll work. Come on." He motioned for her to follow him and climbed out of the boxcar.

"Oh, sheesh. I can't believe you agreed to that." It was too simplistic. It wasn't going to work. There were too many things that could go wrong.

She climbed out with far less grace than Ryan displayed. "Which way is the exit?" she asked as he helped her down.

"That way." He pointed with his gun. "Get behind me."

She did what he said and faced the other way. Walking backward was not easy, but Ryan took it slowly. She had stepped on his heel only a few dozen times when he broke the silence.

"See anyone so far?" he asked.

"Nope. Oh, wait." She saw a glimpse of red hair behind an ancient caboose. "I see Brandy."

"Where?"

Brandy slid around the side and spotted her. Michelle gave a nod of acknowledgment. Damn, even Brandy looked good in the stupid goggles. "Behind the faded red caboose. I don't see Clayton anywhere."

"I can't look behind me," Ryan reminded her. "Give me her clock position."

"What are you talking about?"

"Picture a clock and I'm at the twelve position," Ryan suggested patiently. "What position is Brandy?"

Michelle made a face. She was twenty-five years old and playing army with a bunch of overgrown boys. "Five o'clock."

"Any authorities?"

She glanced around. "Mmm—nope." Her attention went back to Brandy. Her eyes went wide as the redhead cocked her gun and aimed. Directly at her. "Oh, shit."

"What?" Ryan stopped and Michelle collided into his back. "What's wrong?"

"Five o'clock!" She pushed Ryan to the ground. "Get down!"

Ryan rolled onto his back as he heard a shot. It ricocheted wildly on one of the boxcars. "What was that about?"

"Brandy just took a shot at me!" Michelle jumped to her feet with amazing speed and aimed at five o'clock. "She's going down."

Ryan sat up. "Don't waste your paint."

"Why not? She did." She put her gun down. "She's gone. The one time I could hit her right between the eyes and I miss that opportunity."

"I'm sure you'll get another chance." Ryan got on his feet and looked around. They were lucky no one fired on them while they were distracted.

"Are those train tracks under that train?" Michelle asked, pointing at the series of boxcars next to them with her gun.

"Yep." It was probably how they moved the cars to the train yard.

"Let's crawl under this train." Michelle's voice wavered with excitement, the first time he had heard it since they walked into the yard. "It will give us the cover we need."

"It's too low." They would be on their bellies, making them far too vulnerable.

"We'll crawl on our elbows like they do in the army. Ooh, won't that be fun?"

Ryan raised his eyebrow at Michelle's sarcasm. "We won't be able to see our surroundings as well as our opponents."

"And they probably won't have as good a shot."

He didn't think it was a good idea, but he didn't have another one to counter it. "Might as well."

He crawled under the train after Michelle. At this level he could see a lot of ground. But only in front of them. Ryan decided it wasn't worth pointing out the disadvantage. Michelle had already started crawling on her elbows, determined to make this work.

"This is harder than it looks," Michelle said between grunts.

"Don't think about that," he suggested as he kept an eye out for any sudden movements and listened for telltale sounds. "Think about something else."

"Like why I'm doing this? Why am I spending a beautiful autumn day under a train with freaks shooting paint at me? Sorry, Ryan, that doesn't give me much of an adrenaline boost."

"How about why does Brandy hate you so much?" The redhead seemed to be Michelle's mortal enemy. That had to get her blood pumping.

"I don't know." Sure enough, Michelle's next move was quick and clean. "It's always been that way, but it got worse after I won Miss Horseradish."

"She really wanted that title."

"Well, yeah. But she didn't think I deserved it." Michelle suddenly shot ahead of him on the track.

"It doesn't matter what she thought," Ryan said as he caught up with her. "You won."

"Honestly, I didn't deserve it, but most people are too polite to say anything. I was aiming for one of the top five spots and to get some scholarship money. But Brandy was doing some horrible stuff to her true competitors and they were firing back. All the antics basically leveled the playing field. No one expected me to win. I sure didn't."

And he sure didn't expect the topic of Brandy would make them move so fast. "You don't think we have a chance of winning this hunt. You could be wrong again."

She scoffed at the idea. "I don't think so."

"But you're getting your mojo back."

"I'm beginning to regret mentioning it." Her eyes narrowed as she looked at him. "You just like saying the word."

"It's what brought you back to Carbon Hill, you know."

"What did?" she asked, her pace slowing down.

"Your mojo. You lost it. Couldn't find it, so you came back where you last had it."

"Sshh . . ." She held up her hand.

They froze as they heard footsteps racing around them.

Ryan hated not being able to see. Hated the vulnerable position they had put themselves in. They waited, guns ready, until the scuffling footsteps faded.

"I did not leave my mojo here," Michelle said as they went back to crawling on their bellies. "I think I would have noticed it was gone way before now."

"When you lived in Carbon Hill, you went after whatever you wanted and you got it." Did she know how unusual that was? She might take that for granted. "You made things work your way."

"You can't beat that feeling," she said with a wistful smile. "But Carbon Hill has nothing to do with it."

"Okay, from the way you're explaining it, the moment you leave town, that mojo starts to fade." Something niggled in the back of his mind. He had a feeling they shouldn't discuss this.

What if the mojo had started fading before she left town. After all, her first time wasn't perfect. Did he have something to do with this? Was he going to have to fix it?

Michelle paused from crawling. "I like who I was back then. I felt like I could do anything."

So did he, but he found this version of Michelle even more fascinating. "You liked it when life came easy."

"That, too." She sighed and collapsed on the track. "Well, thanks a lot, Ryan," she said, her voice muffled against her arm. "You have totally depressed me."

"What's your problem?" Ryan looked around them. "You don't like things too easy."

Michelle groaned but didn't look up. "Think again."

"Back then, if there was an opportunity, you went for it, and you gave it your all. And guess what? You got everything you wanted. Probably because you weren't dreaming big." Unlike Ryan, who dreamed too big. But at least he knew it.

"You make it sound like that's a bad thing," Michelle

said, lifting her head. "My dad was out of a job and we were barely making ends meet. There was no point in dreaming big."

"Exactly." She should be reaching for the stars, but she was pulling herself back.

"Then everyone in town backs me up, and all of a sudden I'm not in control of my goals. The dream starts getting bigger and bigger."

"Hold that thought." He pointed past her. "The exit is right there."

She looked at where he indicated. "How are we going to get there? There's no cover."

"We run like hell."

Michelle looked back at him. "That's it? Just run? It's out in the open."

He waggled his eyebrows. "Makes things exciting, don't you think?"

Michelle snorted. "You mean harder."

"Same thing."

She sighed and got into a crouching position. "You better watch my back." Michelle closed her eyes, muttered something that could have either been a prayer or a curse, and stepped out from under the train.

Ryan didn't realize he had been holding his breath until he stretched to his full height and no one took a shot at him. No reason to test his luck any further. "Ready? Run!"

Michelle grabbed his shirt before he could move. "This is your idea of strategy?" she asked, her eyes wide with disbelief. "We could get ambushed."

"The strategy is simple. Don't get hit."

"Stop." She held on tighter. "The exit is right there, and they have no one covering it. Don't you think that's weird?"

"Yeah, now that you've mentioned it." There were mountains of boxcars and parts on either side of the path to the exit. No telling what could be lurking in the shadows.

"Okay, new plan. Keep your back against the wall and look out for the authorities."

"Got it." She hurried to the closest wall and slammed her back against it. The sound of metal reverberated around them. "Sorry."

"If there's anyone lurking," Ryan said, walking down the middle of the pathway, his gun ready, "I'll draw them out, and then you shoot them."

"Me?" She almost dropped her gun. "I've never shot one of these things."

He pivoted on his feet and looked for any blind spots. "You were ready to shoot Brandy."

"That's different."

It probably was. She didn't have to think about it. Didn't have to gear up for it. "Then channel that feeling and aim it at the authorities."

"I'm not experienced with this thing." Her voice wavered with nervousness. "Let's switch."

"Michelle"—he looked above her, but didn't see anybody—"I wouldn't ask you to do it if I didn't think you could."

"Ryan! Over there! Uh . . . uh . . . one o'clock!"

He didn't look. He reached, ducking, and rolled out of the line of fire. But the guy didn't let up. He was spraying paintballs and Ryan didn't know which way to run for cover.

"Bulls-eye!" Michelle yelled with victory.

Ryan kept rolling as the rainfall of paintballs stopped. He lay on his back, trapped against the wall, the gun on the ground where he first rolled. Damn!

But the baller didn't shoot. Ryan was unarmed and vulnerable. What was going on? Ryan looked at where the shots were fired and saw their opponent inspecting the smear of paint on his leg.

"Whoo-hoo!" Michelle ran for Ryan. "I did it! I did it!

Uh-huh, uh-huh." She did some sort of dance move that was relegated to wedding receptions, and only when everyone was drunk. "Did you see that?"

"Lucky hit," the guy called out.

"Aw, don't be a sore loser. You are out. Uh-huh, Uh-huh." She did that weird chicken dance again and raised her fist above her head. "I'm king of the—"

He heard it. Saw the cloud of paint fanning around her back. Michelle's mouth sagged open. She didn't look behind her. It didn't matter anymore.

"I've been hit."

"Do you watch football?" Ryan asked Michelle as the paintball referee escorted them to the exit.

"Not if I can help it," she said, looking straight ahead. She didn't need to look at Ryan to know he was not happy.

"Do you know when the player does the touchdown dance? Do you know *why* they call it a *touchdown* dance?"

Michelle clenched her teeth.

"It's because the player has to make the touchdown *before* the dance."

She turned sharply and glared at Ryan. "Are you done?"

"I'm just warming up."

Michelle pointed at the area where she had been shot down. "You should have been watching my back. What happened?"

Ryan's eyes widened at her complaint. "I was *on* my back and I didn't have my gun."

Michelle scoffed. "Excuses, excuses."

"It's a fact. You were there." He gestured at her and then at the spot on the ground. "You saw it happen."

She wasn't listening to him anymore. "And now I have this huge paint blotch on my favorite jacket. It's never going to come out." She could feel it seeping into the fabric, touching her shirt. Michelle quickly shrugged the jacket off.

"Michelle and Ryan, what happened?" Annie's voice was almost a whine. "You were so close to the finish line."

Oh, great. That was going to start Ryan off all over again. "Now what?" Michelle asked as she wrapped the jacket sleeves around her waist.

"Well, in the legend, the authorities chased Homer and Ida to the river bluffs."

"River bluffs?" Ryan's tone was sharp and clipped.

"On foot," Annie added.

Michelle's blisters on her heel started to pulse. "Are you sure they didn't take a car?"

"The authorities did," Annie admitted. "And they will for this reenactment, but Homer and Ida didn't."

"We have to get to the bluffs on foot?" Michelle verified. "And keep from getting caught?"

"That's right. There's a checkpoint where we're going to meet you." She gave them a map. "You'll want to get there before dark, or you'll be communing with nature tonight."

"Fun." Michelle looked at Ryan, who looked grim. Or tired. Probably still pissed off at her.

"At least you're wearing tennis shoes," he said.

And he was still Mr. Ray of Sunshine. Did he do that just to annoy her? Most likely.

Michelle made a face and returned her attention to Annie. "What happens when we get caught?"

"You mean if," Ryan said.

There was that optimism again. He needed to get medical attention for that. It couldn't be healthy.

"Then we'll take you back to this starting point and you'll have to do it again," Annie explained.

Michelle rubbed her forehead as a headache began to brew behind her temples. How had she gotten herself stuck in this? Oh, yeah. Vanessa. The friend who was supposed to look out for her, not throw her to the hungry wolves. Vanessa had a lot of groveling to do after this hunt.

"Anything else?" Michelle asked.

"Yeah," Annie said, not looking her in the eye. "Because you were caught, you are required to take on one more element of the legend."

Michelle winced and closed her eyes. "Tell me it's not a dog." *Please, please, please. No more animals.*

A spontaneous, nervous laugh escaped from Annie. "No, no dog. I promise." She reached for Michelle's right hand and snapped a metal cuff around her wrist.

Michelle looked down, her mouth sagging open, as she saw Annie cuff Ryan's left wrist. Her eyes grew wide.

Ryan yanked away from Michelle, but he didn't get far. The chain was short and strong. They were stuck.

"No, no, no." She refused to believe that anyone would handcuff her. Especially to Ryan Slater! The panic flashed in her chest as she stared at Annie's apologetic expression. "No! You have *got* to be kidding."

Chapter 10

"Stop!" Michelle said as she quit kicking the fallen leaves when she heard the rush of water. She couldn't see it, but they had to be near. And about time, because she was one step away from chewing her hand off to regain her freedom. "I said stop!"

"You keep falling behind." Ryan slowed down and looked over his shoulder. "Are you okay?"

"Oh, yes. Thank you for asking," Michelle said as she brushed the hair out of her eyes. "I'm fine. I would feel even better if a guy wasn't *dragging me handcuffed across the countryside.*" She lifted her right hand and jingled the chain that connected them.

Ryan walked toward a tree stripped of its leaves. "Catch your breath here for a few minutes."

"Minutes?" She leaned against the thick trunk. It was scratchy and leaned at an odd angle, but it was better than walking. "How about a half an hour?"

"We don't need to get caught."

Like she hadn't figured that out on her own. "We are well off the beaten path. What am I saying? There is no path." She rubbed her wrist under the handcuff. The metal chafed her skin.

"I wouldn't be too sure. These guys are following us and there are only a few ways to get to the river bluffs."

Michelle glanced around the ground. "Is there a sharp rock around here?"

Ryan took a step back. "If you try to brain me with anything, then you'll be dragging dead weight. It's best to keep me conscious."

"Don't give me any ideas," she muttered darkly. "I want a sharp rock to break this chain. It would make this trek easier."

Ryan was already shaking his head at her idea. "A rock isn't going to do the trick. You need something that's going to cut through metal."

Michelle groaned and trudged her feet forward. It wasn't as if she had any choice in the matter. Wherever Ryan chose to go, she was forced to follow. "How is it that you make a mistake and we're both punished? It's so unfair."

He stopped abruptly. "Wait."

She lost her balance. Her legs kicked in the air and she caught herself before falling in the dirt. "Hey, stop that!"

"This is my fault?" He sounded incredulous. "Is that what you think?"

Hadn't he been listening? "You were supposed to watch my back," she said as if she were talking to a toddler.

"I did." He tapped his chest with his cuffed hand, Michelle's hand flopping next to his. "But there's only so much I can do when you're doing the chicken dance out in the open."

She cast a withering glare in his direction, but it was useless. The man was immune to them. "First of all, it was a celebration dance. Second, watching my back is watching my back. There are no excuses. It doesn't matter if I was standing still or doing backflips. You were supposed to watch my back."

She walked away, determined to lead them to the bluff. The sooner they got there, the sooner this stupid handcuff would be removed. But Ryan refused to follow. He stood still, and with one sharp move of his arm, she boomeranged back, colliding into his chest.

"Would you stop doing that?" she asked through clenched teeth. She pushed away from him, refusing to notice the solid muscle and heat under her palm.

"Can't blame a guy for having some fun," he said in a low, soft voice.

"Yes, I can." She pulled away but Ryan wasn't finished. Another sharp tug and she was sprawled against him again.

"You need to stop doing that," Ryan told her. "You're going to pull your arm socket out like that."

Michelle's eyes narrowed into slits as she heard his laugh rumble in his chest. "Knock it off," she said as she stepped away from him.

"Or what?"

"Or I'll . . ." What could she do that wasn't going to affect her? Nothing, that's what. And from the smug expression on the rat bastard's face, he knew it.

"Face it, Michelle. This handcuff is an inconvenience"— he held it in front of her face—"but it gives me the power."

A violent jolt of awareness forked through her body. "No, it doesn't," she said hoarsely.

"We are both right-handed, but look at this." He held up their chained hands. "Only your right hand is cuffed. How about that?"

"That doesn't mean anything." Her skin felt hot and tight. "For all you know, I could be ambidextrous."

Ryan didn't seem too concerned about the possibility. "I'm bigger than you." He braced his legs and folded his arms across his chest. "Taller. Stronger."

Did he expect her to get on her knees and sing his praises? She looked at his feet as an idea formed. "You're forgetting something."

He arched one eyebrow. "What's that?"

She dropped to her knees and quickly crawled between

his legs, taking his left hand with her, before he wised up to her plan. Ryan somersaulted and fell onto the ground with a whomp. She could have sworn the ground shook. Her right arm sure did.

She rose to her feet and brushed the dirt off her hands. "The bigger they are, the harder they fall. How about that?"

Michelle shrieked and jumped back as Ryan made a grab for her. "Don't you dare!" She dodged his big hands, but he was fast. Where was this speed when she was getting shot in the back with paint? "Stop it!"

"Michelle," he said as he got to his feet. "You can't get away from me, so stop running."

Like she was going to listen to him. She ran clockwise, and when he made a grab, she went counterclockwise.

Ryan started to laugh. "You look like a tether ball doing that."

"All right, all right." She stomped her foot. As long as he wasn't mad, she'd stop. "Let's start acting like adults here."

Ryan made a face. "Sure, you decide this after you drop me on my ass."

Michelle smiled. It was surprising that maneuver had worked. She was quite proud of it. "Are you going to tell your bowling buddies about that?"

His mouth sagged open. "Hell, no."

"Can I?" She scurried back when he approached her. "Kidding! I swear I'm kidding!"

Ryan's eyes widened. He moved quickly. At her. "Michelle—"

She jumped back. "Stop it—"

"Don't go—" He pounced as she dodged.

"Whoa!" She felt the ground taper off under her feet. She reeled back, trying to get away from the ledge. Ryan made a grab for her, but it was too late. They went tumbling down the grassy hill.

Ryan was suddenly on top of her. His arms cushioned her back, his hands cradling her head. When the ground leveled and they skidded to a stop, she was lying on top of him next to the gurgling river.

"Okay," Michelle said in a squeak. "That hurt."

"Uh-huh." He continued to stare at the sky. The guy looked dazed.

"Are you okay?" she asked as she got off of him in a hurry. "Did you hurt anything?"

"Just my pride."

"How about important stuff?" she asked, looking for any broken bones. "Limbs? Feet? Head?"

He rose onto his elbows. "Clear. What about . . ." His voice trailed off. "Uh-oh."

"What?" She brushed her hand against her mouth and nose. "Do I have something on me?"

"Wait, let me check." Ryan got to his knees, his gaze intent on the area next to her ear.

"What is it?" She cringed and hunched her shoulders. "Is it a bug? Oh, God, is it a spider?"

"Hold still."

She felt his gentle touch against her hairline. "Is it in my hair?" She shivered at the thought. That was one thing she couldn't handle. Michelle raised her hands, ready to scratch whatever it was out of there.

"It's blood."

Michelle's eyelids snapped open. She stared at the red streak on Ryan's thumb. "Blood? Are you sure?"

"Yeah, I'm sure." He reached up and flicked her earlobe with his fingertips. "You have a small cut next to your ear."

How did she manage that? Michelle raised her right hand to check and the metal glittered in the sunlight. "I must have nicked it with the handcuffs."

Ryan stood up and helped her to her feet. "Let's get closer to the water and I'll clean it."

"Clean my cut with *river water?*" All the warm fuzzy feeling of having Ryan taking care of her evaporated. "Thanks, but no thanks."

"C'mon, Michelle," he coaxed as he guided her toward the water's edge.

Didn't this guy know anything about bacteria? Germs? She dug her feet into the ground, but it didn't work as he led her to the water. "Hey, hey, hey. Stop pulling me around. I can still flip you."

His dangerous look made her pulse skip a beat. "Try it and I will flip you over my knee and—"

She gasped as something hot and forbidden flared between her legs. "Try *that* and—"

Ryan looked past her shoulder and tensed. "Uh-oh. They spotted us." He broke into a full-throttle sprint, the jagged pain ripping through her arm as he dragged her behind him. "Run!"

Ryan couldn't believe they didn't get caught. Did he mistake a fisherman with one of the players? Were the opponents disinterested now that they couldn't shoot paintballs at them?

It didn't matter now, and he had a feeling that those guys were done for the night. While he was hiking the bluffs to the top, chained to Michelle.

He had to get to the top before it turned dark. If they were stuck together for the rest of the night, he was in trouble. Nothing, not even a handcuff, was going to stop him from making love to Michelle.

He paused to watch the sun setting over the river. It would be a matter of minutes before it turned dark. They weren't going to make it.

His cock stirred as anticipation filled him. He wanted Michelle more than anything. More than he had five years ago. Or was the need different? The yearning wasn't a dull ache like before. It pierced him like a knife.

"Well, one thing's for sure," Ryan said as he continued up the trail, trying to think of something else. Anything else. "Homer and Ida didn't hide any treasure here."

"Really?" Michelle looked around him, probably wondering what he saw that helped that decision. "How do you know that?"

"Because the commute is insane."

She let out a tired chuckle. "Amen to that."

"There are a couple of other things that wouldn't make it work. All the coming and going would raise suspicion. Not to mention, it would be too heavy to carry items from the tracks."

"True," Michelle agreed.

Ryan stopped and looked at her. "You know, for a minute there it sounded like you believe there's a treasure."

She went a couple more steps before she finally said, "I think there was a treasure. I'm not saying it's still around."

"Wow, I never thought you would say that. What made you change your mind?"

"Because no one—even hardworking horseradish farmers—would put up with all this unless they were protecting something good."

"Yeah, I agree with that." Ryan watched the sun dip past the horizon. Only streaks of red and orange lingered in the evening sky. The excitement simmered deep inside him. "It's getting dark."

"Walk faster," she urged him.

"There's no way we can walk this trail without any light." The moon was probably behind some clouds. At least he thought so. He wasn't one to track the moon on the calendar.

She put her hand on his arm. "Just a little bit farther? Please?"

"Okay." He might be eager over the idea of spending the night under the stars with Michelle, but she would rather face a slippery dark trail. That was a blow to his ego. "We should have reached the top of the bluff by now."

"I know. What if we're on the wrong bluff?"

He didn't even want to consider it. "Michelle, if you have something to say, can you try for something upbeat. Maybe encouraging?"

"Fine." One little word conveyed one big attitude.

"Fine." Yeah, his seduction technique sucked. What was it about Michelle that made him do everything wrong?

"I'll keep quiet, then."

"An even better plan." He squeezed his eyes shut. He was getting worse!

They had walked a couple more steps when Michelle sighed. "Ryan, I am sorry I got you into this."

"You don't need to be. I volunteered." He had been surprised when he did, but now he realized that it all made sense. Michelle Nelson was his weak spot. Always had been, always would.

Did he still love her? He didn't know how to answer that. What he felt for her was different. Before, she had been his muse, his inspiration. He had put her on a pedestal.

Today, she was so off that pedestal. The woman was pushy, sarcastic, and negative. And he wouldn't change a thing, Ryan thought with a wry smile. If he had to choose a partner to be handcuffed to, or to face any challenge, it would be Michelle.

"You volunteered because of me," Michelle said. "And I really owe you after this."

"You don't owe me anything." He didn't want her to hang around because she felt obligated.

"Yeah, I do. I got you into this mess. And then I messed up and got us handcuffed." She jingled the metal to punctuate her statement.

"Which is a nice bonus."

She wasn't listening. "But most of all, I'm sorry I bugged you about your artwork. That was out of line."

His eyes narrowed with suspicion. "What about it?"

"See?" She rapped her knuckles against his shoulders. "You're already tensing up."

He forced himself to relax. "No, I'm not."

"I didn't realize how," she carefully chose her words, "aggressive I was about it. I was trying to be supportive. I'm sorry and I'm not going to say another word about your artwork."

He liked the idea of her support. He wanted it, probably more than anyone else's. "It's not that big of a deal."

"Yeah, it is. Support is a very big deal, but there's a dark side to it. Everyone's been very supportive about my career, but they can be very pushy."

He remembered what she had said while they were under the boxcars. "That's what you meant about the dream getting bigger and bigger."

"There's a lot of expectation," she admitted. "Sometimes it's different from your own, and you don't know which direction to go."

"You'll find your way." She might take some wrong turns, but Michelle wouldn't take long to figure out what she wanted or how she was going to get it.

"How can you be so sure?" Her voice was quiet and hesitant.

"Because I watched you for years, and I see what you're capable of. You can do anything." He used to think it came to her effortlessly. He never looked behind the image to see the hard work she put into it. "It's not luck, or what you call mojo. It's you."

She didn't reply. Ryan suspected Michelle didn't believe him. "I know what it's like not meeting expectations. Or worse, *not* having expectations."

He looked out into the darkening sky and saw a few stars sparkling back at him. "You could never sit back and let it be. I should be more like that. I should keep at my goal until I accomplish it."

"What have you failed at? Is this why you aren't pursuing your art? Whoops." She clapped her hand over her mouth. "Sorry."

"You were there." He stopped and turned around. "It was that night behind the pinsetters."

Michelle looked away and took a step back. "I don't want to talk about it."

He took a step toward her. "Guess what. We are going to talk about it."

"No, we are not." She stuck her fingers in her ears. "La-la-la-la-la. I can't hear you."

"It was all my fault," he admitted.

She pulled her fingers away from her ears. "What was that?"

"Your selective hearing is amazing," he said with a smile. "You're right. You were too sexy for me."

"Oh!" She growled in the back of her throat and pushed at him. "I knew you were going to tease me about that. Just forget I ever said that."

"I'm not. You should have seen yourself that night." His heart pumped faster as he remembered. "You were a goddess."

Her jaw shifted to the side. "Stop teasing me."

"I'm not," he said. "There you were, the one girl I thought I couldn't get, let alone keep, and—"

"You couldn't get me?" She shoved her hands into her hair. "Hello! I was the one trying to catch you."

The corner of his mouth lifted into a crooked smile. "You weren't trying very hard."

"You weren't trying at *all*."

He was guilty of that, but for a good reason. "Because I didn't think I could get you."

"Okay, we definitely need to work on this." She shook her head in disbelief. "From now on, when you want something, go after it. Don't wait for it to come after—"

He swiftly cornered her. He stood in front of her and the river bluff was at her back. Ryan held her hands above her head and nudged his knee between her legs.

". . . you . . ." she trailed off.

"Like this?"

"Of course," Michelle said, swiping her tongue across her bottom lip, "there are times when you might want to ask."

"I want to kiss you." He lowered his head, blocking out everything but him. She felt contained. The bluff at her back and this hungry, determined man in front of her.

"*Ask,*" she emphasized, trying to appear cool as excitement crawled up inside her, ready to burst from her skin. "Nicely."

"Kiss me." His mouth grazed hers.

She noticed he didn't ask. He was a slow learner. Michelle wanted to turn her head and make him ask exactly as she wanted. She wanted to see what he would do. Or even better, what he would make her do. But she sensed that his will would prove stronger this time around.

"Remember to say please."

His fingers flexed against her hands. "Please," he said gruffly against the corner of her mouth.

She closed her eyes, surrendering to the moment. "Yes," she whispered.

His kiss was fierce and rough. The stubble on his chin pricked at her skin. The edge of his teeth dug into her soft mouth.

Already, this wasn't anything like their last time.

Ryan nestled between her legs, his cock pressing against her stomach. He reached down and grabbed at the jacket wrapped around her waist. One short pull and it flapped to the ground.

Sliding his hand under her shirt, he spanned his fingers against her warm flesh. Her stomach muscles twitched and bunched under his palm before his hand trailed up and cupped her breast.

Her nipples tightened under his touch. Her breasts felt heavy and full. He shoved her bra up and the cold breeze made her nipples furl into hard buds. Ryan teased the tips of her breasts with his fingers. Each pull and squeeze plucked deep inside her.

Ryan dipped his head and drew her nipple deep into his mouth. Michelle's staggered groan echoed in the air. She fought to remain upright as her knees threatened to crumple.

His free hand trailed down her stomach. The light, purposeful touch tickled. Her blood roared in her ears as his fingers brushed against the snap of her jeans.

Fire, thick and rushing, pooled low in her belly. Her heart slammed against her rib cage. But she didn't stop him. Didn't say a word.

He flicked open the button and yanked down the zipper. Dipping his hand into her jeans, he pressed his hand against her underwear and cupped her mound. Michelle moaned and sagged against the bluff. He pressed the heel of his hand against her and she flexed her pelvis against him.

"Ryan," she said, closing her eyes, licking her lips.

"Yes?" He traced his finger along her wet slit. Michelle strangled back a moan.

Ryan lazily drew his finger toward her clit, slowly drawing circles around the swollen nub. He licked one of her nipples with the same lazy, slow circles.

Michelle couldn't stand it anymore. All she could think

about was the aching center of her body. She had to have him. Inside her. Right now. She grabbed his hand and slid his finger beneath her panties.

And whimpered when he withdrew. Ryan pulled her hands above her head and held her fast. "Michelle," he said as he leaned into her.

"Hmm?"

"Sometimes it helps if you ask nicely," he said as his free hand skimmed down to her breast.

"This is me being nice."

His husky chuckle made her want to sigh with pleasure. "Politely," he continued as his knuckles swept down the curve of her waist.

She didn't think she could do politely. Not right now. Not when she was straining against him.

His fingertips glided along the edge of her panties. "Saying please."

She arched and rubbed against his thick, hard cock. She twisted against his big hand, but he wouldn't let go. She had to do as he asked.

"Please." The word dragged out of her.

His fingers slid past the silky fabric and threaded along the wet curls. Michelle shuddered against his hand, her body trembling as her self-restraint slipped.

Ryan dipped his finger into her wet core. Her inner muscles gripped him tightly, drawing him in deeper. He pumped her, fast and furious.

The heat inside her coiled tighter and spun. She knew it was too soon, but she couldn't stop it. She didn't want to. She was ready to yield to the inevitable.

She peaked quickly. Violently. The sensations ripping through her, leaving her weak and clinging. Her skin stung, her body pulsed, as she lay weakly against the river bluff.

"Michelle," Ryan roused her. He lowered her hands and she felt the sparks zipping across her bound hand. It blended with the dull ache between her legs and at the tips of her breasts. Even her lips tingled from his whiskers.

"Five more minutes," she told him groggily.

He pressed a kiss against her cheekbone. "It's too dark to keep walking," he decided, straightening her clothes. "We need to find shelter."

Find shelter? It slowly dawned on her. She was alone in the wild with Ryan. She was handcuffed to the sexiest guy she knew and he was hungry for her.

It was official. Vanessa was the best friend *ever!*

Chapter 11

Then again, the wilderness was not all that it was cracked up to be. She stared at the area Ryan wanted them to camp in. "I'm not going in there!"

"It's not that big of a deal."

"Ha!" She pointed at the cave, the opening yawning at her like a giant mouth, ready to take a bite out of her. "That hole is huge."

"Michelle, we can't go any farther on the trail because we don't have a flashlight. This is our only option. It's going to be okay."

She knew everything Ryan said was true and reasonable, but her gut instinct told her to keep moving. "You want me to sleep in a *cave?*"

"Technically it's not a cave," Ryan said as he patted the rocky ledge jutting out. "Think of it as an alcove."

"I'm thinking of it as unacceptable. There could be a bear in there. Or a wolf."

She wasn't sure if bears and wolves were indigenous to the area, but she was certain a bloodthirsty creature with really sharp teeth lived in that cave. If for no other reason than that was how her luck was running.

"There aren't," Ryan said, his patience wearing thin. "I promise."

"What about bats?" She shivered at the thought. Oh,

man, she wished she hadn't thought about bats. They were creepy. There was no way she would lie down in that cave, even with Ryan there to protect her.

"Come on, Michelle." He tugged on their bound wrists. "We have to. I can't see where we're going on the trail."

"We can sit on the trail." It wasn't much better, but it didn't mean dealing with bat droppings.

"This cave will keep us warmer. It will also protect us from the wind and rain."

Michelle ground her back molars. This was not the night of hot wilderness sex she was imagining. She wanted raw, primal passion, but instead she was searching for a dry safe place to sit.

"People are not meant to live in caves," she complained. "I mean . . . you know, people who aren't cavemen." So much for arguing her case.

"I heard people camped out here during the Depression," Ryan said as he crouched down. She had to bend down with him or risk losing an arm. "They were here for months. Years."

Michelle shuddered. She couldn't imagine and she definitely didn't want a taste of that kind of life.

"I'm asking you to stay here for one night," Ryan said, coaxing her inside. "Not even that. A couple of hours until the sun comes up."

"Fine," she said as she crawled under the rocky ledge. "But if I see one bat, we are so out of here."

"Okay. Come here." He pulled her against him until she was settled between his legs. With her back against his chest, and his arms around her, she did feel safe.

"I wish I had my cell phone," she said as she huddled against Ryan. She was feeling the withdrawal in full force. "We could have called Annie and found a way off this bluff. Ordered a pizza. Played solitaire. Something!"

"I don't think they deliver this far."

"Brandy is going to pay dearly for this." The redhead had gone too far this time.

"Let it go."

She considered doing that. She had heard holding a grudge required a lot of energy. She could take the higher road. Or plot her next move against Brandy. That was infinitely more entertaining. "Nope. Not going to."

They sat in front of the opening, looking up at the starry night. "I'm hungry," Ryan said suddenly. "Are you hungry?"

"Not really. Here." She dove her hand into her jacket pocket and pulled out a hard candy.

"A mint?"

"That's all I have, unless you prefer eating paper."

"You're supposed to be a cook," Ryan said as he unwrapped the candy. "You should be able to make a nutritious and filling meal out of bark."

"I'm a pastry chef, not a Green Beret."

"Mm. Yeah." Ryan chomped down on the candy. She could hear it splintering under his teeth. "That hit the spot."

Michelle smiled and snuggled into him. She needed the warmth, but she needed the closeness even more. She loved the feeling of being surrounded by him. Protected. Cherished.

It was just an illusion, but she didn't want to wake up. Not yet.

She couldn't see very much of the cave and decided that was a good thing. The inky darkness and earthy scent were enough for her to keep her eyes directed to the stars in the sky.

Michelle settled against Ryan, her heart thudding against her breastbone. She felt the pull of each breath she took. The metal rubbed against her wrist.

But she was more aware of Ryan. The mint tingled her nose. His heat shrouded her. She closed her eyes as she felt the steady rise and fall of his chest.

The anticipation built gradually inside her. Low, low in

her belly. It grew heavy and hot. It started to ache. She rocked her pelvis forward, but the dull throb wouldn't disappear.

Why wasn't Ryan making his move? She was right there. Ready, primed for action. Nothing and no one would interrupt them. It was just the two of them under an endless night sky.

Yet Ryan sat still, content while she was ready to burst from her skin. He stroked her short hair with his big hand. The flyaway ends slipped between his fingers with agonizing slowness.

She shivered as his palm brushed her neck over and over. She arched into his hold. The fine hairs on her skin stood to attention, ready for him to cup his hand against the side of her throat. To hold her still, to turn her whichever way he pleased.

To take charge.

He didn't seem interested in the idea, yet she could feel his arousal pressing against her. Why wasn't he interested? Why wasn't he reading the signs?

Or, maybe he *was* reading the signals and choosing to ignore them. Why would he do that? He had seemed interested in making love during the hunt. Had even suggested it!

So what was the problem?

Unless . . . no. She pushed the possibility away. Far, far to the edges of her mind only for it to zing right back to the forefront.

It was possible. There was a chance. She hated to admit it, but she really might be too sexy for him.

Michelle cringed at the phrase. Too sexy. There was a positive spin on it, even though "too" anything meant it was negative. She might as well call it as it was. She was too *sexual*. That was more accurate.

That was one of the problems she had encountered with him behind the pinsetters, and it was something she'd had to hold back and hide from the other men whom she invited into her bed. It was never enough that a guy she was attracted to had kissed her. She wanted another kiss. A deeper kiss. A kiss that would make her head spin.

She was definitely one of those women who could never get enough. Guys might *think* that was a trait they wanted in a bedmate, but they gave up real fast. It was too much work. Too much expectation. Simply too much.

Even now, after what happened on the trail, she was ready for more. Did Ryan think that some impromptu, incomplete lovemaking would take the edge off of her desire? She wished.

It only whetted her appetite. Ryan might be satisfied stroking her hair and staring at the stars, but she was about ready to yank his hair, pull him underneath her, and have her way.

Which he may or may not be ready for.

One thing for sure, he was not going to make the next move. It was up to her. The sense of power was mind-boggling. She sucked in the cool air, steadying her nerves.

She moved forward and felt the bite of metal on her right wrist. Ryan's left arm wrapped around her. More out of comfort than design.

What was she going to do about the handcuff? That was going to be a problem. The scrap of silver was the power equalizer. She couldn't have that.

Michelle was ready to work around it. With the handcuff if she had to. But what would be her first move?

She would have to meet him head-on. No flirtations, no innuendo or hints. Face-to-face. No other way would work.

Michelle rose to her knees and the top of her head skimmed the cave ceiling. "Ow." She moved to check the tender spot with her right hand.

Ryan's arm clipped her chin and her head jerked up. The silver chain caught her hair. "Owww!"

"Hold on." He brought his other hand to her waist and carefully turned her, maneuvering her around the handcuff. "What are you trying to do?"

"Turn." She couldn't see his face, but she had a feeling he was smiling and his blue eyes were shimmering with amusement. "Where is the moonlight when you need it?"

"How badly are you hurt?" His free hand touched the crown of her head, even though there wasn't much space between her and the ceiling.

"I'm fine." She placed her hands on his shoulders and lowered her head. The tip of her nose bumped against his as her lips found his mouth.

The tight coil around her ribs gave way as she tasted the lingering mint. She closed her eyes and savored the firm, masculine mouth.

Ryan cupped the back of her head with his hand as he kissed her. Slow, wet kisses that made her pulse skitter. She explored the curve of his bottom lip with a few nibbles and licks. He tasted exactly as she remembered.

She dipped past his lips and teased his tongue with her own. Ryan seemed determined to win. His hand braced against her head as he caught her tongue and drew her in deeper.

Michelle sank against him, her hands slipping from his shoulders to his chest. She smoothed her fingers against the soft cotton stretched across his muscles. She could feel the heat and power trapped underneath. She wanted to unleash it and test her own strength.

Bunching his shirt up, she heard the metal cuff around her wrist jingle with each awkward move. She flattened her hands against his hair-roughened chest, flexing her fingertips into the sculpted muscles.

He was beautiful. She moaned her appreciation against his mouth. She didn't need to see him to know. She could feel it. The bold lines and sleek curves. The indentations of his ribs and the sharp jut of his hip bone.

But she still yearned to see him. She wanted to explore every inch with her hands and mouth. The need sparked inside her. It pricked and burned until she couldn't think of anything else. She had to taste him.

Michelle dropped her hands down to his jeans. Her fingers had bumped against his belt buckle when Ryan tore his mouth from hers.

"Michelle." Her name came out like a groan.

"Hmm?" She wrestled with the leather strap. She was usually more graceful and quicker about this.

"We can't do this."

She pressed her hand against his cock. Her womb clenched at the touch of his hard and thick length. "I think we can."

He yanked the chain that attached them at the wrists, startling her. "You don't get it. I don't have any condoms."

Michelle froze. The need for him flared until she wobbled from the fierce, intense pain.

No condoms. He had *no* condoms. How could he say he wanted her, torment her with his hands and mouth, and not be prepared to back it up with a condom?

"They are back at the bed and breakfast." Ryan's voice was close to a growl.

She couldn't move. She wanted to yell. Scream. It was so unfair! She was never going to know the pleasure of riding him hard. She would never get to experience the pure ecstasy that pressed under the surface between them, desperate for release.

"You don't know the pain I'm in," Ryan said, his voice low and shaking with restraint. "There is nothing more that I want to do than toss you onto the ground and hold you down with my body—"

She closed her eyes and pressed her lips together.

"—strip you naked—"

Her hands clenched his leather belt.

"—and drive my cock into you."

She bit back the whimper as she squeezed her thighs together.

"But I can't." Agony blurred his words. "No matter how much you tempt me, I won't give in."

Michelle licked her lips. She heard the challenge and she desperately wanted to test it. She wanted to see how powerful she was against his determination.

She wanted to, but she wouldn't. He was protecting her. He could have easily flipped her on her back and settled between her thighs and to hell with the consequences.

Ohhh . . . Michelle winced as her core pulsed. *Stop thinking like that.* She should be thankful Ryan was being considerate. Thoughtful. Responsible.

And once the throbbing disappeared she might start feeling thankful.

But right now she felt as though someone just stole the last bite of chocolate cake she had been saving. Her mouth still watered for it and she wasn't going to be satisfied until she had it.

She shouldn't be greedy. She knew that. She really did. After all, Ryan didn't have any of the cake.

Now *that* she might be able to fix.

She slid the button free from his jeans and grasped the zipper when Ryan yanked the handcuff hard. She found herself batting her right hand in the air.

"I mean it, Michelle."

"I know you do." She lowered his zipper with her other hand until he grabbed her wrist and held her immobile.

Soon enough he would figure out that this was for his pleasure and his pleasure only. She wanted to please him as much as he had pleased her. Okay, and maybe throw in a little tormenting. After all, she was going to be suffering until they got back to the bed and breakfast thanks to his lack of foresight.

She lowered her head and rooted for the zipper with her mouth. It was harder than she expected and she was relieved that the darkness cloaked her movements.

"Michelle!" Ryan flexed his pelvis against her. She knew from the instinctive move that he liked it. The inflection of his voice hinted that he was intrigued and willing.

Michelle dragged the zipper down with her teeth. She inhaled the masculine, musky hot skin as her nose pressed against his naked erection.

She wanted to breathe a sigh of relief or cackle wickedly. She didn't have to deal with another barrier of clothing. *This is going to be so easy.* She could take him in her mouth right now if she wanted to.

"Ryan," she said, her puffs of breath making him shiver. She nuzzled against his protruding cock. "I already had my turn. I want to give you yours."

His fingers relaxed around her wrists before he regained his firm grip. "I don't believe you," he told her, his voice gravelly. "You're trying to lower my guard."

"You'll find out soon enough." She bathed his cock with the flat of her tongue, starting from the base and working to the tip. His cock beat against his stomach by the time she swirled her tongue along the domed head.

Ryan's fingers pinched her skin. His shallow breaths echoed in the cave. Her heart pulsed to the same beat as the throbbing between her legs as she inhaled his scent.

She kissed and licked his cock, wanting more. She wanted to grasp the base and pump him with her hands. Cup his balls and squeeze them gently.

Michelle inched down and covered one sac with her mouth. Ryan turned out to be more sensitive than she had anticipated. He flinched and jerked against her mouth. She suckled and licked him until he released her hand. She immediately cradled his balls.

Ryan grabbed the back of her head and silently urged her upward. She smiled against the nest of his wiry hair.

"Let go of my other hand," she whispered. The sense of power flooded her when he immediately complied.

She grasped his cock with both hands and pumped him fast and rough. Ryan twitched and swayed underneath her touch. She would have loved to have seen the pleasure rippling across his face. *Next time . . .*

Michelle covered the head of his cock with her lips and relaxed the muscles in her throat. She inched down his length and drew him in, building a rhythm that was too much for him. Ryan jerked and his guttural groan reverberated against the cave walls.

Later Michelle faced the wall of the cave, determined to get some sleep as her body ached for its own release. It didn't help that her back was pressed firmly against Ryan's chest or that she was cradled into his loose embrace.

He lifted his head and murmured sleepily in her ear. "Didn't you say something about not having sex with me?"

"That sounds vaguely familiar," she whispered as she sought a comfortable spot on his arm for her head. Why was he asking?

"You don't even like me anymore," he teased.

She jabbed her elbow into his ribs. "Stop that. It's not true and you know it."

"What do I know?"

"I like you. Now go to sleep."

Like him. She rolled her eyes at that statement. What a euphemism. The truth of the matter was, she wasn't sure how she felt about him. It was more than like. Right there on the edge of falling in love.

Oh, who was she kidding? She had already fallen, and hit the ground hard. *Ker-splat.* Ryan Slater had been her first love. Okay, her only love. She had been crazy about him. Lusted after him.

And she had never quite gotten over him. Funny, she thought she had. It was odd that here she was, right by his side, after all this time. She hadn't thought that would happen.

But why not? Michelle frowned at her wandering thoughts. If she loved him, why did it seem so weird that she was with him now? Come to think of it, she had never once thought of them having a future together. Why was that?

Unless Vanessa was right. Michelle's eyes widened. Her fling with Ryan had been a part of her to-do list.

All the fragments that she never allowed herself to look at suddenly came together and crystallized. She didn't like what she saw. She didn't like the facts pointing at her. Because she had meant for that disastrous night to be a one-night stand. She had considered having sex with him being the end of the relationship.

Michelle's body tensed as the truth hit hard. She really *was* shallow. If a guy she dated thought having sex was the end of the relationship, she would hit him upside the head.

"What's wrong?" Ryan asked, his voice laced with exhaustion.

"Nothing," she said calmly as her mind screamed, *I messed up! I completely messed up!*

She had loved him for what seemed like forever, but she had never thought what they had would last forever. Why? Her eyes darted around the cave as her mind went into a tailspin. Why did she think that?

Had she fixated on one level of the relationship and needed to complete it? Had she looked at Ryan and thought he would suit one purpose and only one purpose?

No. Yes. Maybe it had been all of that or none of it. It

176 / Susanna Carr

was more than going after the sex. She had been after the fantasy.

And it had been that way with her ever since. Even her French lover. And the one after that. And then there had been that guy she met on vacation who was still under the illusion that she was a flight attendant.

Oh, my God. Michelle wanted to bolt up. Run from the cave. Her arms and legs shook as she forced herself to lie still.

All of those guys were her fantasies, and once she slept with them, the fantasy was over. Reality set in. A relationship had been made and then the hard work had started.

Kind of like her career. No, she didn't want to think about it. Michelle shifted and turned, pressing her face against Ryan's chest. The powerful beat of his heart giving her some comfort.

She loved the idea of being a chef. Loved the work. Enjoyed going to Europe, working with amazing people and in fabulous restaurants.

Now the hard part was starting. It had nothing to do with her mojo. She had to dig in and maintain the dream. Make it work.

Because fantasies and dreams were not the same. A fantasy came easy, was perfect, but unattainable. A dream could be achieved if you put your heart into it.

She had really fucked up.

Finding her mojo wasn't it at all. Michelle closed her eyes, wishing she could block it out. Her mojo happened when everything around her was new and exciting.

The excitement disappeared when everything became routine. When she saw the unglamorous structure holding up the fantasy. She needed to face reality. Dig in at work. Put her heart into it.

She needed to do that in all aspects of her life. Both in her career and in her relationships. She had to stop running.

But what about Ryan? Michelle nestled in closer to his chest. Was he her fantasy lover or her dream lover? After tonight, did she want to have a relationship with him?

And if so, what was she going to do about it?

Chapter 12

As they made it to the top of the bluff bright and early the next morning, Ryan felt torn about seeing the other players at the checkpoint. He was relieved the level they were stuck on was finally completed, but he also preferred having Michelle to himself.

"Ryan! Michelle!" Margaret hustled over to them, her face lined with concern. "We were worried about you two. Are you all right? Where were you?"

That was going to be a sticky answer. He was prepared to be vague when Michelle spoke.

"We were still on the trail when it turned dark," Michelle explained. "So Ryan made us sit in the cave all night."

Ryan wanted to pull her aside and warn her. She was dancing on the edge of being talked about. Obviously she had been living in the big city too long.

Margaret looked properly horrified. The older woman scanned their wrinkled clothes that were streaked with dirt. "That's terrible."

"I know!" Michelle agreed fervently. "It was!"

"It was?" Ryan asked, arching an eyebrow. To hell with discretion and propriety. The night wasn't all that bad.

"It was," Michelle said, giving him a look of warning.

Ryan decided not to pursue it. The tips of her ears turning bright pink were enough for him. He'd like to know if she blushed like that all the time. One of these days he was going to make love to her in full sunlight.

"Where did you guys stay?" Michelle asked Margaret.

"We were fortunate to make it to the checkpoint right before it turned dark. Dennis and I were so exhausted, we couldn't eat dinner. We went straight to bed."

"How did you get here on time?" Michelle asked. "Didn't the handcuffs slow you down?"

"Handcuffs?" Margaret's eyes widened when she saw the bound wrists. "Oh . . . I see . . ."

Yep. He and Michelle would give Carbon Hill something to talk about tonight. Michelle didn't seem worried about it, but then again, she didn't live here anymore. It was going to be up to him to protect her name. He'd do it, too.

"You *weren't* handcuffed?" Michelle asked, finding it hard to believe.

"No." Margaret slowly shook her head. She couldn't take her eyes off their wrists. "What did you two do to deserve this?"

"We got hit in the paintball level," Michelle admitted. "I take it you didn't."

"No, we didn't get hit, although there were quite a few near misses." She looked over at a picnic table where the others sat. "Clayton and Brandy weren't handcuffed, either."

Michelle turned to Ryan. "We were the only ones who got hit. The *only ones* who were handcuffed."

"I guess we're special." What was she getting all upset about? They had experienced one of the most memorable nights of his life because of it.

Well, okay, they did have to spend it in a cave, which was worse than behind the pinsetters, but he was willing to make that up to her. She could name the time and place and he would be there.

"Where is Annie?" Michelle asked, struggling with a polite smile. "She would have the key to set us free."

"Try by the van," Margaret said, pointing at the vehicle parked next to the road. "That's where I saw her last."

"Thank you!" She tugged at Ryan. "C'mon, no time to dawdle. We can finally get this thing off of us."

"I'm in no hurry," he said, refusing to do more than stroll toward the van. "I'm getting used to it."

"You would." She kept trying to make him move faster, but he wasn't going to give in. "Annie might have coffee waiting for you. And breakfast."

Michelle knew him too well. "Well, why didn't you say so in the first place?" He broke into a full run, dragging her behind him.

"Hey, guys," Annie greeted them with a smile as she stepped out of the van. "Glad you finally made it."

"Do we get released now?" Michelle asked hopefully, the metal clanking as she shook her bound wrist.

"You sure do." Annie dug the key out of her jeans pocket. "Oh, Michelle! What happened to your wrist? It looks bad."

Ryan glanced down at Michelle's arm. It did look red and chafed. Did that happen when he held her against the bluff? Or was it when he took her on the cave floor?

The guilt ripped through his gut. He didn't know he hurt her and she didn't say anything to him. Why not?

But there was a darker emotion swirling with the guilt. One he was least comfortable with. He felt a primal satisfaction of seeing his brand, his mark, on her.

"Nothing," Michelle said dismissively. "It was difficult keeping side by side hiking the bluff."

"I never thought about that," Annie said as Ryan took the key from her. "But, yeah, I guess that would be a problem."

Ryan turned the key, releasing Michelle from the cuffs. His hand dropped to his side as she pulled away. "You're free now," he said.

He released the latch and removed the metal from his wrists. He gave it back to Annie, his hand feeling too light. As if something was missing.

"And, Michelle, before I forget." Annie reached for the dashboard. "Here's your phone."

"Yes!" She grabbed it with both hands and clasped it to her chest. "Thank you! Where did you find it?"

Annie bit her lip, as if she wasn't sure what to make of it. "It was on your bedside table."

"Oh, really?" Her voice was flat and controlled as she shared a look with Ryan. "Interesting."

"And your mother keeps calling every fifteen minutes."

Michelle cringed. "I should have known. Did you tell her where I was?"

"I told her that you were in the middle of completing a challenge." Annie's face was suspiciously blank. "She didn't get any more information out of me."

"Thank you." Michelle backed away. "I better call her back."

He watched Michelle retreat. Last night might have brought them closer, but how was he going to keep Michelle by his side after the hunt? It might call for some desperate measures.

"So, Annie," Ryan said, leaning up against the van. "Where'd you get those handcuffs?"

Michelle found a private spot on the grounds, away from her competitors and the group of men who seemed to be building something. She dialed her mom's phone number and prepared herself for the lecture of all lectures.

"Michelle Louise Nelson," her mother said by way of greeting. "Where have you been?"

Apparently once she entered the city limits, it didn't matter that she was twenty-five and had been living on her own for quite some time. "I've been completing a level."

"In the middle of the night? With *Ryan Slater?* The boy no good mother would let her daughter go out with? Did anyone see you?"

"No," Michelle assured her. "And before you ask, this is the last day. It shouldn't take all night."

Her mother gasped. "It better not! You still have to judge the horseradish recipe."

Michelle winced. She had forgotten about that. Eating horseradish in front of a crowd was going to get the better of her. She'd rather go back to the cave.

"Michelle," her mother's voice rose. "You didn't forget, did you?"

"Of course not."

Her mother didn't believe her. "It's a good thing I called. You have to be there. You cannot be late. Do you understand?"

"I'll be there. Promise." But that was all she could promise. She had no idea what the next level would be or how long it would last.

"Good." Her mother gave a deep sigh. "Now, what do you plan to wear?"

Michelle pulled the phone from her head and stared at it before putting it back to her ear. "I don't know! I'm still wearing the clothes I wore yesterday."

Her mom was silent for a few heartbeats. "No one has seen you yet, right?"

She didn't have the patience to have this conversation. "Oops, my phone's battery is running low. I forgot to charge it."

"Michelle?" Her mother's voice was low and urgent. "Is the *Herald* there taking pictures?"

If her bed head made the front page, in color, her mother would go into hysterics. "I gotta go."

"Remember, you have a station!"

"Love you. Bye!" She turned off the phone and walked to the picnic table where Ryan sat. "What does this outfit say to you?" Michelle gestured at her jeans, jacket, and T-shirt. "Former Miss Horseradish or hobo?"

Ryan's gaze slowly traveled up and down her body. Michelle's breasts felt heavy and tight and her cheeks grew hot by the time he gave his opinion. "You look beautiful."

Good answer. She rested her elbows on the picnic table. "I forgot about the horseradish recipe competition," she admitted in a low voice. "Just for the record, I don't like horseradish. I hate it."

"I wouldn't have guessed it."

"And now I have to judge the finalists." She closed her eyes in dread. "I'm not going to survive it."

"You've ridden a horse. Been shot at. Slept in a cave. Stuff you didn't think you could do. So what's the big deal? A mouthful of horseradish is nothing."

"Well, when you put it that way, how about you judge the competition?" she answered brightly. "I'm sure you'll love the cottage cheese horseradish gelatin thing."

"That gelatin thing is not half bad. I think it's a Carbon Hill classic. I can't judge it for you, but I'll be there to watch."

Michelle sat up straight. "You will? Why? The hunt will be over."

"Why not?"

Huh. There it was. The relationship stuff. The couple-dom. The expectations were already building. She wasn't sure if she liked it.

And why did they have to start now? At a horseradish contest, of all things. Come to think of it, why would he want to be there? *She* didn't want to be there. "You don't have to go. You'll be bored."

And that was the crux of the matter. He was going to get

bored fast. With them and the idea of them. With her. He was going to find out that she was an ordinary woman. Not a goddess. Not a beauty queen. Not his fantasy.

"I'm going."

"Going where?" Brandy asked as she sat down next to Ryan. A little too close to him. Her perky ponytail swatted against his shoulder and lay there.

Michelle tried to hide her irritation. Her nerves were already on the edge. Her manners were touch-and-go. She didn't want to be anywhere around this woman.

"Michelle is supposed to judge the finalists for the horse-radish recipe contest," Ryan said as he took another sip of his coffee.

"Is that right?" Brandy's eyes narrowed as she looked at Michelle. "Because you're a cook, or because you're a former Miss Horseradish."

"Both, I imagine," Ryan answered for her.

Michelle wanted to kick Ryan under the table. Didn't he see the steam coming out of Brandy's ears? Or how the woman was turning green with envy. Talking about this in front of her was like waving a red cape in front of a blood-thirsty bull.

"Michelle doesn't seem to understand that the Carbon Hill women have given her an honor."

"I see it," Michelle replied, wondering why Ryan was telling Brandy all of this. "But I don't think I'm the right person to judge."

"I agree with her," Brandy said as she inspected her damaged manicure. "The women of Carbon Hill are very particular about who gets the blue ribbon for the horseradish recipe."

Great. Michelle felt the pressure building. She was going to walk right into a political minefield. Why did her mom want her to do this?

"*Very* particular," Brandy continued. "They aren't going

to be happy to hear that the final judge spent the previous night handcuffed to a man she isn't married to. Not happy at all."

Michelle propped her head on her fist. She had seen this coming and there was nothing she could do about it now. Any arguing, pleading, or response would give Brandy ammunition.

"Then again," Brandy paused as she gave some more thought to the matter. "Even handcuffs among married couples would be enough to freak them out."

Michelle tilted her head and flashed a tight smile at Brandy. "Well, who is going to tell them?"

Brandy smiled back, baring her teeth. "You know how these things get around."

Michelle looked at her straight in the eye. She hoped she was giving the image of not caring. She didn't want Brandy to get wise to the fact that she was figuring out the mathematical formula of picking the woman up by her ponytail, twirling her around a couple of times, and throwing her off the cliff.

Unfortunately, math was never her strongest subject.

Well, her mom would never forgive her after this hunt. She would probably start wearing sunglasses and a scarf whenever she went out. The disguise only looked good on Audrey Hepburn—which her mother would point out frequently. Probably for the rest of Michelle's life.

"I know what you mean," Ryan said as he set down his coffee cup. "It's amazing how some of these rumors get started. Like that one about you."

Brandy looked at him from the corner of her eye. "There are a lot of rumors about me, and most of them were started by my pageant competitors. They couldn't handle the pressure. The more pageants I win, the more friends I lose. That's the price I have to pay for my success."

Was this her way of saying "don't hate me because I'm

beautiful"? Michelle was thankful she hadn't eaten anything yet. That would have definitely caused her to gag.

Ryan leaned over and whispered something in Brandy's
ear. Michelle was surprised to see the woman's eyes widen.
The red head turned pale. Even her freckles lost color.

"That's . . . that's . . ."

"That's what I said." Ryan took another sip of coffee as
if they had been discussing the weather. "I said no way
would Brandy do *that*. But, it turns out someone had taken
pictures at the party."

"Those pictures are doctored. I keep telling people that."
Brandy bolted from her seat. "I was young . . . impression-
able . . . and . . . and . . ."

"Double-jointed," Ryan finished for her. "Let's hope the
women of Carbon Hill don't find out about it."

They watched as Brandy whirled around and flounced
off. "She's not going to say a word," Ryan told Michelle.

Michelle leaned forward. "What's the rumor?"

"Uh-uh. No way." Ryan's smile crooked to one side.
"I'm not telling you."

"Oh, then it's really good." She shifted on the bench, getting ready for the story. "Don't hold out on me. What did
she do?"

Ryan leaned forward. "You know, Michelle, I'm a firm
believer that what happens between consenting adults should
stay between them."

"I agree. I noticed you didn't say *two* consenting adults.
Are there more involved with the Brandy thing?"

"I'm not telling you anything."

"I won't tell anyone," she promised. "Cross my heart
and hope to die, and all that other stuff."

"Yeah, right."

"I never told anyone about us," she informed Ryan.

Ryan's expression showed that he found that hard to believe. "No one? Not even Vanessa?"

"Not even her."

"Hmm."

She wasn't sure what that "hmm" meant, or what he was reading into her answer. "So what did Brandy do? And with whom? And where?"

"I'm still not telling."

Michelle narrowed her eyes. "I'm going to get it out of you. Take my word for it."

Ryan's bright blue eyes twinkled. "I'm looking forward to your methods."

"Michelle?" Clayton said as he approached her at the picnic table. "What's wrong with Brandy?"

"I wish I knew."

"Huh." Clayton looked at his team member and clucked his tongue. "She's usually sweet and cheerful, but she's been acting different during the hunt."

"Stress does that to people," Michelle responded, as if she were an expert on the subject. It was either that or yell at Clayton to open his eyes.

"It's probably a combination of stress and exhaustion," he decided. "Everyone is wiped out. I'm tempted to call in sick all next week."

Michelle nodded, although she didn't feel the same way, which was strange. She could use a nap, but she felt the energy pulsing inside her. She was ready to take on the next challenge. Ready to take on the world.

If she didn't know any better, she'd say she got her mojo back. And it felt good.

"What are we waiting for, anyway?" Ryan asked Clayton.

"They're still setting up something on the course," he answered, nodding at the other side of the street.

"Course?" Michelle looked at the wooden structures she had seen earlier. "What kind of a course?"

"Obstacle course." Clayton shrugged. "Challenge course. Endurance course."

"Well," she prompted Clayton. "Which one?"

"What's the difference?" he muttered as he walked away. "They are all designed to bring pain and suffering."

Michelle exchanged a look with Ryan. His eyebrow quirked up. "Ready for it?"

"Bring it on."

Chapter 13

"We came in first!" Michelle jumped on Ryan at the obstacle course's finish line. She threw her arms around Ryan's shoulders and held him tight. She felt as if she was going to burst with pure joy. "Can you believe it?"

"No."

"That ten-foot wall with the knotted rope almost killed me," Michelle confessed. "I mean, what the hell was that about? It isn't romantic. It isn't horseradishy. What were these hunt organizers thinking?"

"Who cares? We came in first!" His arms went around her and he twirled her around. She squealed as her legs went horizontal in the air.

"Congratulations," Annie said as she walked a wide berth around them. "Because you came in first, you get to go first on the final challenge."

"Did you hear that?" Michelle asked as Ryan lowered her down to the ground. "The final challenge."

"We're almost done." His smile was tired but relieved.

"No, besides that." She leaned forward and whispered, "We could actually *win* this thing."

His blue eyes twinkled. "I thought you weren't in it for the prize."

"I'm not. This was for Vanessa. But after all we've been through, I want to take home the prize."

"Let's go find out more about this final challenge." He looped his arm around her shoulders and tucked her against his side. Michelle was getting kind of used to this closeness and intimacy. Okay, she was quickly becoming addicted to it.

"You guys have done a great job," Annie said to everyone as Michelle and Ryan walked to the group. "There were times when I expected someone to drop out. I know I would have! But you all have seen it through and now you are ready for the last level."

The last level. It was music to Michelle's ears. She was ready to attack and conquer the last challenge.

Annie pointed at a wooden structure with steps. It was like a tower or a fort. At the top was a pole with a wire stretched tautly that went over the bluff's edge.

"In the legend," Annie said, "Homer and Ida Wirt fell into the river and drowned. Don't worry, we're not asking that from you."

"Good to know," Clayton said.

"We're asking you to do a variation of that jump. Each team member will take their turn and climb up that tower to the zip line."

"Zip line?" Margaret asked. She looked around at the group. "What is a zip line?"

"It's basically a trolley with a handle on it that is fitted against a metal cable," Annie explained. "You're going to grab the handle and zip down the line, over the bluff, across the river, and onto the lower bluff on the other side of the river."

Annie paused and looked at the six slack-jawed expressions. "You're going to wear a harness and a helmet," she quickly added.

Michelle exchanged a look of disbelief with Ryan. She must be misunderstanding this level. Did the organizers really want them to swing down the bluffs across a river?

"Let me show you," Annie said as she gestured everyone to follow. "It's not as bad as it sounds."

She guided them to the edge and Michelle saw a group of spectators waiting at the top of the bluff on the other side. The crowd shouted and clapped as they saw the competitors. She felt Ryan's hand tighten on her shoulder and he maneuvered her away from the edge.

"There's going to be a group of people who will catch you and slow you down." Annie pointed at a team of muscular men waiting at the end of the zip line. "So you don't have to worry about slamming into the ground on the other side."

"Thanks for that visual," Dennis said with a nervous chuckle.

"Oh, and you see near the end of the zip line?" Annie pointed at something metallic that caught the sunlight. "There are three keys on brass rings. You need to let go of the handle, grab one of the keys, and bring it to the bluff you're landing on."

"Why?" Brandy asked. "What's so important about the key? And why is it hanging in the air?"

"Each key goes to a treasure chest that is on that bluff." She pointed at three chests that sat next to the end of the zip line. "One of those chests holds the grand prize."

Michelle looked up at Ryan. "When I signed the medical waiver, I thought it was a precaution," she whispered. "I didn't think I was going to dangle over a freaking river."

"So . . ." Brandy looked over the edge and then turned to Annie. "We only have to pick one person from each team to do this, right?"

"Nope, everyone has to participate on this challenge or their team forfeits. Okay," Annie said and clapped her hands. "Let's get to it. Michelle and Ryan, you guys are first on the zip line."

"That's not fair!" Brandy declared. "What about all the

times we've come in first? Shouldn't that count for something?"

"Take it up with the organizers," Annie said without looking at Brandy. "Now listen closely. Only one team member is allowed on the zip line at a time. Pick the person who has the best chance of getting the key first. If he or she doesn't get the key, then the second member of the team will have to do cleanup duty and get it."

"What if neither person gets the key?" Dennis asked.

"Then you don't have any chance of getting the big prize," Annie said. "I know, I know, after all you guys went through, it all comes down to a second."

Everyone turned and looked at the keys glittering in the sun. Michelle felt the pressure building inside her. She could win or lose the hunt in a second.

"Any more questions?" Annie asked. The group was silent. No one said a word. Crickets chirped.

"Okay, Michelle and Ryan. I'm not going to tell you again." She swept her arms in the direction of the wooden structure. "Climb that tower and get suited up."

Michelle ran to the structure, her heart pounding with excitement and nerves. She sensed Ryan right behind her. He didn't show any emotion. The guy was a rock. She should take lessons from him in displaying outward calm and serenity.

"This is great!" Michelle squealed as she climbed up the rungs to the top of the tower. "We have just as much chance of winning as everyone else."

"Michelle."

"In fact, we have an even better chance because we have first pick of the keys." Michelle knew her smile turned downright wicked. "No wonder Brandy was livid. Heh, heh, heh."

"Michelle."

She paused from climbing and looked down at him. "What is it?"

Ryan stopped. He dipped his head as his shoulders sank. "I don't think I can do this."

She frowned. "Do what?"

"Ride the zip line." He said it through clenched teeth. "I can't do it."

"Oh, sure you can." It definitely promised a wild, crazy, and fast ride, but they only had to do it once. "I tell you what. I'll go first and grab the key."

Ryan shook his head.

"Or would you rather I do cleanup?" She'd prefer to go first rather than be required to absolutely, positively grab that key or lose everything, but she would do whatever it took to complete this level quickly and cleanly.

"No, Michelle." Her stomach twisted with dread as he shook his head slowly. "We need to forfeit."

"No, no, no." Michelle's eyes widened in alarm. "Ryan, no. We can do this."

"I can't." He wanted to, he really did. If only to erase that look on Michelle's face.

"Why didn't you tell me you were afraid of heights?" she whispered fiercely.

"I'm not." He had never shown the signs, but then, he had never done anything like this before. "At least, I didn't think I was. Then I looked over the bluff and it hit me."

"Vertigo?" she asked as she climbed the remaining rungs of the tower.

"I guess." He didn't like the word. It sounded sissy. He was feeling bad already admitting he couldn't do this. He wanted to be strong and invincible in Michelle's eyes. Why did she always see him at his worst?

She paced the small confines of the tower, dodging him and the guy in charge of the zip line. "Okay, Ryan. You're going to get through this. It's really no big deal. Just shut your eyes and you'll be fine."

"That's not going to work." It wasn't that easy. When he stood on the bluff's edge, every muscle froze. His gut instincts screamed for him to move back. He broke into a cold sweat.

"I'll get the key on the brass ring." She grabbed the helmets and slapped one into his hands. "You won't have to do a thing."

Ryan kept shaking his head. Michelle wasn't getting it. What made it so difficult to understand?

"I'll go first," she offered as she put her helmet on and fumbled with the clasp.

"I can't do it," Ryan said. He slumped against the tower wall. Maybe she didn't want to understand. Was the prize more important to her than his feelings?

"I really hate bringing this up," Michelle said, her voice shaking. With impatience or with anger? "But I rode a horse because you made me."

"I know." He stared at the helmet in his hands. "And I feel bad about making you do that."

"Yeah, now, when you know turnabout is fair play." She grabbed his helmet and set it on his head. "Come on, Ryan. I didn't think I could do it, and I did. The same will happen with you."

"It's not the same thing."

Michelle's jaw dropped in surprise. "It is, too!"

He grabbed her wrist and pulled her hands away from his helmet. "Falling off a horse is way different than plunging off of a river bluff."

"Ryan, look at me." She held on to his gaze. He could feel her willing him to follow her lead. "Forget about winning. Forget about this hunt. Just grab on to the handle and push off."

He dropped her wrists. "Forget it." That was his final decision and she was going to have to accept it.

Her fingers bit into his arms as she tried to keep her patience. "You are going to be angry with yourself if you let this opportunity go by."

"No, I'm not." He was going to be relieved that he didn't allow himself to get talked into this insane challenge.

"You're letting your fears get the better of you."

"I can live with that."

"Can you really?" Michelle let go of his arms. "Because that's how you've been living these days. That's how you've been dealing with your talent. Hiding it. Backing away. Refusing to make a choice."

"I don't believe this." He turned to the harness guy who was doing his best not to listen in. "I'm standing here sweating blood and she decides this is the time to launch into a philosophical discussion."

"What I'm talking about here," Michelle's voice held a sharp edge, "is fear. I'm talking about pushing out of your comfort zone. And, you know what? I am personally tired of living afraid."

"And you're going to prove this by jumping off of a cliff?" He motioned at the bluff's edge. "How is that going to change anything?"

"If I can work through this, I can work through anything I face. And believe me, I'm afraid of a lot of things. And not just horses and bats and things like that. I'm talking about everyday stuff."

This he knew wasn't true. Michelle Nelson was the boldest person he knew. "Like what?"

"I don't know, lots of stuff." She tossed her arms up in exasperation. "I'm afraid I'm not going to ever repay what Carbon Hill did for me. Or that I won't become the success everyone wants me to be. Or fulfill every expectation that is placed on me, even the ones I put on myself."

Ryan rubbed the ache that formed in his temples. "That fear is different than what is going on here."

"Fear is fear." She poked her finger against his chest. "Your mind and body react to it the same way."

"No, they don't."

"I'm afraid of what's going to happen to us after this hunt. It leaves this hollowness in my stomach." She tapped her midriff. "I'm scared to death and my body is reacting to the fear just as if I was about ready to jump off a cliff."

Ryan closed his eyes in defense. "Michelle."

"I'm afraid that if I try to hook up with you, you're going to find out I'm not the fantasy you want." She flattened her hands against the base of her throat. "Just thinking about it makes my chest tighten and my throat squeeze up."

"You're not going to die from it."

"My mouth goes dry and it hurts to breathe when I think about telling you that I still love you."

Whoa. Did she say she loved him?

"Don't tell me that those aren't signs of fear," Michelle continued. "Don't you dare."

"Is everybody okay up there?" Annie called up.

Michelle leaned over the railing. "We're fine," she replied with a frantic smile. "We're talking strategy."

She said she loved him. Why did she say that now? Why did she choose *this* moment to tell him?

"You don't need to cover for me," Ryan told her coldly. "They're going to figure out that I'm not doing this."

"Ryan Slater," she said as she stepped into the harness. "I expect you to do this challenge. And you know why? Because you *are* afraid."

He glared at her. "I don't like to be pushed."

"No, you're not used to it," Michelle said as the guy adjusted her harness. She kept her eyes locked on Ryan. "No one pushes or challenges you. You've gotten along well enough with a wink and a smile."

Her dead-on analysis rubbed him the wrong way. "And

what happens when you go down there and you see that I'm not right behind you? No wink and a smile will make it better."

"You got that straight."

Whoa. No assurances that she would love him. That she would respect him in the morning no matter what. "Then what? Is that it between us? Are we through if I don't meet your expectations?"

"Is that what you think of me?" She clucked her tongue in disgust. "Whatever you do about this challenge is not going to affect my feelings toward you. I don't do emotional blackmail."

He spread his arms wide. "What do you call this?"

She held her hand up. "You don't seem to understand what I'm saying. I feel that if you don't do this, it's going to feel a hundred times worse than the fear you're feeling now."

Ryan didn't know what to say to that. He had a feeling she was right, but he didn't want it to be true.

"I'm not too thrilled about doing this." She pointed at the bluff's edge. "But I expect it of myself to finish this hunt. If I don't, I will regret it."

"You were ready to give up the minute you saw Lucifer," Ryan felt compelled to point out.

She nodded. "I was. And I would have regretted it. It was a good thing you were there. You finally got me on that horse and you looked after me."

The harness guy interrupted. "Are you ready?"

Michelle paused and gave a sharp nod. "Ready." She looked at Ryan. "All I can say is that I'm going to be there for you, no matter what you decide."

He needed to hear that. But he didn't know if it was true. He didn't know if pride and respect were wrapped around that love and he didn't know if he could fight through this choking fear to make her proud.

Michelle took a deep breath. "Now, are you going to give me a push?"

She screamed the whole way down. Michelle didn't think she would do that, but the ride down the zip line went fast. Way too fast.

Everything was bumpy and shaky. She didn't see the river below her. Her eyes were on the prize. The keys. She was going to get one if it meant defying the laws of nature.

The keys were suddenly coming up. The light hit her in the eyes and she automatically squinted. She panicked for a moment and made herself uncurl her fingers from the handle. She was going to get this, damn it.

Reaching out quickly, Michelle closed her hand into a fist. Her fingers fumbled and she missed one. She made a quick, desperate grab. She clenched her hand and felt the cold metal biting her palm.

Her stomach did a wild flip as the bluff came up fast. What if they miscalculated? What if—

The group of men caught her. The stop was abrupt and jarring. She wobbled and fought for her balance, but her mind was on the key, snug in her grip.

The cheer from the crowd came at her like a crashing wave. She had been so focused on the keys that she didn't hear the onlookers at all on her ride down. Michelle gave a wave to let them know she was okay.

She clumsily stepped out of her harness, thankful for the men helping her out. Michelle turned around and faced the other bluff. The zip line was empty. She peered in the tower, but didn't see Ryan's familiar silhouette. She didn't see anything.

He'll come. Just give him a minute.

She unbuckled her helmet with shaky fingers and nervously fluffed out her hair. *Come on . . . come on . . .*

Nothing.

Michelle dipped her head, determined to put on a brave, unconcerned face. She knew Ryan thought this was all about the winning. He didn't get it, no matter how many times she tried to explain.

It wasn't about the hunt. It was never about this stupid challenge. She had already gotten her prize. She had a second chance with Ryan.

But she had failed him. She wanted to tell him it was okay to give up and forfeit. It would have been the easy route. She had tried to be tough and strong for the both of them and it blew up in her face.

She thought she could help him work through his fears because she loved him. How arrogant was that? All he thought now was that her feelings were contingent on how he handled the challenge. He probably felt as if he had failed her. How was she going to convince him otherwise?

"Mojo!"

Michelle jerked her head up as she saw Ryan sailing along the wire. She slapped her hand over her mouth as tears burned her eyes. Her heart swelled at the sight of him racing down the wire.

"Is he saying Geronimo?" one of the men by her side asked while the crowd cheered.

"Nope. He's saying"—she arched her back, threw her hands in the air, and screamed—"Mojo!"

Chapter 14

Michelle launched in on Ryan the moment he touched the ground. His face was pale, his mouth pinched with tension. Guilt and relief slapped up against her so hard it knocked her silly.

"You did it!" She gave him a fierce hug that made him stumble back. "How do you feel?"

"I'm never doing that again."

"You don't have to. I promise." She waited until he took off the harness and then she pulled him to the side, away from everyone. "Once is more than enough."

She noticed he wasn't smiling. Far from it. His eyes looked glassy. "Really, Ryan. Tell me the truth. How are you feeling? Are you okay?"

He nodded dumbly and looked straight ahead. "I'm okay."

"I kept thinking I pushed you too hard." She held her hand against her sternum. "That you would never forgive me. But we're good now, right?"

"Ah, no." Ryan turned and looked directly in her eyes. "I'm still pissed off at you, and nothing is going to make that change. Not even if you deep throat me again." He paused and reconsidered. "Although you could try."

Okay, Ryan was slowly coming back to his normal self. She exhaled a shaky sigh of relief.

"And once I stop feeling like I'm going to puke, I'm going to let you have it."

She playfully gave him a shove. "You are so full of it. You're feeling pretty good about yourself. I can see it in your eyes."

He curled his arm around her shoulders. "Whatever you say, Mojo."

Michelle's eyes widened. "Mojo?" Did he rattle his brain on the trip down?

"I decided you need a nickname." His sly smile made her tingle. "Michelle is way too long."

"You are *not* calling me Mojo. I *forbid* it. Mojo is what someone would call their pet dog. I—" She stopped and turned around when she heard a scream.

Brandy careened down the zip line. While her long red ponytail slapped against her face, her knees were ramrod straight and perpendicular. She made a wild grab for the keys and missed.

"Ooh." Michelle flinched and bit her bottom lip. "That can't be good for Clayton. It's all up to him."

"Pressure." Ryan didn't sound sympathetic at all.

"He's going to feel horrible if he doesn't get the key. Brandy will eat him alive. Chew him up one side and down the other."

Ryan gave a sympathetic cluck of his tongue. "I know how he feels."

Michelle looked at him, startled. She glared at him when she saw the unholy glow in his eyes. "Don't compare me to Brandy!"

"Clayton has to know that she's going to dump him right here and now if he doesn't deliver."

And he put her in the same category? The nerve! "I'm not dumping you. I never said I was dumping you."

Ryan cupped her cheek with his hand and gazed into her eyes. "I know. I just wanted to hear you say it."

Michelle stuck her tongue out at him. "Oh, you are not so easily forgiven. Comparing me with Brandy. I can't believe it."

"I like to live dangerously." He held her close, but she refused to relax against him. She wasn't going to sink into him. She folded her arms across her chest for good measure.

Ryan's hold tightened around her as Clayton went down the zip line. As much as Ryan acted as if the other guy annoyed him, she felt the nerves grip him the moment Clayton grabbed for the keys.

"He got it." Michelle let out a long breath. "It is really hard to get those keys."

"I'll take your word for it."

"Michelle!"

Michelle turned to see her best friend running toward them. "Vanessa!" She gave the blonde a hug. "Where have you been?"

"I have been running around like crazy from one event to the next." She released Michelle and looked at her from top to toe. She then gave a covert glance to Ryan who stood back, but made his possessiveness clear. "You made it to the end. I knew you would," she said with unshakeable confidence.

"Oh, sure you did." Michelle made a face. "You have no idea what you've put me through. Have you tried *any* of these challenges your committee put together?"

"No," Vanessa admitted. "We all got drunk one night and brainstormed."

Michelle and Ryan looked at each other. His eyebrow quirked up as if to say, *That would explain a lot.* She had to agree.

"I'm kidding!" Vanessa swore.

"I don't know about that," Ryan said as they turned to watch Margaret swinging wildly from the zip line. Michelle was surprised at how the older woman grabbed the key from the air, making it look amazingly easy.

"By the way, the scavenger hunt has generated a great deal of business for the Horseradish Festival," Vanessa informed them with great pride. "It'll be a while before we get the final tally."

"That's great. You got this festival back on its feet," Michelle exclaimed.

And it was great. Not only had her hard work paid off, but Vanessa had achieved her goal. Rising to power in Carbon Hill might not be Michelle's dream for Vanessa, but it was important to her friend. That was important enough for her.

"I guess the hunt will be one of the festival's new traditions," Vanessa said. "Are you guys interested in doing it next year?"

"No!" they said in unison.

Vanessa's smile widened. "Yeah, I had a feeling you were going to say that, but I thought I'd check." She looked in the direction of the river. "Here comes Dennis. I better get to the treasure chests. Good luck, you guys!"

Ryan watched Dennis safely hit the ground before he turned to Michelle. "Do you have the key?"

"Right here." She jingled it from the brass ring. "I haven't let go since I got it. I think it's permanently imprinted on my palm."

Ryan reached for her hand and slowly uncurled her fingers. He looked at the key and glanced up at her. Energy crackled from him. "Mojo, I think we're going to win."

"It doesn't matter, and stop calling me Mojo."

"Whatever you say." Ryan lifted her hand and kissed her palm. "But I still think we're going to win."

"Contestants," Vanessa called out, her voice loud and clear without the aid of a microphone. "If you would please gather around the treasure chests, we will find out who is the big winner of Carbon Hill's First Annual Horseradish Festival Scavenger Hunt."

"She's getting a little ahead of herself, isn't she?" Ryan asked as she strolled over to the treasure chests.

"There's no such thing as advertising too early," Michelle said loyally as they approached the chests that were lined up in a row facing the bluff's edge.

"Each key has a colored handle," Vanessa told everyone. "This color matches with the lock on the treasure chest. Find your treasure chest, but don't open it yet."

The warning was loud and clear. Ryan looked at the key clenched in Michelle's hand. The green tip matched the lock to the treasure chest in the middle. "Over there." He pointed it out and escorted Michelle to the chest.

He noticed that the Aschenbrenners were crouched in front of the chest to the left of him. Clayton and Brandy were to the right. The crowd stood in an arc in front of them, impatient to discover the winner.

Michelle knelt down in front of the chest and Ryan followed her example. He was surprised by the jitters. He watched Michelle wiping her palms against her jeans. Didn't matter if they won, huh?

Why was he nervous? He got his wish. He got to say sorry. He got a do-over. He had everything he wanted.

But he wanted more, he finally admitted to himself. Ryan wanted Michelle by his side and in his life. He had to come up with a plan to make that happen.

No matter whether they won or lost, he was going to pursue her after this hunt. He would make Michelle his. The way he should have done it years ago.

"Ready?" Vanessa called out to the contestants. "One . . . two . . . three! Open your treasure chest!"

Michelle shoved the key in the lock and gave it a firm twist. It mirrored the twist in his heart.

No matter what happens . . .

Michelle stared at the contents in the box. She blinked.

She blinked again. She couldn't believe what was sitting in front of her.

And then the disappointment hit her like a fist. A big, fast one. She rocked back on her knees and her shoulder bumped against Ryan.

"That's a lot of horseradish," Ryan said beside her.

A shriek pierced the silence. Michelle turned in time to see Margaret tossing her arms around her husband. One quick glance at the gold and glitter in the Aschenbrenners' treasure chest and she knew they had won.

"Okay, so we got a lifetime supply of all the horseradish you can eat," Ryan said as he helped Michelle up to her feet. "That doesn't erase the fact that we did pretty well on this hunt."

"You're right. We were a great team." Her eyes wandered back to the box. "And all we have to show for it is a bunch of roots."

"That's all we got out of the hunt?" His eyes twinkled mischievously. "I wouldn't say that."

Michelle felt the heat rise in her cheeks. "Let's go congratulate the Aschenbrenners," she suggested primly.

She waited until Margaret and Dennis stopped jumping up and down to give them a warm hug. She found herself truly happy for them. "It was a well-deserved victory."

"Thank you," Dennis said as he shook Ryan's hand. "We needed this win."

"Is the ring in there?" Michelle asked.

"The ring!" Margaret wiped the tears from her eyes and peered into the chest. "I forgot to look."

"Here it is." Dennis reached in and picked up the velvet jewel case. He reverently removed the ring and slid it on his wife's finger. "I promised I'd get you diamonds some day, didn't I?"

Michelle felt the tears clawing up her throat. She wiggled

her nose and blinked. She wasn't going to cry. Nope, wasn't going to.

"Excuse me," Vanessa said to the Aschenbrenners as she placed her hand on Dennis's arm. "The *Herald* would love to get a picture of you for the front page."

Michelle sighed and sniffed as she watched the older couple get their picture taken. She couldn't stop smiling at the joy stamped on the winners' faces.

"I never would have guessed it," Ryan said as he laced his fingers with hers.

"What?" She looked up at him. It felt good to have him beside her. She didn't realize she'd been missing that.

"You haven't pointed out the negative," Ryan said, his mouth twitching with a smile. "Not one snarky comment about their win."

She thought about it and realized she didn't have anything snarky to say about it. "Mmm, nope. Nothing comes to mind."

"Nothing like, 'I'd hate to see the taxes on that prize.' Or 'There's no place to wear that ring in Carbon Hill.' "

"Okay." She nodded reluctantly. "I would have gotten around to that eventually."

"Glad to hear it." His hand tightened against hers. "It's not like you to get mushy and sentimental about a bunch of diamonds."

"I don't get mushy. Especially over diamonds." She glanced at their treasure. "Or horseradish."

He stared at their box for a long moment. "That is a lot of horseradish."

"You want my share?" Michelle asked out of the corner of her mouth.

Ryan chuckled. "No, thanks. Hey, what did Clayton and Brandy win?"

"I don't know." She turned to the other treasure chest,

but it was closed shut. Brandy and Clayton weren't nearby.

"Where did they go?" Michelle searched the crowd. Brandy was nowhere to be found. Clayton had broken away from the crowd and was walking toward the parked cars. From his slumped posture and slow gait, he looked like the poster child for defeat and dejection.

"Oh, poor Clayton. We should go check on him." She didn't get far when Ryan's hand held her back.

"Leave him be." His tone held a hint of steel.

Now was not the time to get all jealous and territorial. Clayton had tutored her in history and nothing else. "But look at him."

Ryan shook his head. "He wants to lick his wounds in private."

Michelle tilted her head and winced at the sadness radiating from Clayton. "I don't know . . ."

"Take my word on this."

Michelle sighed. He was probably right. Men were a strange breed. "Okay, okay. But Brandy's timing sucks."

"I wouldn't say that," Ryan disagreed. "Had they won, Brandy would have fleeced him for the whole prize and then dumped him."

He had a point, but it didn't make her feel any better. "She is evil." Her eyes narrowed as the anger flashed through her. "Are you sure you don't want to share the dirt you have on Brandy?"

"There's dirt on Brandy?" Vanessa said, popping up next to Michelle, and grabbed her arm. "Brandy Rasmussen? Tell me everything."

"I wish I could, but no one"—she darted a meaningful look at Ryan—"is telling it to me."

"Well, probably because they know better." Vanessa ruffled her friend's hair and grimaced. "You're lucky your mom isn't here to see you."

Michelle swatted her friend's hands away. "It's not that bad."

Vanessa's expression said otherwise, but she immediately changed the subject. "I'm done here, but I have a few more events to hit. Do you guys need a ride?"

"Yes, because now I get to judge the horseradish recipe contest."

"Oh, yeah." Vanessa smiled sheepishly and checked her watch. "Well, you can rant all you want while I drop you off at your parents' house to clean up. What a deal, huh?"

"Make it the bed and breakfast," Michelle said. "I still have my overnight bag there. If I go back to my parents' house, I'll come out dressed as my mother."

A look of horror flashed across Vanessa's face. "Bed and breakfast it is."

"Of course," Michelle said in a wheedling tone, "if you accidentally make a detour and I can't get to the fairgrounds on time . . ."

"Now, Michelle," Ryan interrupted. "You're tired of living afraid, remember?"

She cast him a dark look. "Shut up, Ryan."

"You need to face your fears." He pumped his fist in the air. "Conquer them."

"I don't believe this," she muttered to no one in particular.

"And I'll be there to see you through each bite of horseradish . . ."

Michelle's jaw tightened. "What did I do to deserve this?"

The fairgrounds was still packed with people during the final hours of the Horseradish Festival. Ryan couldn't remember the last time he attended the annual event, but he was surprised at seeing it so crowded. When did the horseradish become so popular?

He dodged a group of boys running in different directions before opening one of the doors to the Hall. "After you," he said to Michelle.

"Ryan, I appreciate the thought, but you really don't need to watch me judge the contest." She fluffed her hair with her fingers again, a sure sign that she had a bad case of the nerves.

"Are you trying to get out of this and you don't want any witnesses?" he teased and gave her a wink. "If you need an accomplice, why didn't you say so?"

"The thought did not cross my mind," Michelle responded as she tugged the hem of her sweater over her dark blue jeans.

"Are you sure about that?" He glanced around as they walked by the Horseradish Still Life art competition. "No one has spotted us. We can make a break for it."

"I am staying. You can leave anytime."

"How about if I take you somewhere? Like, oh, I don't know, my place." *Or my bed. My car. Anywhere we can be alone.*

Michelle cast a look from the corner of her eye, but he couldn't decipher it. Was she tempted? Was she ready to continue what they had started on the bluff?

He didn't even get a chance to lure her near a bed when they returned to the bed and breakfast. After a quick shower and change of clothes, Michelle and Ryan had to jump back into Vanessa's car and race to the fairgrounds.

But he didn't need to rush her into his bed. He didn't need to seduce her in less than a second. Michelle said she loved him. This gave him something to build upon, to work with before she returned to Chicago.

Then again, she had loved him the first time around. Ryan winced as the sour taste of fear filled his mouth. Michelle hadn't backed up her declaration of love that last time, now, had she?

Ryan bumped against Michelle when she stopped short and stared at the Canning and Pickling Contest. She looked around frantically. "Where is the recipe contest being held?"

Like he would know? "Let's try over there." He pointed at the far end of the hall.

"I'm late, I'm late," she chanted under her breath.

"They will forgive you." He placed his hand against the small of her back.

"Ha!" The word burst from her lips and she shook her head. "You have no idea." She zigzagged past old ladies and women pushing strollers. Ryan was finding it difficult to keep up with her.

"There you are, Michelle!" Mrs. White's voice carried over the hum of the crowd.

They looked over to where the very proper woman stood. She wore a mottled brown dress with a high ruffled neckline that reminded Ryan of a turkey.

"Hello, Mrs. White," Michelle said with a firm smile. "Oh, this is Ryan Slater. Ryan, this is Mrs. White of White Motors."

Ryan greeted the woman who interestingly didn't have a first name. His hand flexed against Michelle's tensed back. He couldn't help it. Mrs. White always gave him the hives.

"We've been waiting for you."

"It's my fault," Ryan said before Michelle could say anything. "We just finished the scavenger hunt."

"Oh, did you win?"

"No, the Aschenbrenners did."

Mrs. White gave a twitch to her nose. Margaret and Dennis were probably not in her elite circle of friends. Her eyebrows rose higher when she noticed Ryan standing closely to Michelle. "You competed together?"

"Yes." Michelle looked up at him and gave him a smile that made him feel strong and invincible. "Ryan was my partner."

"As a couple?" She leaned forward, as if she was trying to comprehend. "A *romantic* couple?"

The back of Ryan's ear started to itch. Okay, now things were going to get sticky. Ryan wasn't sure how to handle this line of questioning.

"Are the two of you"—Mrs. White paused as if she couldn't quite believe it—"dating?"

Chapter 15

"Yes," Michelle answered. She didn't hint at the shock zinging inside her. What really surprised her was that she didn't even hesitate with the answer.

"No," Ryan answered, just as swiftly.

"Hmm-mm." Mrs. White looked at Michelle, then at Ryan, and back again at her. "Well, that's enough chitchat for now. Come along, Michelle. We need you to judge the horseradish recipes."

"There wouldn't by any chance be a Bloody Mary in the finals?" Michelle asked.

Mrs. White stopped and pivoted on her chunky high heels. "Excuse me?" she asked icily over Ryan's chuckle.

"Never—" Michelle stumbled into silence as she watched Mrs. White pull something glittery out of a plastic shopping bag. "Is that my crown?"

"Yes!" The older woman showed a glimmer of enthusiasm. "Your mother found this and your sash. She gave them to me for the judging. Isn't that wonderful?"

Define wonderful. Michelle's calm and serene smile was firmly in place. "You want me to wear them? Now?"

"Of course." Mrs. White gave her a strange look as if Michelle was a bit touched in the head. "You need to hurry because the newspaper reporter is waiting."

She was expected to wear a tiara and sash over her

sweater and jeans? And then get her picture taken for the paper? And why did Michelle feel as though her mom would give her full approval? Hmm . . . three guesses . . .

"I don't think the crown will work with my hair." Not to mention she was going to look like a freak.

"It's a shame you had to cut your hair." Mrs. White tsked and handed Ryan the rhinestone tiara. "I'll go find some hairpins."

Ryan waited until the woman disappeared into the crowd before he asked, "Why did you tell her we're dating?"

"Because we are," she answered as she slipped the sash over her head and settled it against her hip. "We're a couple. Starting now."

"Michelle."

"Can you hand me the crown?" she asked politely, reaching for the glitter and paste monstrosity.

"How can we be a couple?" he asked in a low voice as the crowd bumped and moved around them. "I live here and you live in Chicago. You've made it clear since you've been back that Carbon Hill is too small for you."

"What about it?" She set the crown on top of her head. It immediately tilted and slid over one eye. That couldn't be good.

"Don't expect me to follow you," he said as he took a step back and slid his hands into his back pockets.

"I'm not." And really, what made her think he was going to act differently? He had never pursued her and he had no reason to do so now.

"I feel like we're right back to square one," he said, looking away. "You had no problem leaving the last time we were dating."

"This is different." This time she knew what she was up against. Her fears as well as Ryan's. It wasn't going to be easy to conquer them, but recognizing them was half the battle.

"And I had no problem letting you go," Ryan seemed insistent to point out.

"Yes, you did. Just like you are now," she said as she readjusted her crown, the glitter coming off on her hands. No telling how much was caught in her hair.

Ryan's eyebrows dipped into a V as he frowned. "What makes you think that? You can go. I'm not stopping you."

"Let me put it to you this way. The scavenger hunt is over. Why are you still hanging around?"

Ryan's smile was wry and self-deprecating. He wasn't going to win this argument and they both knew it. "Maybe I'm here to see the events."

"Yeah, you're really the type to see if a kid can conduct electricity from a horseradish." She gestured at the science fair projects. "Just to let you know, he can't. There's no citrus in horseradish."

"Since when are you an expert on horseradish?"

"I'm not. I'm making a wild guess." She tapped the crown and prayed it wouldn't move. "How do I look?"

Ryan reached out and straightened the crown. "Just as I remember," he answered in a rough voice as nostalgia tugged at his smile.

Just as she was five years ago? "Is that good or bad?" She'd like to think she had improved with age.

"It's very good. And don't listen to anyone else about your hair," he told her. "I happen to like it."

Michelle smiled back at him, reluctant to leave his side. *Yep, he's a keeper*. "Now don't go anywhere."

"Me? Nah," he said as he rocked back on his heel. "I want to see you eat horseradish and smile."

Michelle gave a small groan just as Mrs. White approached her. "Here are some pins. We can anchor the crown here and here."

Michelle winced as each hairpin made skid tracks in her

scalp. She schooled her expression as Mrs. White studied her with a frown.

The older woman gave a long-suffering sigh. "It will have to do. Let's hurry."

Michelle decided she wasn't going to let it get to her. She wasn't a beauty queen and she wasn't going to try and meet these women's unrealistic ideals. So there. And she was going to keep this attitude. At least until she caught a glimpse of herself in the newspaper looking like a schizophrenic fashion victim.

She walked to the table decorated with plastic table cloths and swags. Michelle gave her queenly wave as the women applauded, scanning the dishes that had made the finals. There was a small blip in her shoulder-shoulder-elbow-elbow-wrist-wrist move when she saw the five dishes. Five very unusual looking and pungent dishes.

And not one of them looked like a Bloody Mary.

At least there was some good news. The gelatin mold hadn't made the cut. And that was about as good as it was going to get.

She sat down as gracefully as one could with a tower of rhinestones anchored to one's head and smiled. Sometimes she had to do things she'd rather not do, but expectations had to be met. It was a fact of life.

Michelle looked over the crowd and spotted Ryan. Even he had expectations of her, but was he going to have to stand in line and wait his turn? Was he going to get tired of waiting for her to fulfill the expectations already placed on her? Or was she going to find the courage to put him as top priority and blow off everyone else.

If only it were that easy.

"Michelle Nelson," Mrs. White said by way of introduction, "is a former Miss Horseradish and currently a chef in Chicago."

The women in the crowd oohed and ahhed while a few

took pictures. She was so tempted to tell everyone the life of a chef was not all that it was cracked up to be, but that statement would reek of ingratitude.

"She has graciously accepted our invitation to sample the recipes," Mrs. White continued before turning away from the crowd and deigning Michelle with a regal nod. "Michelle, please sample the recipes."

"Thank you." While she was tempted to reach for the least scary dish, Michelle forced herself to go in order. She kept her face completely blank, fighting her way through a professional analysis of each dish.

"Have you determined a winner?" Mrs. White asked after Michelle reluctantly went through the samples a second time. She owed it to the contestants to make a thorough decision, even if her stomach would never forgive her.

"Yes, I have." Michelle discovered her voice was hoarse and cleared it. One of those dishes had been very . . . piquant. "The third prize goes to the delightful Tuna-Horseradish Salad."

There was a shocked silence and a twitter in the audience. Michelle gave a quick look to Ryan. He shrugged, unclear about the response. She braced herself as she saw the mayor's wife slowly walk to the stage and unsmilingly receive her green ribbon.

Mom is so going to kill me. If her parents both got jury duty this year, they'd know who to blame. Michelle kept her smile bright even though the politician's wife's handshake was like holding a dead, floppy fish.

"The second prize," Michelle continued as if she hadn't rocked the foundation that Carbon Hill was built on, "goes to the Cole Slaw with Horseradish."

An even larger gasp rang out. Michelle didn't blink. Didn't close her eyes. She instinctively sought out Ryan, who was suspiciously rubbing his hand over his mouth.

A very old woman with lavender hair hobbled to the

front of the crowd and grabbed the red ribbon from Michelle's hand.

"You don't know nothing," the geezer told Michelle, by-passing her outstretched hand. Michelle moved her foot right before the woman could impale her with her cane.

Okay, why did her mom want her to do this judging? Did she have a death wish for her one and only daughter? "And the grand prize goes to"—Michelle braced herself for the imminent apocalypse—"the Horseradish and Apple Salad."

The crowd was deathly silent and then a startled smatter of applause rang out. Michelle flinched when she heard a squeal of unbridled delight. She stood very, very still as a young girl ran up to the stage.

"Oh, my gosh," the girl screamed and squatted before jumping up and down. "I can't believe I won."

She gave a quick look at Ryan, who was leading the ap-plause. *The women of Carbon Hill are going to run me out of town.* "Congratulations on your win," Michelle told the young girl who couldn't be older than twelve.

"I can't believe I won," the girl kept repeating. She pressed her hands against her bright pink face. "I have to call my best friend."

Yeah, that can wait until after I make a fast getaway. She gave the winner the blue ribbon and asked, "Did you create the recipe?"

"Well, kind of." The girl shifted from one foot to the other. "This is something my mom always throws together when we have leftovers."

Michelle nodded as if she were interviewing Julia Child, all the while thinking, *I am so beyond dead.*

"Only this time"—the girl rubbed her nose with the back of her hand—"when I put the cinnamon back on the shelf, it tipped over and spilled into the salad."

Deader and deader. Michelle continued to nod as if her life, doomed as it was, depended on it.

"So I tried to take out most of the cinnamon," the winner chattered on. "But I couldn't start over because I didn't have more ingredients."

Michelle was aware of the grumblings in the audience and hoped the girl was oblivious to it. As much as her decision would bring trouble on Michelle's head, the girl won fair and square and she wasn't going to shortchange her of the spotlight.

"Well," Michelle said when she realized the girl had finished, "sometimes the best ideas come from accidents, or making do with what you have on hand."

"Oh, yeah. That was the other thing." The girl smacked her hand on her forehead. "The apples. I usually make the salad with Granny Smiths, but all we had in the house were the Golden Delicious."

"Really?" *Nail my coffin shut.*

"I can't believe I won." The girl did that squat-jump-squeal routine again. "I thought for sure I'd lose. Man, I'm going to use goldens from now on. They are what probably got me the grand prize."

"Are you ready to pose for the paper?" she asked, guiding her to face the newspaper reporter, who snapped a series of shots with his digital camera.

The girl giggled as she held her ribbon close to her face. "My best friend isn't going to believe this."

Yeah, she's not going to be the only one. Michelle saw the photographer scribbling furiously. She could almost see the headline. "Goldens Got Her the Real Gold."

Golden . . . Michelle gasped as it hit her.

Ryan pushed off from the wall as Michelle hurried over to him. "What's up?" The Carbon Hill women might hate her right now, but there was no need to find a fast getaway car. The women couldn't move that fast in their high heels and girdles.

Michelle leaned close to him and bunched his shirt in her fists. "I know where the real treasure is," she whispered as she looked around her in case of eavesdroppers.

"Wait a second." Ryan peeled her fingers away, one by one. "You don't believe there is a treasure. You said it was long gone. Remember?"

"Okay, I did say that. But listen to me now. We need to go back to the bed and breakfast." She started to move toward the exit. "And we need a shovel. A big one."

"Oh, now I see why you're dragging me along," he said as he strolled leisurely behind her. "You want someone to do the hard labor."

"No. I want you there because I think we make a damn good team," she answered with more than a trace of irritability. "I want you there because you said you like the idea of a treasure being found. If you like the idea so much, then do something about it."

Michelle winced as she realized she had dug up the old accusation. "Never mind." She held up her hands in apology. "That's not what I meant. If you want to go on another treasure hunt, then you know where I'll be." She turned and disappeared into the crowd.

Ryan was immediately at her side before she could go far. "You're going to need me," he announced.

"I do need you." She leaned her head against his shoulder and knocked him on the cheek with her crown.

"Ow." He rubbed his chin. The tiara should be registered as a lethal weapon.

"Sorry." She clawed at the hairpins and removed the tiara before she poked someone's eye out.

"You need me for a ride," he clarified and caught her

eyebrow waggle. "We'll stop by the bowling alley and get some shovels."

"We just need one," Michelle said as she pulled off her Miss Horseradish sash.

"You're the one all into 'one must act.' You want action?"

"Yes, please." She batted her eyelashes and Ryan's gut twisted with desire.

"Good," he said hoarsely. "Then you're going to shovel."

Michelle watched the muscles ripple in Ryan's bare back as sweat trickled down his bronzed skin. "Why was there no shoveling task in the scavenger hunt?" she asked him.

He grunted as he tossed dirt out of the giant hole they had created in the bed and breakfast's backyard. "Less talk and more shoveling."

She couldn't work. Not when Ryan was standing in front of her, shirtless and gleaming with sweat. While she watched the fading light play along the lines of his body. Forget the treasure. She was ready to pounce on Ryan and take him in the dirt.

A shadow crossed over her and Michelle guiltily glanced up. Annie stood by her as she stared at the hole with growing trepidation. A purse was slung over her shoulder and she held keys in her hand.

It was obvious to Michelle that the bed and breakfast proprietor was stepping out. It was also apparent that she wasn't waiting breathlessly for the treasure chest to reveal itself anytime soon.

"We'll clean up once we're done," Ryan promised as he paused from scooping up more dirt with his shovel. "I'm being careful with the apple tree roots."

Annie nodded. "I'm going to leave for a while. The back door is open if you need inside." She eyed the hole again. "How long will you guys be?"

"Not much longer," Ryan said as he leaned against the shovel.

"Don't forget," Michelle said as the enthusiasm trickled into her voice. "You will get a third of whatever we find."

"Uh-huh, okay." Annie nodded. "See you."

Michelle watched the woman walk away until she was out of hearing range. "She thinks I'm nuts, doesn't she?"

"Yeah, pretty much."

"The treasure is here," Michelle insisted. "I know it. I feel it in my bones."

Ryan parked his shovel in the dirt. "I know you feel that way, Michelle, and I think that's great . . ."

She knew that tone. Knew what was coming. "Don't give up now," Michelle pleaded. "We are so close."

Ryan gestured at the hole with outstretched arms. "It's not here."

"Yes, it is."

Ryan shook his head. "I give up." He tossed his shovel onto the grass and hoisted himself out of the hole.

"Maybe it's a little to the right." Her hands fluttered above the freshly made ditch. "Or to the left. I don't know, but it is here." She didn't know why, but it was very important that he believe with her.

"For someone who used to hate fairy tales, you're making up for lost time."

She had to make him believe and do it quickly before he gave up. Michelle placed her hands on her hips and launched into her argument. "I know it's here and I can give you two very good reasons."

Ryan didn't take the bait. He silently found his shirt on the ground and shook the dirt off of it.

"First of all, the marker is for their dog's burial site," Michelle started. "Homer and Ida loved their dog. Everyone says so, yadda, yadda, yadda. But do you know what?"

"The dog was still alive when the Wirts died," Ryan answered as he pulled his shirt back on. "Yeah, I know. You said that on the way here. And I'm telling you, someone else buried the dog."

Michelle scoffed at the possibility. "No one would have given it an expensive grave marker."

"You don't know that."

Okay, he was right on that point, but she wasn't going to admit it yet. "Which brings me to point number two." She held out two fingers. "There are no remains of a dog. No box. Nothing."

He looked at the hole and shrugged with indifference. "It disintegrated."

"I don't think so," Michelle said and shook her head. "There would be at least something."

"Okay. Okay. There was no dog here. I'll give you that. But that doesn't mean the treasure is here."

"Then why the marker?" She pointed at the marble slab. "The very expensive and personalized marker?"

"I don't know, and you know what? I don't care," Ryan announced as he picked up the shovel. "Come on, we need to shovel the dirt back into the hole."

"There is a reason for the marker," Michelle said urgently. She couldn't have him throw the dirt back in there when they were so close. "It's because they had to remember where they stashed the treasure."

"Like you said, nothing is here." He dug the tip of his shovel into the mound of dirt by the hole. "No dog and no treasure. If there had been something, it has already been found and spent."

"It has to be here." Michelle jumped into the ditch and grabbed the other shovel. "It just has to be."

Ryan exhaled slowly and tossed the shovel to the side. "Okay. What's going on?"

"I'm finding the damn treasure." She dug up some dirt and tossed it out of the hole. "With or without you."

"This is not like you." Ryan sat down on the edge and let his legs dangle into the hole. "Did you get addicted with the scavenger hunting and now you can't stop?"

"No." She kept digging. Quickly, fiercely. She had to show him the proof before he left.

"Did you start to believe in the legend? You, Michelle Nelson?"

Michelle paused from digging and looked up at him. "Maybe I like the possibility of a treasure," she said, repeating his earlier words. "I like the idea of possibilities."

"I think there's something more." His lean legs swung gently against the dirt wall. "Why do you suddenly want to believe in it?"

Michelle kept shoveling. Was that what was going on? Did she believe it, or did she want to believe it?

"What do you want to do with the treasure?" Ryan suddenly asked.

She hesitated. What did she want? She hadn't really allowed herself to consider the answer. "A couple of things," she hedged.

"Like what?"

Michelle scooped up some dirt and tossed it into the growing pile. "I want to pay back the people who gave to the scholarship fund."

"You don't owe them anything." Ryan's voice rose in anger. "They donated. That's the key word: 'donated.' "

"It was also an investment." She dug her shovel in for another scoop. "One that hasn't paid off yet."

Ryan rubbed the stubble over his jaw. "Then that's a lot of money to pay back."

"No shit." She tossed the dirt with a sharp jab to the shovel.

"Anything else?"

"A nice retirement package for my mom and dad would be good. Throw in a long, long vacation for my mom. That way they won't have to wait and worry for me to do something special." She dug her shovel in deep. "Lucrative."

He nodded in understanding. "Gotcha."

Michelle leaned against her shovel and looked past the wide-open spaces and out into the evening sky. "And then if there's any money left—"

Ryan held his head with his hands. "Hold on. How much do you think there is? Remember, you're only getting a third."

"I'd sock some away and keep it safe." She thought about it some more and nodded. "Yep, that's what I'd do."

"Okay, now this sounds like the Michelle I know. Don't you want to splurge it on a dream home?"

"I haven't thought in terms of a dream home." A nicer, bigger apartment, sure. But a home? She wasn't in that frame of mind yet. She might never be.

"How about a dream car?"

She made a face at the suggestion. "That's a guy thing."

"Dream vacation?"

"No, not really." There were a few places she'd like to go, but nothing that made her lie awake at night, wishing she had the money to make a visit.

"Dream?"

Michelle stopped and slowly stood to her full height. That was it and she hadn't seen it for herself. Nope, Ryan had to rip the veil from her eyes and reveal the truth. Make it stare at her right in the face.

"The money would give me the freedom to dream," Michelle admitted as she stared into the ditch. "Something that didn't have an obligation pinned to it."

"Okay."

She looked up at Ryan and found him smiling. That crazy smile that always did wild things to her pulse. "Okay, what?"

"Okay. I'll help." He grabbed his shovel and jumped back into the ditch.

That's it? That's all she needed to get him back to helping her? Something didn't add up. She watched him suspiciously. "You're going to help me because I don't have a dream?"

"No," he said as he went straight to work in digging the hole. "I'm helping because I want to give you whatever you need to dream."

Michelle leaned into him. The support meant more than he would ever know. She pressed her lips against his cheek and gave him a soft, gentle kiss. "Thank you," she whispered, her throat tight with emotion.

Even if they didn't find the treasure, she had found someone who would keep her dreams safe. In her opinion, that was just as rare a find.

"But I'm warning you," he went on. "There's a very real chance that there is no treasure."

"And I'm warning you," she countered as she dug up a huge pile of dirt, "there is an equal chance that the treasure is here."

"Think about it, Michelle," he said as he shoveled with a lot more expertise than she displayed. "Homer and Ida needed something close enough they could keep their eye on it, but it had to be hidden so no one else saw it."

"Yeah."

"They also needed something they could get to easily. They couldn't dig a hole every time they robbed a train."

Michelle leaned back against the ditch and looked around. "You have a point," she admitted with great reluctance. "But I know it's here."

Ryan looked over the hole and studied the trees. "Unless . . ." He hoisted himself out again.

"Where are you going?" It was going to take forever to lure him back into the ditch.

"The tree." He went directly to the tree behind the marker.

"What about it?" She felt her eyebrows shoot up as he

inspected the trunk. "Oh, come on, Ryan. They couldn't hide it in a tree."

"Why not?" he asked without looking back at her.

"First of all," Michelle said, "trees don't have secret compartments."

She noticed that what she had to say didn't stop Ryan from jiggling the roots.

"Trees get diseases." She ticked that fact off another finger.

He started knocking on it.

"They die."

He kept knocking.

"Get struck by lightning."

Knock—knock—knock.

"Burn. Get . . . get climbed on by obnoxious, curious children." She watched him tap the trunk. Lower and lower. "It's a tree! It grows apples. It—"

Ryan turned to her, about to say something, but the words vanished. His perpetual smile disappeared as his eyes widened with disbelief.

"What?" Her stomach twisted so hard it burned. "Don't tell me there is something there in the trunk. I won't believe you."

"I won't say it." He motioned with his head. "Look behind you."

She turned around and faced the garden. It was the formal garden filled with overgrown plants and wildflowers. There were just as many ornate statues and yard ornaments. "What?" She didn't see anything out of the ordinary.

"You must be too low. Let me help you out of the ditch." He went to the edge and offered his hand. "I'm serious. I need to show you something."

She took his hand and climbed out. "This had better not be a trick to make me stop digging. Because I'm not going to stop."

"Lie down by the marker," he told her. "On your stomach."

"Lie down?"

"Trust me." He guided her down and she felt goofy lying down with her hand dangling over a ditch.

"Fine, fine." She wasn't going to take much more of this nonsense. She had a treasure to discover. "I'm sitting down. Are you satisfied?"

"Not yet." His voice buzzed with excitement. "Look at the garden."

"I'm lookin—" From the level where she lay next to the marker, she saw that statues of varying heights and lengths created an illusion. It looked like a cross with the ornate birdbath in the center.

Michelle slowly turned to Ryan. "No. Way."

Ryan's smile dazzled her. "Who would have thought that 'X' marks the spot?"

Chapter 16

Ryan's hands shook as he gripped the basin of the marble birdbath. He twisted it one way, putting all of his strength into it. It didn't budge.

"Didn't anyone try to look in the statues?" Michelle asked nearby as she studied a partially nude Venus.

"I guess not," he said through clenched teeth as he tried to turn the basin from the other direction. "Why would they? Buried treasure makes most people think it's underground."

The basin gave way and water sloshed over the rim. Ryan paused, his eyes widening as excitement pinged against his ribs. And maybe a hint of nerves.

Michelle was suddenly at his side, the garden art forgotten. "Need help?"

"No, I got it," he said softly as he kept pushing. Hell, why was he whispering?

Because he was scared, that's why. What if there was nothing there? He wouldn't know how to handle Michelle's disappointment, let alone his own.

But he would eventually get over it. He knew that. And he also would believe that the treasure was somewhere else, waiting for him. Maybe he would look for it some other time, or maybe he wouldn't.

The treasure didn't matter. He wasn't going to sacrifice

everything for it. It was a bit of fun. A distraction. A diversion.

But what if the treasure was inside? What if all of his wildest dreams could now come true? His heart jerked at the possibility.

Michelle grabbed his upper arm in concern. "Are you okay?"

He nodded as he pulled the top from its pedestal. The water splashed onto his jeans and the weeds at his feet. Michelle grabbed the other side and helped him lower the basin onto the ground.

She peered into the birdbath stand. "Are you going to put your hand in there? There might be bugs. Or spiders." She shivered at the idea.

"I'm not going to let something like that stop me now." Dipping his hand into the wide and short pedestal, his fingers brushed against something soft and slick. He pulled back in surprise.

Michelle yelped and hopped away from the birdbath. "What?" She held her hands up. "What do you feel?"

Plastic? No, Ryan shook his head at the thought. That wasn't right. Oilskin? Something like a bag?

His heart froze. This was what he was afraid of. From this moment on, everything was going to change. Life as he knew it was never going to be the same.

"Do you feel something?"

Yeah. He felt his old life crashing around him, falling to his feet in jagged shards. He had been doing just fine until Michelle came back to town. He had made peace with life's expectations and limitations.

"Ryan?"

Now it was all shot to hell. He shouldn't feel like this. He should be thrilled. Beyond thrilled. "There's—" He cleared his throat, pushing down the chaotic and undefined emotions swirling inside him. "There's something in here."

He didn't have to look at Michelle to know she didn't have the same reservation he did. She vibrated with excitement. The cool air crackled with energy.

Why wouldn't she? This was the answer to all her prayers. He may want this, but she needed it. And he wasn't going to make her wait one more second.

Ryan grabbed the sack and slowly pulled it out of the base. Michelle clapped her hands over her mouth. Her eyes bugged out as she saw the size of the bag.

It wasn't as big as it was heavy. It also smelled musty and earthy. Michelle grabbed the drawstring and pulled it over the pedestal's edge. It took some grunting and straining from both of them before they could lower it carefully onto a dry patch of ground.

Michelle overcame her rare lapse of silence and reverently pulled open the bag. "Oh, my God." She rocked back onto her heels and fell into an awkward sitting position.

The top of the bag almost overflowed with gold coins peeking through wads of crumpled money. He caught a glimpse of some official-looking paper that said bearer bonds, whatever those were. Jewelry that sparkled with diamonds and colorful precious stones.

"Oh. My. God," Michelle repeated, unable to take her eyes off of the bag.

"That looks like more than I expected." He had also expected a treasure *chest*. Not that he was complaining. He'd take what he could get.

"I . . . I . . ."

"Yeah, me, too." Ryan rubbed his hand over his chin. He couldn't estimate what it was worth. He wasn't used to thinking of numbers that big.

Michelle pulled her gaze from the treasure and looked at him, her forehead lined with worry. "What are we going to do?"

Ryan dipped his chin and stared back at her. Michelle

didn't know? She didn't have a plan? Then they were both up a creek without a paddle. "I vote for counting it."

"Right. Yeah. Good idea." She delved into the sack, scooping up the money and letting it fall through her fingers. She pulled her hands sharply out of the bag. "But not here."

"Why not?" It was going to get dark soon, but they could grab a flashlight.

"It's not safe here." Michelle scanned the backyard, her gaze pausing at every shadow. "It's too much out in the open."

What was she talking about? Too much out in the open for what? "And the problem with that is?"

She rose to her knees and put her hands against the lumpy bag. "We need to handle this like those lottery winners."

Okay, now she was talking in riddles. He'd had enough of that on the scavenger hunt. "What does that mean?"

"First, we keep it a secret. We need to hide this." She closed the bag with a quick, decisive move.

Hide it? After all they went through to find it? Ryan exhaled a long sigh. "It's not going to be easy stuffing this back into the birdbath."

"No. Not there." She stared at the marble pedestal, but Ryan had a feeling she wasn't looking at it. He sensed the wheels in her mind were spinning wildly.

"Annie probably told a few people what we were doing," Michelle said. "Most of the town will just laugh it off, but not everybody."

He knew she was talking about Brandy. He didn't think the redhead was going to do anything about it, but then again, he hadn't predicted some of her tactics. "Where are you going with this?"

"If word leaks out that we found the treasure"— Michelle turned to him, her gaze intense and serious—"or at least are on the trail, someone will come sniffing around and they might stumble on it."

"You are paranoid."

"No"—she pulled the bag's drawstring tight—"I'm cautious."

"How long do we have to hide this?"

"Until I get a lawyer on the job. I'm going back to Chicago tomorrow anyway. I'll get some referrals, and we can decide which one to go with."

"You're leaving? Tomorrow?" The news hit him like a punch to the stomach.

"Well, yeah." She frowned at him. "I have a job I need to get back to."

His head spun. She couldn't leave now. Not after what happened between them. Not after finding the treasure. "You trust me alone with this?"

"Absolutely."

Okay, that didn't work. "You don't have to go back. You're a millionaire." He gestured at the bag.

"We don't know that yet. There might be some legalities."

Michelle was already in planning mode. Assessing the risks, considering options. While he was sitting on the ground wondering what hit him.

"I'd rather be safe than sorry." She stood up and brushed the dirt off of her jeans. "Okay. Now we need to come up with a good hiding place."

"Good luck with that. I think the Wirts found the only good hiding place in Carbon Hill. Everyone knows everyone's business around here."

"Not always." She pursed her lips and she thought about the problem. Her expression brightened. "There is *one* place no one goes to."

Ryan grunted as his strained muscles shook. "This is too risky."

"Oh, come on," Michelle coaxed him with a tired smile. They had only a little farther to go. They could do this. "You know you want to."

"We're going to get caught." He gritted his teeth and squeezed his eyes shut.

She watched the play of his muscles under the dim light and felt the tug of desire deep in her belly. "We're not doing anything illegal," she responded in a husky voice.

"I wouldn't be too sure about that."

"Aw, come on, Ryan." She didn't want to look at the bad side of this. Of the possible pitfalls and problems. She wanted to enjoy this one moment. "Where is that positive attitude?"

"I left it in the ditch."

Michelle had a feeling she was going to hear about the ditch digging for a very long time. So that part of the plan had turned out to be a waste of time, but now everything was working in their favor. "You have to admit, this is a good idea."

"No, it's a risky idea." He sagged against the open door and wiped the sweat from his forehead with the back of his hand. "It'll be a good idea if we pull it off."

"Which we will." She knew it. Felt it deep in her bones. The kind of feeling she'd had when she realized where the treasure had to be hidden. She felt confident and bold. Felt as though nothing could go wrong. It was an amazing feeling.

Ryan grumbled under his breath before he grabbed the bag filled with treasures and pulled harder.

"We're following the same principles as Homer and Ida," she said, pushing the bag from the other end. Who knew gold was so freaking heavy? "It will always be out of vision, but never out of your sight."

"There are more people crawling around here than there ever were on their farm." He scooted the sack another inch across the floor.

Michelle immediately closed the door behind them. "And you can grab the bag quickly if you need to."

"Are you kidding me? Did you see how long it took for us just to move this bag from the car? The two of us?"

She dismissed his concern with the wave of her hand. "This is the only place that Carbon Hill doesn't know about."

"Behind the pinsetters?" He gestured wildly at the high-tech machines in the small room. "Are you kidding me? They know it exists."

"They don't know what happens here. No one knows what happened here between us," she pointed out. They had managed to keep something private that occurred in this room a secret and they could do it again.

He didn't say anything as he pulled, pushed, and kicked the bag into the corner by the door.

"It's going to work," Michelle told him.

"I'm not so sure." Ryan stood still with his hands on his hips. His chest rose and fell with every hard breath as he stared at the sack. "I haven't had much luck in this room."

"How can you say that? You got me." Okay, that might pale in comparison to the big prize in the corner of the room, but she was trying to make a point.

Regret tugged the corner of his mouth. "Not the way that I wanted."

"Really?" Her pulse jumped and skipped. She took a step toward him and placed her hand on his arm. "How did you want me?"

A dimple played against his cheek. "In awe."

She leaned against him, enjoying the feel of his strength lurking under his warm skin. "Show me," she whispered.

"Show?" He dropped his hands to his sides and glanced around. "No, I don't think so. Not here."

"Why not?" She stepped in front of him.

Something close to panic flickered in his blue eyes. "I don't want history repeating itself."

"It won't," she promised, curling her arms around his shoulders before lacing her hands behind his neck.

"It already is. You're leaving first thing tomorrow."

"I'm coming back." She pressed her lips against the hollow at the base of his throat. She felt his pulse beating rapidly.

"No, you're not." The certainty in his voice sent a warning skittering down her spine. She ignored it as he continued, "This town is too small for you. Too confining."

"You can come with me this time," she suggested, her lips trailing up the column of his throat.

His Adam's apple bobbed under her mouth. "I don't know," he said hoarsely.

Michelle wanted to convince him. Wipe away any doubt about her, or about them. "Kiss me." She tilted her face up to his.

He brushed his mouth against hers before pulling back slightly. "You can't distract me with a kiss."

Distract? More like make a promise. But would he understand? No, he would just argue some more. "Kiss me just because."

"Because why?"

She looked at him from beneath her eyelashes. Her chest and throat squeezed, the blood roaring in her ears as she made a leap of faith. "Because you love me."

The pause screamed at her. Her heart stopped. Her throat tightened and she was about to pull back when he reached for her and slammed her against his chest.

Ryan's mouth went down hard on hers. He tasted hot and wild. On the edge.

She was going to take that as a yes.

She returned his kisses with abandon. This would erase what had happened between them. This would be the new beginning.

Michelle threaded her fingers through his hair and she

clenched the back of his head as he deepened the kiss. Her lips felt swollen. Raw. She felt as if she was being devoured and taken.

Ryan's hands swept along her shoulders and back, bunching her shirt in his fists. She wanted him to rip the shirt off and take his along with it. Press her skin against his as she watched the play of his muscles when he thrust into her.

Okay, that did it. She needed him underneath her, as in now. To rock against him. Have him look at her in awe.

Her hands dropped to his belt and his fingers covered hers. She frowned, unable to understand why he was slowing her down. Stopping her. A horrible thought hit her. She stared at their hands. "You better have a condom this time," she warned him.

"I do"—he pulled her hands away from him—"but we're taking this slow."

"Oh, we are?" Not if she had anything to say about it. They didn't have all night.

"Yeah." He traced his hands along her face and neck. Her skin tingled until the cool air stung. Ryan then gently trailed his fingers down her shirt. The soft touch tickled and she found it almost too much to bear.

Now would be a good time to rip off her shirt, Michelle decided as her choppy breaths echoed in her ears. *Right now. Right . . . now.*

His hands skimmed under her shirt and he caressed her waist, slowly moving his way up to unclasp her bra and cup her breasts.

Okay, enough teasing. She shucked off one shoe and then the other. They went skittering across the floor. She knew her sudden move surprised Ryan.

But didn't he get it? She couldn't take any more of this. She grabbed the hem of her shirt, yanked it over her head, and tossed it on the floor. Her bra followed quickly behind.

Her hands trembled as she unzipped her jeans. By the time she kicked them into the pile of clothes and stripped off her panties, the boldness had disappeared. She fought the instinct to cover herself with her hands as Ryan's hot gaze swept over her body.

Her skin felt tight, waiting for his next touch. Her nipples furled into hard buds. The vulnerability crashed over her. She didn't feel powerful or beautiful. She didn't feel anything like a goddess.

She was standing naked in front of a fully clothed man. Presenting herself and waiting for him to accept the offer. She was suddenly and completely afraid to look at him.

Michelle slowly lifted her gaze and met his. She froze when she saw the feral hunger in his eyes. Color streaked across his cheekbones. His head shook as his restraint started to slip. This was definitely a man who had been pushed to the edge.

"I . . . I'm trying," his voice was a low, dangerous growl, "to go slow."

She rolled her shoulders back. "Take me now."

He lifted her against the wall and she wrapped her legs around his waist. He probed her with his finger and found her wet and ready. Her flesh gripped and surrounded him and she whimpered when he retreated.

Michelle slathered his face with kisses as he grabbed for the condom. She captured his earlobe and bit down hard as he cursed and ripped open the foil. Jabbing her tongue in his ear, she waited impatiently for him to slide the latex over his cock.

And finally his hands were on her thighs. She had no time to think, to breathe, before he drove into her.

She gasped and arched against him. The wall bit into her back as she raked her nails across his shoulders. Michelle flexed against him, again and again. She couldn't stop.

Wouldn't stop as she chased the sensations ripping down her body at each thrust.

The white-hot sparks danced across her pelvis and gained speed before sweeping through her veins and shattering through her mind. She closed her eyes as she succumbed to the intense pleasure. Everything stopped. And then she felt herself falling and held on tight to Ryan's shoulders, pressing her lips against his throat as she groaned.

She found herself on her knees, straddling Ryan. His hands roamed her breasts as his eyes glittered with desire. Michelle rocked against him. Flexed and rotated her hips. She grinded against Ryan as his thrusts grew harsher and his hands pinched her breasts.

His thrusts grew deeper. His cock pressed firmly into her core. She moved against him fast and furious until he thrashed underneath her. He froze, his mouth sagging open, but no sound emerged.

Michelle slowed her hips as she watched him slump against the floor. The look of sated pleasure on his face made her smile. She leaned forward and kissed his lips softly. "Next time, we'll need to put down a blanket."

He didn't say anything. Didn't open his eyes. Didn't smile.

A sense of unease prickled at her. "I am coming back," she insisted.

Ryan showed no expression. He didn't nod his head. Didn't open his eyes. "I'll believe it when I see it."

"I will come back."

Famous last words. Michelle shook her head in disgust as she opened the security door to her Chicago apartment. She was cold and tired. Drained from a crazy, full day, just like yesterday and the day before.

She couldn't believe her newest creation was causing a buzz. The traditional cake with small treasures baked inside wasn't a brand-new idea. Who knew that it would create a sensation?

Of course, it helped that the pastry chef had found a real buried treasure.

The cake was popular for the Christmas holidays. Christmas. Michelle paused on the steps to her apartment. She couldn't believe it was already December. She had told Ryan she would be back. That hadn't happened yet, although she called frequently.

But the calls weren't enough. They had become shorter and shorter. Tense. Silent.

It was her fault, she admitted as she trudged on to her apartment. She had promised she would come back. She wanted to. Just for Ryan.

But she was becoming something of a coward. She didn't like that part of her personality and was finding it difficult to gather the courage to fight it.

Lost in her thoughts, she didn't realize someone was waiting by her door until she almost tripped over the familiar tennis shoes. She did a double take.

"Ryan!" Without a second thought, she launched into his arms. Tears filled her eyes when she fell into his embrace. She inhaled his scent, her throat hurting.

Michelle noticed he didn't say anything. He just held her. She pulled back, not sure what to do, or how to greet him. She wanted to jump on him and kiss him breathless, but the expression on his face made it hard to figure out how he felt about seeing her. "What are you doing here?"

"I decided you weren't showing up." There was a hard edge to his teasing smile.

She ducked her head and made a show of finding her keys in her purse. "I wanted to come back. You don't need to escort me back to Carbon Hill."

"Don't worry," he said softly. "I'm not."

Oh, God. What did that mean? Her hands shook as she grabbed her keys. "How's your family?" she asked brightly.

"Good."

"They're keeping the bowling alley?" She busied herself by opening the door to the apartment.

"Yeah, for old-time's-sake. Fully remodeled this time around."

And that was where his life was going to be. But could she go back? It was a nice place to visit. Briefly. Like a weekend. "How's everyone else doing?"

"Had you come back, you wouldn't have to ask," Ryan said as he walked behind her and entered her home.

She was going to let that rebuke go. Because she knew she had been in the wrong. "And how is Annie?" Michelle asked as she hung up her purse and tossed her keys on the table next to the door.

"Hugs me every time I see her." Ryan looked around the cheerful apartment. "She just can't seem to get over the fact that she's an instant millionaire."

"And . . . you?" she finally asked as she removed her coat.

He turned and met her gaze head-on. "I missed you."

Michelle closed her eyes at the pleasure and pain the words brought. "I missed you, too."

"Then why didn't you come back?"

She hung up her coat and leaned against the wall. "I can't live in Carbon Hill. Not anymore." She shook her head with regret. "It's where my family is, and it's where my roots are, and it's where you are, but it's—"

"I know." He said it gently, which seemed to hurt even more.

Of course he did. He understood her more than she understood herself. And he wasn't giving up on her. That was the real surprise.

And that was why he had been so sure she wasn't coming. She had meant it. Was determined to follow through, but had ultimately failed.

She had failed them both. Showed her shortcomings right in front of Ryan, the very last person she wanted to disappoint. All because she couldn't face her fears. She didn't live up to her own expectations and hated it. "I'm sorry you came all this way to hear that."

"That's not why I came."

She gnawed her bottom lip. "It's not?"

"No, I'm here to stay."

"Stay?" She jerked her head up and saw him shrug off his coat. "Stay where?"

"Chicago."

She frowned as she tried to comprehend what he was saying. "Where-what-no." She held her hands out, halting her chaotic thoughts. "Why are you staying?"

Ryan looked away and his smile was almost shy. "I'm enrolled in an art program starting in January."

No. Way. She couldn't believe it. "You are not."

"Am, too." He glanced back at her, his eyes twinkling. "Wanna see the acceptance form?"

She shook her head. "I'll take your word for it. But what happened to the no-need-to-pursue-my-art spiel?"

"Well"—he scratched the stubble forming on his chin—"I met this really annoying woman who made me realize that the gnawing in my stomach had more to do with my art than what I thought was boredom."

"Really?"

"Yeah, really. So, I'm going to do it. Find out how far I can go. See what I can do." He took a big sigh. "And what I can't."

Michelle walked over to him and held him tight. She was thrilled for him. Proud. She felt as though she had influenced him and it would enrich his life.

"I might find out that I suck."

Maybe too much of an influence. Michelle pulled away and gave him a punch to his ribs. "Stop it."

Ryan smiled and dodged her next punch. "But I need to know that I gave it a shot. That I'm not going to regret missed opportunities."

"Sounds like a good plan." She lifted her eyebrow. "You do know that you're staying with me."

"I don't know." He looked around. "Is this what multi-millionaires can afford in Chicago?"

"I've been too busy to apartment hunt." She had been hiding. Avoiding. It sounded as if Ryan wasn't going to let her get away with that anymore.

"That reminds me." He stepped away and pulled a jewelry box from his coat pocket. "I have something here for you."

Michelle opened it up and smiled when she saw the golden chain. "It's the necklace! You remembered."

"I also bought that purple triangle pendant thingy," he said proudly.

She looked in the box, but there was no pendant. She looked back up at Ryan.

"Guess you're going to have to hunt for it."

She snapped the jewelry box closed. "Aren't you going to give me a clue?"

"I love you," he said in a rush.

She froze and the box fell from her hands. Her heart raced at warp speed. What did he say? "Is that the clue?"

"Yes. No," he blurted out. Ryan shook his head. "I mean both. I mean . . . Michelle, I love you."

She placed both hands against his face and kissed him. The joy kicked inside her and she kissed him again. She leaned into him to deepen the kiss. Placing her hand against his chest, she felt the pendant under her palm.

Ryan groaned against her mouth and pulled away.

"How did you find it so fast? I guess I'm not good with clues."

"Yeah, you are." Her hands crept along the back of his neck and she tilted his face down so her mouth could brush against his. "But I know how you think. That's why we make a good team."

"Good?" He swept her into his arms. "Michelle, when we're together, we're the best."

Nonstop international action and one of the
hottest heroes ever from Amy J. Fetzer.
Don't miss this sneak peek from
HIT HARD,
available now from Brava . . .

Viva's gaze slid over his bare chest, his hair still damp from a shower. The towel looped around his neck, he gripped the ends. Did it get any sexier?

"You're one terrific guy, ya know."

He smiled gently.

"I've seen courage before, but you take the cake." She let her feet touch the floor.

"Give yourself some credit."

"For trouble, sure. But nothing like what I've seen." She pushed his hair back off his forehead. He had hero written all over him, she thought. "Do you *fear* anything?"

Sam stared into her soft green eyes, and saw the truth. "Only you."

"Why?"

"You do things to me."

Her lips curved. "Screw up your mission, force you to come rescue me, twice?"

"Who's counting." He leaned in.

Viva felt swallowed up by the look in his dark eyes, intense, for sure, but something else she'd never seen in a man.

"You make me want to crawl inside your skin and find out what makes you tick."

Tears blurred her vision and she inhaled sharply, a perilous feeling tumbling through her. "No one's ever tried," she whispered, touching the side of his face.

"Lucky me."

She smiled softly, a tear falling.

"Don't cry, it tears me up to see it."

"So now it's all about *you*, huh?"

He chuckled. He never knew what to expect from her. She was the most unpredictable woman he'd ever known, and she fascinated the hell out of him.

She grasped the ends of the towel, pulling him near, and his hands on either side of her slid along her thighs, her hips.

"This is dangerous," he said, his face nearing hers.

"Define danger." Her mouth lingered over his and she slipped off the chair, straddled his lap.

God. He could feel the heat of her through his jeans. "You, in *any* form, me hot as hell to have you."

"And time alone with no one shooting at us," she finished. "And let's not forget I'm naked under this robe." Her mouth trailed his throat, and she caught his earlobe and nibbled.

Sam felt himself go cross-eyed with desire. "Oh, Jesus. You're making me come apart again, Red." He kissed her hot and quick.

"Is that all?"

He gripped her hips, ground her to him, and proved she had him in her grasp.

"You've had a rough couple of days, and—"

Her gaze flashed to his and he saw it, the memory, the moment when Ryzikov violated her, when she felt she'd die. "I know my own mind, Sam, and I think—yours."

But she didn't.

She had no idea how close she came to *not* dying today.

Ryzikov had plans for her, a personal brand Sam had seen once before. The bastard would have taken her to the edge of her life, then jerked her back; a reprieve that would have lasted only till the son of a bitch wanted to witness his control again. The marks on her neck were only the first layer.

Seeing them made him relive his fear, admit he'd never been so scared in his life than when he couldn't find her, couldn't protect her. It ate him alive. She had no training, no defenses, nothing to help herself, and then, she proved him wrong—again.

"Sam?" She frowned, wondering what he was thinking about so hard. "This zoning-out thing is not a good sign and my ego is terribly fragile. I might not recover."

He smiled slow and broad, then cupped her jaw in his broad palms and kissed her. Really kissed her. Not like he hadn't done a damn fine job before but this time, he was full of patience when she wanted to plow ahead. Each roll of his mouth made her toes curl, her skin tighten. Her soul opened.

"I can't ignore you, baby," he said against her lips. "It's physically impossible."

Her body reacted with quick shivers, her hands spread wide over his chest. "Mmm, command of the body. It's a good start."

He met her gaze, something battling behind his dark eyes. "You and me, we're more than that." His fingers flexed on her jaw.

Viva went still inside, and swore her heartbeat just plain stopped. Was he for real? No one had ever spoken to her like this. She covered his hands, pulling them from her face and gripping. "Seriously?"

"I don't say anything I don't mean."

"Me, either." Her gaze lingered over him, her hand spread

over his bare chest, the contours of muscle defined and rippling. It made her hot to see all that man, and know he was hers for tonight. She lifted her gaze to his as she tugged at the robe's sash. She'd never been shy, never let what she wanted escape.

Yet he hesitated. "Me or erasing his memory?"

She smiled with feline grace and spread the robe, exposing her breasts and loving his jaw-dropping look. "Oh, if you don't know that by now, we really aren't communicating well enough." Her hand went behind his neck, and she drew him close. "Let me fix that."

Her tongue snaked out and slicked his lips and he groaned as he sank into her. The terrorist's touch evaporated with each press of his mouth on hers, in the way he touched her, as if he'd never get the chance again. It was a rare sensation for her, and the bounty of it flowed into an empty place in her, in the scattered loneliness she'd lived for years. And she ached for more, greedy woman. There was no question in her mind when she slid the robe off her shoulders, and let it pool at her hips.

He swallowed, his gaze riding over her body. "Oh, man, you're—"

"Ready and willing?"

"Beautiful."

Her heart just got lighter, she thought, sliding her arms around his neck and sinking her fingers into his hair. Her breasts grazed his chest, and in his ear she whispered hotly, "Wanna rock and roll with me?"

"Jesus." Sam slammed his eyes shut.

Then she kissed him.

Pure heat and wild hunger. And more. Sam felt the power of it speed down his body and fight for escape. Instead it built, a need like sucking in a lungful of air that wouldn't come, and he struggled. It almost scared him, opened up feelings he'd buried for the missions. Fighting it was impossible. Viva made him feel. Just by her very existence. She was her own adventure, her own ruler, and the thrills in a high-speed chase in a tight cockpit didn't compare to the ecstasy of Viva.

Romantic. Passionate.
That's Sylvia Day's
ASK FOR IT,
available in August 2006
from Brava . . .

Marcus studied Elizabeth from the doorway of his bedroom. She slept, her beautiful face innocent in slumber. Despite her betrayal, his heart swelled at the sight of her cuddled peacefully in bed. Next to her, on the small table, sat two open packets of headache powder and a glass of water, half full.

Slowly she stirred, the force of his presence and the heat of his gaze penetrating her sleep. She opened her eyes and focused on him, the instant tenderness of her gaze quickly shielded by guilt-heavy lids. He knew in that instant the reports were true. He held himself upright by will alone, when all he wanted to do was crawl to her and bury his pain in her arms.

"Marcus," she called in the soft, throaty voice that never failed to arouse him. Despite his anger and torment, he felt his cock stir. "Come to bed, darling. I want you to hold me."

Traitorously, his feet moved toward her. By the time he reached her, he had removed his coat and waistcoat. He stopped at the edge of the bed. "How was your day?" he asked, his voice carefully neutral.

She stretched, the movement of her legs pulling down the sheet so that her torso was exposed through the thin shift she'd worn to sleep. He grew hard, and hated himself for it when his thoughts drifted to the secrets she kept. Nothing could temper his response to her. Even now, his heart struggled to forgive her.

Wrinkling her nose, she said, "Truthfully? It was one of the most horrid days of my life." Her mouth curved seductively. "But you can change that."

"What happened?"

She shook her head. "I don't want to talk about it. Tell me about your day instead. It was certainly better than mine." Pulling back the covers, she silently invited him to join her. "Can we have dinner in our rooms tonight? I don't feel like getting dressed again."

Of course not. How many times would she want to dress and undress in one day? Maybe she hadn't undressed at all. Maybe St. John had merely pushed her skirts up and . . .

Marcus clenched his jaw and willed the image away.

Sitting on the bed, he yanked off his shoes. Then he turned to her. "Did you enjoy your trip into town?" he asked casually, but it didn't fool her.

Elizabeth knew him too well.

She made a great show of sitting up in the bed and fluffing the pillows into a comfortable pile. "Why don't you simply say what you mean?"

He tore his shirt over his head, then stood to remove his breeches. "Did your lover not bring you to orgasm, love? Are you anxious for me to finish what he started?" He slid into bed next to her, but found himself alone. She had slipped out the other side and stood at the foot of the bed.

With hands on her hips, she glared at him. "What are you talking about?"

Marcus leaned back against the pillows she had so recently arranged. "I was told you spent some time with Christopher St. John today, in my carriage with the curtains closed. He gave you a touching kiss goodbye and an open welcome to call on him for *anything* you might need."

The violet eyes sparked dangerously. As always, she was magnificent in her fury. With a chemise so finely crafted as to be nearly transparent, he could barely breathe from the sight of her.

"Ah," she murmured, her lush mouth drawn tight. "Of course. Despite your insatiable appetite for me, which often leaves me sore and exhausted, I find I still require further sexual congress. Perhaps you should commit me?"

Turning on her bare heel, she left.

Marcus stared after her, agape. He waited to see if she would return and when she did not, he pulled on his robe and followed her to her room.

She stood by the hall door in her dressing gown, telling a maid to bring up dinner and more headache powder. After sending the servant away, she slipped into her bed without looking at him.

"Deny it," he growled.

"I see no need. You are decided."

He stalked over to her, caught her by the shoulders, and shook her roughly. "Tell me what happened! Tell me it's false."

"But it's not," she said with arched brows, so damn collected and unruffled he wanted to scream. "Your men related the events exactly."

He stared at her in shock, his hands on her shoulders beginning to shake. Afraid to do violence, Marcus released her and clasped his hands behind his back. "You have been meeting with St. John and yet you won't tell me why. What reason would you have for seeing him?" His voice hardened ruthlessly. "For allowing him to kiss you?"

Elizabeth didn't answer his questions. Instead, she asked one of her own. "Will you forgive me, Marcus?"

"Forgive you for what?" he yelled. "Tell me what you've done! Have you taken a fancy to him? Has he seduced you into trusting him?"

"And if he has?" she asked softly. "If I've strayed, but want you back, would you have me?"

His pride so revolted at the thought of her in the arms of another man that, for a moment, he thought he would be violently sick. Turning away, his fists clenched convulsively at his sides. "What are you asking?" he bit out.

"You know very well what I'm asking. Now that you are aware of my duplicity, will you discard me? Perhaps now you'll send me away. Now that you no longer want me."

"*Not want you?* I never cease wanting you. Every damned moment. Sleeping. Waking." He spun about. "And you want me too."

She said nothing, her lovely face a mask of indifference.

He could send her with his family. Distance himself from her . . .

But the mere thought of her absence made him crazy. His ache for her was a physical pain. His pride crumbled beneath the demands of his heart.

"You will stay with me."

"Why? To warm your bed? Any woman can do that for you."

She was only an arm's reach away and yet her icy demeanor had her miles from him.

"You are my wife. You will serve my needs."

"Is that all I am to you? A convenience? Nothing more?"

"I wish you were nothing to me," he said harshly. "God, how I wish you were nothing."

To his amazement, her lovely face crumbled before his eyes. She slipped from the bed and sank to the floor. "Marcus," she sobbed, her head bowing low.

He stood frozen.

She wrapped her arms around his legs, her head resting on his feet, her tears slipping between his toes. "I was with St. John today, but I didn't stray from you. I could never."

Near dizzy with confusion, he lowered slowly to the floor and took her in his arms. "Christ . . . Elizabeth . . ."

"I need you. I need you to breathe, to think, to *be*." Her eyes, overflowing with tears, never left his face. Her hand moved to cup his cheek and he nuzzled into her touch, breathing in her scent.

"What is happening?" he asked, his voice hoarse from his clenched throat. "I don't understand."

She pressed her fingertips to his mouth. "I will explain."